SNOOKERED

# Snookered

## DONALD TRELFORD

*faber and faber*
LONDON · BOSTON

First published in 1986
by Faber and Faber Limited
3 Queen Square London WC1N 3AU

Photoset by Parker Typesetting Service, Leicester
Printed in Great Britain by
Redwood Burn Ltd, Trowbridge, Wiltshire
All rights reserved

*British Library Cataloguing in Publication Data*

Trelford, Donald
Snookered.
1. Snooker
I. Title
794.7'35'0924      GV900.S6

ISBN 0-571-13640-0

To my mother and father,
but for whom I might have
had a misspent youth.

# ACKNOWLEDGEMENTS

No one can write about snooker without owing an immense debt to Clive Everton, whose knowledge and wisdom about the game are unparalleled. He has encouraged and assisted me throughout this enterprise (though any mistakes are mine). Thanks are due also to those who made me welcome on the circuit, especially to Janice Hale and her colleagues in the press room, and to the officials, sponsors, broadcasters, managers and players who talked to me so freely. Barry Hearn, Dennis Taylor, Brian Wray, Peter Dyke, Trevor East and Nick Hunter deserve a special mention, as do Faber and Faber and Brian Wenham of the BBC, who concocted the idea between them. Quotations are gratefully acknowledged from the *Sunday Mirror*, *Sunday Telegraph*, *Daily Mail*, *Yorkshire Post*, *TV Times*, *The Observer*, and from books by Jean Rafferty, Angela Patmore, Trevor Fishlock, Ted Lowe and the others listed in the bibliography. Jeffrey Care and his staff in the *Observer* library were as helpful as ever. Without the tenacious zeal of my secretary, Barbara Rieck, the book would never have appeared at all.

# CONTENTS

# FOREWORD by DENNIS TAYLOR
## (*World Snooker Champion*)

It was my manager, Barry Hearn, who first commended Donald Trelford to me. 'It isn't often,' he joked in his inimitable style, 'that you get somebody writing about snooker who can read and write and makes no spelling mistakes.' I had heard, of course, about this eminent newspaper editor who was writing a book on the game. But it was only when I met him that I understood why Barry had accorded him the rare honour of membership of the Romford Matchroom.

Not only did he have an undisguised enthusiasm for the game, but he was obviously there to listen and to learn. In no way was he condescending. He also laughed at my jokes! Unlike some journalists I'd better not mention by name, he didn't claim to know it all. He certainly knows a great deal now. He wouldn't expect me to agree with all that he says about the state of the game or with all his comments on the leading players, but I wholeheartedly commend his book to everyone who cares about this obsessive sport of ours.

Snooker has grown so big so fast, attracting so much public interest and so much money, that it is right that it should be examined by an independent mind at this stage of its development. We are lucky that in this case it is a mind – and pen – as sharp, as thorough and as entertaining as Donald Trelford's.

His researches into the curious history of the game, his character sketches and his detailed match reports will not only give hours of pleasure for those engaged in the game at all levels, but will fill out the knowledge of those many millions who have come to it through television. His story of the final at the Crucible is a classic piece of sports reporting – it even made my

hands sweat as I relived every moment! He opens a door – a
green baize door, if you like – for those who have only seen the
game on the box.

I remember driving with him once from my home town at
Coalisland, County Tyrone, down to Dublin, where I was due to
play some exhibition matches. 'Would you like to come along to
watch?' I said. 'I'd love to,' he replied, 'but I have a lunch date in
Dublin.' 'Who with?' I asked. 'With the prime minister,' he said.
It was true, too. Donald Trelford is one of the few people I've
ever met who would be equally at home at both occasions.

## Chapter One

# A PRIVATE OBSESSION

Norfolk Street, winding crookedly down from Sheffield Town Hall to Roxy Nite Spot on the ring road at Arundel Gate, is blessed with an unusual variety of churches, all in the space of a hundred yards. The most handsome of them, built in 1700, is the Unitarian chapel, where a notice board proclaims a quotation from Thoreau – 'Goodness is the only investment that never fails' – seemingly directed at the building societies on either side, and the monumental Trustee Savings Bank across the road. Then, in processional order, come the Sheffield Centre for Religious Education; Cathedral House, leading through an alley to St Marie's Cathedral (shortly to receive a most unexpected communicant); the Central United Reformed Church; and Victoria Hall, the Methodist Church, which exhibits a rather exasperated sign: 'Why will people go astray when they have this blessed book to guide them?'

The question appears to be addressed to the Crucible Theatre opposite. Of Norfolk Street's many temples, it is to this, the only secular one, that the congregation are streaming. The crowds – undeterred by the message 'Slow Me Down, Lord' in the Victoria Hall window – are not here for South Yorkshire Opera's production of *Aida*, nor for Noel Coward's *Present Laughter*, *Woza Albert*, the *Rocky Horror Show* or *Joseph and the Technicolour Dreamcoat*, all of which are listed among the Crucible's coming attractions. They are here for the snooker, which packs out the theatre for a run of two to three weeks every spring.

What brings all these people to Sheffield is nothing less than the biggest tournament of the snooker year, the pot of pots, the championship of the world. I am reminded irresistibly of the headline on a front-page editorial I was once asked to write when I started as a journalist in this city: 'Sheffield – Centre of the Universe'. At the time it had seemed ridiculous, a certifiable case of provincial *folie de grandeur*, ordered by an editor who had dined not wisely but too well, with a gravy-stained waistcoat to prove it. And yet twenty-five years later, not only had the world finally come to Sheffield but, through more than one hundred hours of television, Sheffield was going out to millions of people around the world.

It was in this same Crucible Theatre, just after Easter 1984, that I decided to embark on the sporting adventure charted here. Like thousands of other people in recent years – 64 per cent of the British population, according to a survey – I had developed a growing interest in snooker (described by *Private Eye* as my 'strange, obsessive passion'), induced by its hypnotic rituals on television. The BBC began giving daily coverage to the world championship in 1978, Ray Reardon's year. Another Welshman, Terry Griffiths (this one fair instead of dark), won at his first attempt the following year; I remember being glued to that match while staying in Guernsey. Then, in 1980, came the famous clash between Canadian Cliff Thorburn, the eventual winner, and Alex 'Hurricane' Higgins, when the climax was interrupted by live coverage of the SAS raid which ended the Iranian embassy siege in London. Snooker fans were outraged. By this time the game had so fired the public imagination that the one event seemed almost as dramatic and exciting as the other.

Snooker could have been designed for the TV screen, down to the rounded corners on the table. The camera not only captures the colours of the balls and the subtle texture of the play in its entirety, unlike the larger arenas of soccer or cricket: it also catches the moods and personalities of the players, the telltale twitch or swagger as the game develops, building up their characters in a national soap opera. And the cast is suitably colourful too. No script writer could have invented the wild Irish gunslinger or the Tooting tearaway, both with kamikaze tendencies; the huge Canadian bear with an epic thirst for lager; his compatriot with the cool air of a riverboat gambler, settling down for the heat of the night; the tall tense Englishman with the Samurai's self-discipline and dedication; the Welsh Dracula, the Prince of Darkness, the man of many masks.

In the Crucible Theatre for the classic, electrifying final of 1984 between Steve Davis and Jimmy White – the Samurai versus the Whirlwind, or 'the Engineer and the Poet', as *The Times* saw it – I was suddenly enthused with the idea of knowing more about these people at first hand, in rising from the TV armchair, so to speak, to go through the green baize door, and enter the closed world behind the screen, beyond the reach of the cameras. What was the inside story of the snooker boom? How would the reality compare with the myth? Would the characters turn out to be larger or lesser than life?

The Crucible Theatre itself was the first of many surprises. It was indeed the secular temple it had promised to be from outside. Its steeply banked seating made for mesmeric concentration on the altar-like table, tended by black-tied gladiators with finely honed weapons and a red-coated referee in white gloves, all going about their curious, priestlike tasks before a hushed congregation. Even on TV, as Clive James pointed out, you can hear the tension before the picture forms: the sound of the Crucible is a hiss that clicks. This aptly named theatre, set in the city of steel, puts men's characters to the test: 'The champion is the man who can stay incandescent longest without losing shape.'

In the 1984 final it was Steve Davis, the Samurai, who just held himself together when the heat became overpowering in the final frame. Jimmy White, with the pale cheeks of a James Dean and the 'nervous system of a fighter pilot on amphetamines', finally bombed out after a brave fightback in the afternoon. But the echoing cheers as he left the arena still drowned Davis's moment of glory. Even as the champion held the trophy aloft, with the cheque for £44,000 already in his back pocket, the crowd were saluting the loser as Davis himself, ever the realist, knew more keenly than anyone else.

Neither Steve Davis nor any of us could have imagined that this memorable, nerve-tingling final ('heart-stopping' was the phrase used in *The Times*) would be upstaged in 1985 by one that was even more thrilling – indeed, in the judgement of qualified observers like Ted Lowe, the 'voice of snooker', the greatest competitive match of all time. A final that would create a new people's champion in Dennis Taylor and bring Davis himself to the brink of despair on the blackest night of his life.

I had first become aware of snooker long before it was fashionable, glamorous and rich. Those were not the first adjectives that came to anyone's mind about Radford Social Club in bomb-scarred Coventry in the decade after the Second World War. My father must have introduced me to the game as soon as I was old enough, in my early teens, to be allowed inside the drinking parts of the club. His own venerable cue in its black metal case is dated 1953, so it must have been about then. The club holds other, more unsettling memories for me. It was there, at an even earlier age, perhaps nine or ten, that I was taken to learn the rudiments of the noble art of self defence from a tough-looking ex-Army sergeant who had just spent the war training Chindits or Gurkhas or some such fearsome fighting force. His pained expression on first examining my frail physique – I was under four feet high and little over five stones in weight – is one I shall always remember with discomfort, along with the smell of wintergreen ointment, the boxing steps that were drilled into us by numbers, and the ironic nickname I acquired in the gym – 'Bruiser'. The rudiments were all I ever seemed able to absorb, though I must have absorbed something, since I find I slip naturally into the correct pugilistic posture at the first hint of family horseplay. A more receptive pupil at the time was a battered young fighter called Pat Poacher, who later became a contender for the British light-heavyweight title.

My grounding in the rudiments of snooker was sadly less professional, with the result that I have never set the green baize alight (or even singed it, to be honest). But the huge enjoyment I get from the game, and the fanlike respect I have for its more highly skilled practitioners, dates back to that early introduction at the Radford Social Club. Like golf, snooker is a game that people badly want to play well, and indeed one can play it well, if only for a few shots at a time – just enough for a tantalizing glimpse of the radiance, the winning glow, that keeps one playing on in hope through a lifetime of near misses and best forgotten disasters.

My father and I went back recently to the Radford Social Club for a game. The room had changed – four tables instead of eight and no man in charge to keep the waiting list and handle the betting slips. They have a 50p meter on the wall. But the atmosphere and the look of it were much the same; even the same cryptic sign, 'Smoking and the tossing of coins is forbidden.' The accents are much the same, too – mostly the thin nasal whine of the Midlands, but more Irish and fewer Geordies than I recall, and still no blacks. The members seemed very much older. While I was there, we stood in silent respect in the snooker room in memory of three members who had died that week. The clicking of the balls suddenly ceased and the men (and one woman) stood at attention with their cues at their sides like rifles while 'Abide with Me' creaked through the loudspeaker. My father said the dead were removed from the lists, so that every year, when new membership cards were issued, you found you were several numbers lower than before. When you got down to single figures you were in the Death Squad: he had been a member since 1938 and was now number 63. While he was telling me this, I won our match with a barefaced fluke on the black.

The billiard room at the Eccentric Club, near St James's Square in London, is a far grander place, with three of the truest and finest carved tables in the land, set on three-inch Welsh blue slate. These have drawn many great players to this room, including the legendary Joe Davis, whose cue is still preserved there in a glass case like a holy relic. The club was used chiefly by showbiz figures such as George Robey, Dan Leno and Little Tich. I came across it by accident, through being a member of the Lord's Taverners, who use it by special arrangement. The most eccentric thing in the Eccentric Club is the clock in the bar, which moves anticlockwise, as if reflected in a mirror. The club is on the site of the old Dieudonne Hotel, where Tchaikovsky used to stay. An even more distinguished patron was King Edward VII, who used it as a *maison de rendezvous*. The raffish Edwardian spirit is preserved in the billiard room, where the walls are adorned by risqué posters and pictures, mainly of pneumatic actresses in various stages of undress. When I was last there, someone had casually placed a sign in front of a semi-erotic picture of a naked lady doing her hair in a mirror. It read 'Ties must be worn at all times.'

The Eccentric Club has been closed for some time for refurbishment, so much of my snooker has been played at the Garrick. The snooker room on the top floor has space for only one table and is furnished rather more severely than the Eccentric, with a brown leather bench and a club fender and old prints of actors, rather than actresses, on the wall. A bronze bust of Sir Edward Clarke, KC (1841–1931), author of learned tomes on the Prayer Book and the Church of England, keeps a beady eye on proceedings. If you look more closely, however, there are hints of a racier past. Pinned low on the wall beside Sir Edward's plinth is an undated poster that must go back to the last century. It is headed: 'Rules, Penalties and Customs Appertaining to the game of Savile Snooker as played by members of the Savile and Garrick Clubs on the Occasions of their Annual Games Contest.' There follow references to Pyramids and Snooker Pool, games which were forerunners of snooker. The point of Savile Snooker was to pot the fifteen red balls without touching any colours; if you did, you paid a penalty and a cash fine to all the other side.

'It is usual,' the rules state, 'for keen watchers to summon laggards to the table with cries of "Savile watchers" or "Garrick watchers", as the case may be.' What this rumbustious scene would have been like may be gauged from a large painting on the wall by Henry O'Neil, ARA, a Garrick member who included himself in the canvas along with Trollope and the Marquis of Anglesey. It shows dozens of eager young toffs on a gambling night out, all straining for a sight of the green baize like the crowd round the surgeon's operating table in Rembrandt's *Anatomy Lesson*. The scene is the Garrick in 1869 and shows the men playing with coloured balls, probably Pyramids, one of the immediate precursors of snooker, which wasn't known as such until six years later. If they *were* playing snooker itself – or even Savile Snooker, as they might well have been from the picture – then the official history of the game would need to be rewritten.

It is worth reading on to the end of these extraordinary 'rules' for Savile/Garrick Snooker, even though this can be done only with difficulty by sitting on the floor and peering closely. 'In the event of the yellow ball being involved in a foul stroke,' it says, 'it is the custom for the watchers to cry out the word "Bollocks".' It concludes: 'When the tenth red ball has been potted, a short interval for all purposes is usually permitted. Feelings may possibly have risen high by this time, and, during this brief period of relaxation and refreshment for mind and body, players will have the opportunity of reminding both themselves and each other that Savile Snooker is, after all, only a game.'

There was once a sacrilegious move by certain members to have the Garrick snooker room converted into bedrooms, but a stop was soon put to that. Talking of sacrilege, I took my wife up to play one lively evening in the Garrick soon after we were married, and discovered to my surprise that she could play quite well; she explained that she had been taught by her brother on a table at home. The following evening, as it happened, she was seated at a dinner party next to an elderly man wearing the Garrick's unmistakable salmon and cucumber tie, who mentioned that he was on the club committee. When my wife said she had played me on the Garrick snooker table the night before, she was alarmed to see his face go the colour of his tie. On subsequent visits to the club I have several times caught this man's disapproving glance; whether this was for allowing a woman to play at all on the holy baize, or for allowing her to beat me on the black, I've never been quite sure. On holiday once we found an old snooker table in the basement of the Savoy Hotel in Madeira: some character who was idly watching us play nearly swallowed his cigar as my wife sank a long blue.

More recently, we have had a small table at home, on which the whole family can work off their rivalries, while my younger daughter, aged five, takes the balls out of the pockets and puts them neatly in the box. The first time she ever saw the coloured balls whizzing around she giggled in excitement from her high chair. Even now, when she sees snooker on the television, she can be heard to mutter 'Daddy's balls', which has been known to startle visitors. One of my teenage sons practises hard to beat me and usually succeeds. On one occasion a friend, arriving for Sunday lunch, came down to the basement, looked round the door and retreated in a state of unbelieving shock to tell my wife:

'There's a little old lady down there potting snooker balls like crazy.' That was my mother.

At the *Observer* my interest in snooker is tolerated as a kind of harmless eccentricity, as if I indulged in numismatics or secret drinking, rather as people accepted my predecessor's somewhat obsessive concern for the rights of the Naga tribesmen. 'I don't suppose J. L. Garvin watched much snooker,' Alan Watkins said. Probably not; but I was told that another of my predecessors in the editorial chair, Ivor Brown, the theatre critic and Shakespearean scholar, had been known to spend some time at a snooker room near the old *Observer* office in Tudor Street. Fortunately (unfortunately, my wife would say), there is a club just round the corner from our new office in Queen Victoria Street. It is called 'Duffers' and is tucked under Farringdon railway arches, about fifty yards from Ludgate Circus. The trains can be heard rumbling overhead on their way to suburbia from Holborn Viaduct, to places like Sevenoaks, Beckenham and St Mary Cray. 'There go the commuters,' one of my colleagues is fond of saying, with the smug superiority of the inner city man, as he bends to concentrate on his next shot. 'Duffers', founded by Robin Arbuthnot, is so named because members are not expected to play well. That would be regarded as bad form and might even result in expulsion if a member were to make a fifty break. From what I've seen, there is little danger of that.

The club's list of founding members includes the Maharajah of Cooch Behar (of whom more later), Viscount Arbuthnot, Sir Henry Plumb, Jean-Marc Heidseck of the champagne family, and 'Whispering' Ted Lowe, the TV commentator – an index of its aspiration to be regarded as a gentlemen's club which just happens to be crammed full of snooker tables, and certainly not to be confused with those sleazy saloons over high street shops that have fallen on hard times. The style is red plush and Victorian prints and cartoons. Apart from luminaries from nearby Fleet Street, it is patronized by young men in waistcoats who sound like commodity brokers. I once saw Lord Matthews, then head of the *Express* group, playing there with Lord Marsh when a blonde in a fur coat suddenly materialized by their table to deliver a singing telegram. The press baron, looking vaguely irritated at this interruption to his game, watched without expression as the fur coat was slipped off to reveal skimpy black underwear, then turned back to the table, chalked his cue, and played his next shot. 'No style,' somebody muttered as she shuffled away, and I don't think he was referring either to the embarrassed model or to his lordship's cueing action.

A false rumour was put about that I used 'Duffers' as a form of staff therapy, inviting journalists there when I knew they wanted a pay rise or felt the urge to give expression to some other complaint about their treatment – my supposed theory being that all imagined wrongs would pale into insignificance and all grievances be mysteriously defused by the calming effect of the green baize. Not at all: the therapy is actually for *me*. I can just visualize my hard-pressed executives, at the end of a long day, muttering 'Where the hell's the editor gone?', then rolling their eyes heavenwards in silent exasperation – none more so than my long-suffering deputy, Anthony Howard, whose eyes take on a glaze of boredom at the merest mention of sport. 'Calls it research for his book, I suppose,' he has been heard to mutter on such occasions.

Once, in the early days of a new ownership of the *Observer*, I found myself in a City boardroom defending a particular columnist against adverse comments by some of the directors. One of them asserted decisively, as if to silence all argument: 'I was talking about the *Observer* yesterday to the chairman of a merchant bank. He thought the paper had improved, but mentioned C [the controversial columnist] as one of its least attractive features.' 'That's funny,' I heard myself saying in reply, 'but I happened to be playing snooker last night with the Archdeacon of London and the Dean of St Paul's and they both said C was the main reason they bought the paper.' The board were silenced by this bizarre piece of ecclesiastical name dropping, as well they might be, but more than one of them looked at me curiously with a dawning (and, as it happens, totally unjustified) suspicion that they might have been having their legs pulled. The truth was that Robin Arbuthnot had indeed invited some clerics into 'Duffers' the night before as part of the opening celebrations. He may have been prompted to do this by the fact that the club's showpiece table, with magnificently carved legs, had been acquired from the house of the late Canon Collins, the CND pioneer, in Amen Court in the shadow of St Paul's Cathedral up the road.

None of my colleagues would claim to play with any great distinction – though the News Editor, the Economics Editor, the Industrial Editor and the Sports Editor might dispute that, and we all have our moments. Geoffrey Wheatcroft, editor of 'Londoner's Diary' in the *Standard* and former literary editor of the *Spectator*, is always liable to ring up for a game at the most improbable times of day or night. There is considerable rivalry among critics such as Martin Amis and Julian Barnes. Amis, who takes all games very seriously, is skilled at lining up his next shot but one with his cue in a most professional manner, an art doubtless perfected in his time as a TV critic – or perhaps from reading Stephen Potter on gamesmanship:

In Snooker the usual practice is to walk quickly up to the table, squat half down on the haunches to look at sight lines, move to the other end of the table to look at sight lines of balls which may come into play later on in the break which you are supposed to be planning. Decide on the shot. Frame up for it and then at the last moment see some obvious red shot which you had 'missed', and which your opponent and everybody else will have noticed before you moved to the table, and which they know is the shot you are going to play in the end anyhow.

Once, when I found myself in a regrettable public wrangle with my proprietor, Martin's letter of support consisted of the two words, 'Snooker him!' I also recall with some embarrass-ment a sixtieth birthday party I gave at the Garrick for Kingsley Amis – rather too much of which was spent by the host and the chief guest's son in the snooker room, where people like Clive James, Hugh McIlvanney and Julian Barnes joined us in a game more reminiscent of the lively old Garrick/Savile Snooker than anything practised by the Davis families.

Once, on a train journey to London, my mother-in-law met a young man who politely asked if she minded if he smoked (it was in the restaurant car). She noticed that he had a huge wad of fivers in his back pocket. When she arrived home she startled everyone with the announcement: 'I've just met a snooker player on the train with the most beautiful manners. His name was Higgins. Have you heard of him?' More recently, I was messing around on a table belonging to some friends in the basement of a manor house near Bath, when a village boy wandered in off the street. For his benefit I played a flashy shot which sent the balls crashing around the table and, surprisingly, two or three reds dropped into pockets. The boy looked up in wide-eyed astonishment: 'I know you,' he said. 'I've seen you on the telly. You're Hurricane Higgins!' Of the few bouquets that life has thrown my way, this one smelt the sweetest!

## Chapter Two

# BACK TO THE RAJ

I was making my way out of 'Duffers' one day when the owner, Robin Arbuthnot, called me over and introduced me to a dusky gentleman with whom he was playing an unusual game of snooker. It turned out that it wasn't, in fact, snooker at all but 'Slosh', a game that had evidently found much favour with Indian princelings in the time of the British Raj. This helps to explain why I suddenly found myself shaking hands with the Maharajah of Cooch Behar. 'Slosh', he explained, was an early variation of billiards, using many coloured balls to make it more interesting. The red, for example, scored twenty, which meant that you got twenty points if you potted one – but lost twenty if you missed. In practice, I gathered, it wasn't just points you played for in the old days, but hundreds of pounds, or thousands of rupees, or elephants, or jewels, or whatever happened to be the gambling currency of the time.

The point of games like 'Slosh' was to allow more than two people to play on the table, which was all that billiards (with one red and two white balls) allowed. This was especially appreciated by young Indian Army officers on long rainy afternoons in the mess. Another sociable variation was 'Pyramids', where there were fifteen reds and all the other players handed over an agreed stake to the man who potted one. In 'Life Pool' the aim was to pot your opponent's ball: three pots and he was dead. Then he could buy another 'life' and so on. The white potted the yellow, the yellow the green, etc. The rules for some of these games seemed to be variations of card games. In 'Black Pool' you aimed to sink a black after every red and collected cash all round if you did so. Joe Davis gambled at a similar game with Derbyshire miners in the 1920s; it was called 'Pink Pool'. Alex Higgins was playing 'Life Pool' for cash in the Jampot, the billiard hall in Belfast, as recently as twenty years ago. The scoreboard in Dennis Taylor's snooker room in Blackburn is an old Life Pool marker.

When I asked the Maharajah how he came to know about these games, he answered simply: 'It was my ancestor who first codified the rules of snooker.' Then he waved a hand airily towards a companion and asked me: 'Do you know Jaipur?' It turned out that he didn't mean that beautiful part of India which covers 5000 square miles and contains 2.5 million people, nor even the Maharajah of that ilk, but his brother. Even so, two Indian princes is more than you usually expect to come across in a London snooker club on a weekday afternoon. I found these exotic connections very surprising – a far cry from the normal grotty associations of run-down billiard halls – and decided to check. It was all perfectly true.

The opulent life style of these Maharajahs in their pink and white scented palaces in the foothills of the Himalayas during the days of the Raj is beautifully evoked by Gayatri Devi, who managed to be both the daughter of a Maharajah of Cooch Behar and the wife of a Maharajah of Jaipur (Jai Singh, the polo-playing friend of Prince Philip, who died playing polo in Britain in 1970). Winter in Calcutta, spring in Darjeeling, the gaiety, the balls, the clothes, the fancy-dress parties, the festivals, the riding, the tiger shooting, the accounts at Harrods, the cricket – and always, of course, the billiard room, which had a specially hallowed place in family life.

The princess recalls in her memoirs: 'It was only a generation later, when my mother arrived in Cooch Behar in an open car, that purdah suddenly ended – except, of course, in the billiard room.' Of her grandfather she says:

One conversation with him lives clearly in my memory. I had gone to say goodnight to him. He was, as always at that time of day, at the billiard table. He stopped his game and said, in a friendly way,
  'Ah, I see you're off to bed. I hope you have a good sleep.'

I explained to him that there was no question of sleep for some time to come as I had to think about all that had happened during the day.

'No, no,' he said, gently but emphatically.

'If you go to bed, you should sleep. If you are reading, you should read. If you are eating, you should eat. And if you are thinking, then you should think. Never mix the different activities. No good ever comes of it, and what's more, you can't enjoy – neither can you profit from – any of them.'

Then, because he was playing billiards, he turned back to the table and gave the game his undivided attention once more. He lived by the clock all his life and did everything in strict order: up at sunrise, walk or ride, work until lunch, brief rest, work until tea, recreation, evening work, supper, reading. It had been the same for fifty years.

Life was not always so well ordered, however, for her father only became Maharajah after his elder brother had deliberately drunk himself to death on champagne out of frustrated love for an English actress whom his family forbade him to marry. The princess's own parents had eloped for a sensational marriage in London because of family objections. By a curious coincidence, Dennis Taylor found himself seated next to the Maharani at a dinner in India a few years ago, when he was playing some exhibitions there and she was campaigning to become an MP. They got on famously together – so much so that she jokingly asked Dennis if he would campaign for her around the country telling his jokes, but substituting Sikhs for the Irish.

The Jaipur family's connection with billiards went back more than a century. John Roberts, the W. G. Grace of the game, who was the English champion for much of the second half of the nineteenth century, went on a tour of India and, in the absence of a railway, chartered some elephants to carry billiard tables to Jaipur. The Maharajah, a renowned sportsman, not only ordered half a dozen tables, but dubbed Roberts his court billiards player for life, with a retainer of £500 a year and expenses to cover an annual return visit. Roberts and his wife were housed in a palace of their own with a hundred servants. He coached the Maharajah and brought over mutton-chopped billiards players from England, at vast expense, to entertain him. For one of these tournaments the Maharajah shelled out £5000 to bring players over, then abandoned the opening match out of boredom after Roberts had potted twenty reds in succession. His opponent, F. W. Stanley, having come ten thousand miles to play only one shot, never forgave Roberts for this and scarcely recovered from the experience.

Roberts eventually opened a billiard table factory of his own in Calcutta. On one of his visits to the City of Dreadful Night he was introduced to the Maharajah of Cooch Behar, the ancestor of the man in 'Duffers', by a young subaltern in the Devonshire Regiment called Neville Chamberlain. At this historic meeting in the Calcutta Club in 1885, Cooch Behar passed on the rules of snooker, which he had written down, and Roberts took the game home to Britain. That is now the accepted official version of how it all began. Snooker had become the favourite variation of billiards for officers of the 11th Devonshire Regiment stationed at Jubbulpore. Chamberlain, the man credited with inventing the name, recalled for Sir Compton Mackenzie many years later how it happened. A young officer had just arrived from the Royal Military Academy at Woolwich and mentioned to Chamberlain that the slang for a raw recruit there was 'a snooker', meaning the lowest of the low (probably corrupted from the French *neux*, the original word for a cadet). Chamberlain went on:

The term was a new one to me but I soon had the opportunity of exploiting it when one of our party failed to hole a coloured ball which was close to a corner pocket. I called out to him: 'Why, you're a regular snooker!'
I had to explain to the company the definition of the word, and to soothe the feelings of the culprit I added that we were all, so to speak, snookers at the game, so it would be appropriate to call the game Snooker. The suggestion was adopted with enthusiasm and the game has been called Snooker ever since.

All this history came out in 1938 because a *Times* correspondence had been provoked by a controversial claim in the *Field* that the great Lord Kitchener had himself taken out the rules for snooker from Woolwich to the Army in India. (Even as late as 1937, it had been confidently asserted in print that the game was invented by a certain 'Captain Snooker, an officer in the Bengal Lancers'.) General Sir Ian Hamilton pointed out that Kitchener had not visited India until many years after snooker had become established. It was at this point that Compton Mackenzie discovered Neville (by then Sir Neville) Chamberlain, still thankfully alive and living in retirement at Ascot in his eighties. Sir Neville's claim was supported by a whole battalion of distinguished figures, including Major-General W. A. Watson, Colonel of Chamberlain's old regiment, the Central India Horse, Major-General Sir John Hanbury-Williams, Sir Walter Lawrence, and Field Marshal Lord Birdwood, who recalled Chamberlain personally introducing snooker into the mess of the 12th Lancers at Bangalore. These curious facts all emerged in the same year that another Neville Chamberlain, the prime minister (no relation), was snookered by Hitler at Munich.

There can be no room for doubt, in the light of all this evidence, that Chamberlain invented the word snooker in British India and also spread the game wherever he went. But I still have a sneaking feeling that the game of snooker itself (or something very like it) may have started in a London club in the 1860s and then found its way out to India, probably (but not certainly) through the Army, before being taken up there and sent back. Full-size billiard tables, some of them magnificent objects, have been found in all the outposts of Empire, such as tea estates in Africa and Ceylon. That picture in the Garrick Club in London, dated 1869 – sixteen years before Roberts's historic meeting in Calcutta with the Maharajah of Cooch Behar – makes me think we still haven't had the definitive account of snooker's origins. Something new may still emerge from yellowing club files, just as the Chamberlain story itself emerged, almost by accident, in 1938.

Chamberlain was the son of an Indian Army colonel and married a general's daughter. He was with the Devonshires in India from 1873–6 before moving to the Central India Horse and then to the Afghan war, in which he was wounded and decorated. Later he fought the Burma campaign, reorganized the Kashmir Army, commanded the Khyber force, was private secretary to Field Marshal Lord Roberts in the Boer War, in which he again won battle honours, and ended his career as Inspector-General of the Royal Irish Constabulary. He died in 1944 at the age of 88.

Everywhere Chamberlain went on his campaigns he seemed to carry a snooker cue in his knapsack. After he was wounded in the Afghan war in 1880, for example, he was posted to the staff of the Commander-in-Chief of the Madras Army, and went with him when they moved to the summer hill station at Ootacamund. Because of Chamberlain's zeal, snooker came to be the speciality of the Ooty Club, where the rules of the game were drawn up and posted in the billiards room. I first heard of this shrine to snooker from Nigel Havers and James Fox, the actors, who made a pilgrimage there while filming *A Passage to India*. Trevor Fishlock, then *The Times* correspondent in India, recalled turning up at the Ooty Club without a jacket and tie and being reminded by a servant's discreet Jeevesian cough, more than a quarter century after the British had withdrawn, that standards were still standards.

In the Ooty Club, of all places, a game of snooker is the proper *digestif*, for this is the source, the temple. The room itself is entered through a door properly fitted with a peephole, marked 'Wait for Stroke', so that you do not in ungentlemanly fashion cause distress at the table. The room has ceiling beams and white walls hung with the skulls and heads of nineteen beasts and with large pictures of the Defence of Rorke's Drift, the Retreat from Moscow, the Battle of Tel el-Kebir and the Charge of the Light Brigade. There are a number of wicker-backed chairs for spectators and a sturdy chair presented by Captain Winterbotham of the Madras Miners and Sappers in 1875.

It has a handsome table over which, if you are fortunate, you may be permitted to lean and sight your cue almost as a kind of obeisance. The room's furnishings are redolent of leisured snookery evenings, joshing and cigar smoke, as the balls click, spin and glide across the faded baize. On the wall near the cue rack there are framed accounts and letters testifying to the origin of the game and its curious name.

Ootacamund is set a mile above the lowlands of southern India among the Nilgiri Hills. It is reached by rail or a long winding road. In the club there are mounted heads of animals and sepia photographs of the colonels and captains who departed long ago. It is polished as immaculately as ever, with plump sofas and split leather armchairs, copies of old magazines and notices about the Ooty Hunt (which evidently still exists, though in a much reduced form).

When I met Rajiv Gandhi, the Indian prime minister, I told him how the game of snooker had its origins in places like the Ooty Club. He was genuinely surprised and, I thought, rather pleased to learn of this curious fragment from his country's imperial past. He was later pictured opening the World Amateur Billiards Championship in New Delhi with a neat-looking shot across the green baize.

Billiards, of course, is a much more ancient game and is said to derive from field games with balls and sticks originally devised by the Greeks and Romans. The word 'billiard', like the French *billard*, descends from 'ball' words like *billa* (Medieval Latin) and *bille* (French) and 'stick' words like *billart* (Old French). 'Cue' derives from *queue*, French for tail, from the practice of striking the ball with the 'tail' or small end of a mace when the ball was trapped under the lip of a cushion. From about 1400, illustrations show a lawn game, like croquet, called 'paille malle' in which players are using French billiard maces and wooden balls of the type which are familiar in later engravings and woodcuts. Pall Mall, the famous London street, derives its name from this game.

An American, William Hendricks, went to the trouble of compiling *A Compleat Historie of Billiards Evolution*, which he published as a private pamphlet. He shows that Louis XI of France (1461–83) led a fashion for billiard tables among the French nobility. So we must assume that it was between 1350 and 1450 that billiards ceased being an outdoor sport and became miniaturized and converted into an indoor recreation.

By the age of Elizabeth there were many public tables in London, as shown by references in Spenser, Shakespeare and Jonson, as well as private tables in the more advanced country houses. The two social scales on which billiards and snooker have always been played – as a relaxation for the upper class and a gambling game for the lower orders – was there from the start. In 1588 the Duke of Norfolk (whose family were to give their name to the Norfolk Street in which the Sheffield Crucible now stands) was said to own a 'billyard bord covered with a green cloth . . . three billyard sticks and eleven balls of ivory'. A year earlier, Mary Queen of Scots had complained shortly before her execution at Fotheringay Castle that her 'table de billiard' had been taken away. The point of this move became gruesomely clear later when her captors ripped off the cloth to wrap her head in it.

The plural, 'billiards', first appears in English in 1591, according to the *Oxford English Dictionary*. A decade later it appears in *Antony and Cleopatra* (Act 2, Scene 5), when Cleopatra says:

> Give me music – music, moody food
> Of us that trade in love . . .
> Let it alone! Let's to billiards. Come, Charmian.

She makes some dubious-sounding pleasantry about women and eunuchs being unsuitable for the game (which is presumably a ribald quip about balls to amuse the groundlings at the Globe) – then changes her mind and goes fishing instead. As some joker pointed out to me, the Serpent of old Nile does not, as one might have expected, propose that they play Pyramids.

In 1674 the *Complete Gamester* describes billiards as 'a most gentile, cleanly and ingenious game'. By the early eighteenth century virtually every café in Paris boasted a table. The game was transported to America by English and French colonists. Potting and scoring 'in-off' were recorded by 1770, by which time a red ball had also appeared. The 'cannon' (making the cue ball strike the other two balls in the same shot) was imported from Carombola, a game still played in Spain, France and

Belgium. The 'Carom' was a word of Indian origin for a round sour fruit. The Carom or Cannon became such an obsession with the French that they gave up potting balls altogether and designed tables without any pockets. In Britain, however, the cannon did not replace the potting game but was absorbed into it – though some tables with no pockets have come to light here from time to time (the *Birmingham Post* recently showed a painting of one found in Malvern).

The mace turned into a recognizable cue around 1800 and quickly made the game more popular in taverns, coffee houses and public gaming rooms. Thurston, the London furniture manufacturer, went over completely to making billiard tables and equipment in 1814. He made Napoleon's table, which is still intact at Longwood House on St Helena, where Gavin Young saw it recently. Wooden balls were replaced by ivory from the centre of the female elephant tusk; until then ivory balls had been a luxury for aristocrats. By the end of the century about 12,000 elephants a year were being sacrificed for the billiard tables of Britain. Cushions, originally there just to stop the balls falling off the table, were stuffed with cotton to make them rebound and thereafter became an integral part of the game. The value of chalk on the cue was first appreciated by John Carr, a marker at John Bartley's billiards rooms at Bath, who started selling it. Before that players used to twist the point of their cues in the plaster of a wall or ceiling to secure more grip on the ball. Carr and Bartley were the first to use 'side' or spin on the cue ball.

A French infantry captain, Mingaud, experimented with a leather tip while he was in a Paris jail for debt and astounded everyone when he came out with his control of the cue ball. He also invented a way of swerving the ball by hitting it vertically from a great height – a shot known as a *massé* (from mace) – which is still used by professionals to swerve round a ball when snookered by their opponent.

By this time, the end of the eighteenth century, the game had spread more widely on the continent, certainly to Vienna. One afternoon during the 1985 world championship, when there happened to be no play because a match had finished unexpectedly early, I called in at a Sheffield cinema to see *Amadeus*. Part way through the film I was astonished to see Mozart composing *The Marriage of Figaro* on a sort of billiard table. I made enquiries and found that Mozart's addiction to the game was such an important feature of his life that in the *Oxford Companion to Music* Percy Scholes includes a special page, entitled 'Mozart and the Billiard Table'. It carries an illustration specially drawn by the artist Oswald Barrett ('Batt' of the *Radio Times*) of the composer at a table of French design with no pockets.

The entry in the *Oxford Companion to Music* reads:

Ball games, particularly billiards and bowls, were greatly to his liking. There is little doubt that he pursued these games not merely for their own sake but because he found in the movement and control of a rolling ball a congenial accompaniment to the movement within his own copious and productive mind.

Instances are recorded of his stopping in the middle of a game to make notes, or of his humming, as he played, a theme which was later found in one of his works. Moreover, he was particularly fond of playing billiards alone, keeping his notebook handy – though the notes he made were always the briefest indication of an idea, for he did his actual composing 'in his head'.

The ever-flowing rhythms in his mind induced him incessantly to tap his fob, a table, a chair-back, or anything to hand, and there is no doubt that he spent some of his most fruitful hours alone at the billiard table.

From 1826 Thurston in London began to experiment with slate instead of wood as a table bed surface and gradually brought the manufacture of tables to perfection. Slate not only guaranteed a level playing surface but was resistant to wear and easy to handle and cut. The slate used to come from South Wales, but is now mostly imported from Portugal and Italy, where the Mafia is said to have cornered the market. Some early beds were made of iron and can still be found rusting in Ireland. Until recently there was a table with a massive cast-iron bed in a Liverpool staff canteen. The early cushions were strips of felt and other substances, such as hair, Russian duck and white swanskin, were tried before rubber was introduced in 1835. This was affected by cold temperatures, for which cushion warmers had to be made, until the vulcanizing process solved the problem. Queen Victoria took delivery of a table with vulcanized rubber cushions in 1845. The only major improvement to cushions since then has been a steel block behind the rubber to make the rebounds more predictable. The 'spider', a rest with its business end raised up on legs to enable the player to strike over the top of balls obstructing the path to the cue ball, comes from an American word for a sort of long-handled pan on legs.

In 1870 an American, John Wesley Hyatt, the man who invented ball bearings, patented a synthetic plastic, made from collodion, a hardening mixture that printers used to rub on their hands. This was celluloid, and billiard balls became one of its many by-products – others were false teeth and piano keys. Celluloid was much cheaper than ivory and more easy to manoeuvre on the table. One early problem was that it was also highly inflammable, so that a ball struck too hard was liable to explode. Fortunately, the new balls retained the characteristic click of ivory, which had become as vital a part of the game as the sound of a leather cricket ball on willow. The balls were to go through many controversial stages in both size and substance – ivories, crystalate, bonzoloid, phenoloid, vilalile – before they reached their present standard composition.

Today's super-crystalate balls are made by high technology. A number of chemicals are mixed in a huge resin kettle for two days until they are like glue, then poured into glass bulbs, which are baked hard and left to cool. The bulbs are then smashed and the substance inside is turned and ground into a perfectly rounded snooker ball. The balls are then heat treated again, ground again, measured, polished and weighed. They have to be exactly $2\frac{1}{16}$ inches in diameter (the pocket is $3\frac{1}{2}$ inches wide).

Apart from the cloth, nothing fundamental has happened to the technology of the table itself since the introduction of slate by Thurston 160 years ago (though fibre-glass beds have been tried and an all-weather surface of coated steel has recently been developed – it was tried out underwater by two divers in a hotel swimming-pool in Kent). The table first used by the BBC programme *Pot Black* had been made by Thurston's in 1907, and had meanwhile resided at the home of Joe Davis. The woods most commonly used are mahogany, oak and walnut. The 1¾ inch slates weigh more than a ton, so that the balance is unaffected even when a player as huge as Canadian Bill Werbeniuk, who weighs over twenty stone, lies across it to play a shot. The tables are always assembled on the spot for a championship and are taken to pieces and reassembled before the final. Steve Davis has been known to sit in the hall and watch intently as a match table is put together. In recent years a good deal of work has gone into standardizing the size and shape of the pockets, which are undoubtedly more retentive than before the Second World War. (For championships, anyway: there are still plenty of tight pockets left on club tables, especially the ones I always seem to play on.) The main manufacturers of tables now are BCE and Riley, though dozens of others have sprung up in the snooker boom.

The cloth for modern tables is made from fine merino wool imported from Queensland, Australia. The cloth has nearly always been dyed green, presumably to resemble grass, though Cliff Thorburn once played on a red cloth with yellow balls in Canada. Jeremy Isaacs, head of Channel Four, believes the green has been an important factor in snooker's late-night popularity: viewers evidently find it soothing to look at. In 1924 a pro called Tom Tothill – a flamboyant character with an eye for the ladies, who was later taken up by Horatio Bottomley, the infamous charlatan and fraudster – actually introduced a green cue. 'This exciting invention relieves eye strain and sharpens the vision,' he claimed. 'The green tint of the shaft contrasts with the white ball, at the same time hiding the grain of the wood.' It was a commercial flop.

The wool for the cloth is washed in thousands of gallons of softened water, made into threads, sprayed with an emulsion of oil and water, blended, corded, combed out, warped and woven, squeezed under rollers, scoured, milled, layered, trimmed and dyed – among many other mysterious processes which create the perfect nap. The ball runs more truly towards the black spot; a ball played from that end to a middle pocket, against the nap, will curl slightly towards the near jaw, even on a championship table. It is rather like golfers having to read the nap of a putting green, which is why snooker players can be seen staring fiercely at the table from time to time and then removing an offending piece of fluff.

For most snooker players, as with golfers' clubs, the cue is the most sensitive instrument of all. For serious players there is never any question of simply taking any old cue down from the club rack. They have all had the same cue for years and would never dream of using any other; in fact, some would say they were unable to play at all with any cue other than their own. A reporter on the *Observer* was once astonished to hear Ray Reardon say that he might have to cancel an exhibition match at a holiday camp because he had left his cue at home in Wales. Fortunately, his wife came racing down by car with it.

Alex Higgins ran into a period of trouble, both personal and professional, when his cue, a Burwat champion of which he was inordinately proud, was broken a few months after he had won his first world championship in 1972; a hotel porter had trodden on it. 'I'd lost my cue and I'd lost my confidence,' he said. 'I was walking wounded. I was easy meat for anybody. Everything started to come unglued. I've been messing about with different cues ever since, and I've never found anything that I've 200 per cent confidence in. I'm not happy with the cue I've got, though it's just been re-butted and Fred Davis says it's like a piece of steel. I keep harking back to my first and best cue. There are about 40 lying about in my house and I keep on experimenting, doctoring one up at a time and trying it out. But it's like looking for the proverbial needle in a haystack.'

Steve Davis was given his cue at the age of 17 by an old man, Dick Sharples, who brushed and ironed the tables and retipped the cues at Plumstead Common Working Men's Club. It was his most prized possession and he gave it to Steve shortly before he died because he had frequently watched him practise at the club and could see his potential. Seven years later, Davis won the world championship with it. 'I've stuck with that cue,' he says, 'and it's never let me down. It never leaves my side. It's the tool of my trade. I care for it in the same way as Boycott cares for his bats and Borg his rackets.'

Joe Davis bought the cue that he used throughout his fifty-year career for seven shillings and sixpence from an amateur called Fred Fraser in the Parish Church Institute in Chesterfield. 'Over the years,' he said, 'it was a great source of worry to me to know that if anything ever happened to one piece of ash, 4 feet 7 inches long and weighing 16½ ounces, I would be sunk.' In fact, something did happen to it – it was stolen off the platform at Victoria in 1948 and handed in, undamaged, at Tooting police station two days later, amid much press hullabaloo. Manufacturers were always making new cues for Joe Davis to try, including an aluminium one, the Apollo, which was a brief marketing sensation. But he always stuck by his old friend. This is the cue that now rests in a glass case on a wall, like a holy relic, in the Eccentric Club in London. Joe gave his younger brother Fred a cue in 1932 which he has used ever since.

The value of having the same cue is largely psychological, but no less important for that in a game where confidence can be more than half the battle. It is probably no coincidence that a restless man like Alex Higgins should have many cues, while men of steadier temperament like Joe, Fred and Steve Davis and Ray Reardon should stick to the same one. The key elements in a good cue are that it is dead straight (which is rarer than you might think, since no two pieces of timber are the same) and that the length and weight correspond to the height and reach of the player. Many amateurs use cues that are too long for them. Higgins prefers one as stiff as a poker. Silvino Francisco used four different cues in the same match at the Rothmans tournament in 1985.

The best cues are made from sporting ash, though Canadian maple is more popular in North America because of its stable moisture content in centrally heated rooms. Different hard woods are worked into the butt. The cues are sawn, spliced, milled, dyed, glued, aligned, tapered, sanded, sealed, weighed and balanced to perfection. Professionals used to experiment with much heavier cues, but most have now settled for sixteen to seventeen ounces. This may be partly because the balls are lighter these days.

An incident in 1938 forced the introduction of a rule that the cue 'must be at least three feet in length'. This was when a London professional, Alec Brown, produced a tiny ebony cue (called a 'fountain pen cue') from his waistcoat pocket in a match at Thurston's to help him play out of a pack of reds. It had been made specially for such situations by his father, who ran the billiard room at the Piccadilly Hotel. But Thurston's famous referee, Charlie Chambers (whom J. B. Priestley once likened to the Mad Hatter), awarded an historic foul which ended this ploy for ever. In his youth Alec Brown had been the Jimmy White of his day, a deadly potter who missed reaching the very top because of the war. He took up TT racing on the Isle of Man, and when he was forced to retire from snooker because of arthritis he returned to building car and motor-bike engines.

The only major design change has come in the past decade, with the introduction of two-piece cues with a wooden or metal joint in the middle. These are less likely to warp, bend out of true or be damaged in transit. They are easier to carry around, especially in cars or as cabin luggage in aeroplanes. Steve Davis still has a single stick, which he carries around with him every-where in a carefully guarded, elongated gun case, but most of the top players have gone over to the two-piece. John Spencer was the first player to win the world championship with such a cue in 1977 after his own had been smashed into four pieces in a car crash three years before. Even though it was lovingly restored, he never had the same confidence in it and picked up a Canadian cue just before the tournament. Curiously, after winning the world title, Spencer then swapped it for a Japanese cue, another two-piece. Even though Spencer continued winning tournaments for several years, some people say he was never quite the same player after his first cue was smashed (though it was evidently a ram-shackle old thing that nobody else could play with). Dennis Taylor's cue was originally two parts of a three-piece half butt that he joined together. It is two inches longer than the one he had before.

Clark McConachy, a tough New Zealand champion, actually gave his favourite cue away to an attractive lady player, Thelma Carpenter, while staying at her parents' hotel in Bournemouth.

He was too gallant (or too stubborn or too shy) to ask for it back
when he realized, as he soon did, what a terrible mistake he had
made. Joe Davis said later: 'From that moment his play
deteriorated and I do not recall his playing really well again.'

An even worse case was that of Willie Smith, who had his
lifelong cue, known as his 'pit-prop', smashed in his dressing
room in 1929 by a Sydney gambling mob who had risked all on
his opponent, Walter Lindrum. In the event, the match – one of
the most dramatic of all time – was not completed because
Lindrum's wife, Rosie, died in the middle of it, at the age of 20,
after being knocked over by a bus. He had married her during
the match because she was pregnant. He was playing for a one
hundred guinea silver tea service she had particularly asked him
to win. On the day she died she asked him from her sick bed to
make a 2000 break for her. He made 2002, but when he returned
to the dressing room it was to hear the news of her death. Later
he used to say: 'That 2002 was the greatest break I ever made in
my life.'

When he was 90, Willie Smith was asked about losing that old
cue half a century before.

'How long did it take to get used to another one?'

'I never did,' was the old man's sad reply.

# Chapter Three

# THE GOLDEN AGE

We last glimpsed John Roberts impersonating Hannibal by transporting billiard tables across India on the backs of elephants. This act was entirely in keeping with his rumbustious personality. He was one of the many outsize, quarrelsome, principal actors who were to colour the game in the century after the accession of Queen Victoria. His father, an enormous man with a thick long beard, had been one of the first competitive billiards champions, taking over in 1849 from Jonathan Kentfield of Brighton, who had dominated the game since 1820. Even with dead cushions (these were pre-rubber days) Kentfield once potted 57 consecutive reds off the spot, and wrote a 'Treatise on Billiards' which is now a collector's item.

Billiards adopted the style of the boxing prize ring, with challengers taking on the established champion for a purse and sizeable side bets. As in golf's early days, to be champion of England automatically meant champion of the world. The elder Roberts had come to fame as a young man of twenty by beating a renowned Glasgow champion in a marathon match over 43 hours. Despite the fact that Roberts also acted as spot boy and marker, it was the Scotsman who collapsed after 125 games of 100 up.

He once played a big challenge match against a notorious hustler (or, as the breed was known then, 'billiards sharp') called Old Minchey. They were playing a series of eleven games for £20 each. Roberts, holding back until the maximum number of bets had been placed, let Minchey get to 5–5 and 87–35 ahead in the decider. Minchey then left Roberts a double baulk, meaning he had to play up and down the table to hit the ball. Roberts not only hit the red but knocked both it and the cue ball off the table, which then carried no penalty. Minchey wagered against Roberts's doing the same thing again, but he did – five times in succession. Minchey was so upstaged by this outrageous display of skill and gamesmanship that Roberts ran out an easy winner.

The reign of Roberts (senior) finally came to a close at St James's Hall in London in 1870, in the presence of an aristocratic audience that included the Prince of Wales, when he was narrowly beaten by William Cook for a prize of £200. Tickets changed hands on that occasion at £5, a prodigious amount for the time. Two months later, however, family honour was avenged by his son, who, after many epic tussles with Cook and Joseph Bennett – the best of them at the Criterion and Gaiety restaurants – then proceeded to dominate the game for the rest of the century. Not only did he dominate play, but he made the billiard tables and sold the cues, the chalk, the balls, books, cushions, even cigars and crockery. He was champion, manufacturer, entrepreneur and promoter – a redoubtable mixture of Steve Davis, Barry Hearn, Del Simmons, Riley's and West Nally combined. He started the first billiards magazine in 1895. He arrogantly overrode the Billiards Association, which had been formed in 1885, saying he could not regard 'a letter from the secretary of a moribund association as other than gross impertinence'. Not for the last time, the personality of the top player was stronger than the game's administration.

The Association had been called into existence to sort out the rules, because the top players tended to adopt the rules that best suited their own play. Many of the problems that were to destroy billiards as a spectacle in the next century – endless cannons and potting of the red ball from its spot – emerged at this time. There were other rows over push shots and the size of the pockets, depending on whether you were chiefly a potter or a cannon specialist. A dinosaur relic of this period is the beautifully maintained table with tiny pockets at the Victoria Club in London.

Roberts was so good at all aspects of the game that he could win under any rules, but still preferred to impose his own. Sometimes, in the same match, he would play by one set of rules while his opponent played by another. He often boycotted championship matches in protest over the rules. He was clever at keeping the crowd on their toes by appearing to lose position in the course of a long break, then making a spectacular 'recovery' shot from the other end of the table. Roberts was always ready to take a risk to make the game more entertaining for the crowd. Once, when challenged about a shot, he replied: 'I know that such a shot is full of risks, but it is full of poetry, the charming poetry of motion. And, to my mind, playing it or leaving it alone marks the distinction between a workman and an artist.' The surviving sepia photographs show that he had a curious semi-upright stance, very different from the modern players with their chins resting on the cue.

Always on his dignity, Roberts was astonished on one occasion in India to be asked by a marker for a game. 'I'll give you 40 in a 100 start,' said the man. Roberts, deeply affronted, produced his visiting card from his wallet and showed the man where it read 'World Billiards Champion'. 'Ah,' said the man, 'in that case I'll make it 20 start.'

Roberts was an unashamed commercial operator, playing any-where from Indian palaces to shanties in Australian mining towns. He took a snooker circus around the English provinces as well as to Jaipur. Always litigious, he once sued for libel when he was described as 'ex-champion'. In one tournament, when he was being paid by a manufacturer to play with certain balls, the other players thought they should also have a slice of the action, and sent someone called Harverson to remonstrate with the great man.

'We hear,' said Harverson, 'that you are being paid to play with the balls we are using and other players are under the impression that they should have their share of the money.'

'That impression will wear off,' said Roberts imperturbably. 'Good morning, Mr Harverson.'

Roberts played many times to entertain royalty, British as well as Indian, and once contrived to allow Lily Langtry to beat him to please the Prince of Wales. When electricity was just coming in, a set of lights was installed at the Palais Royal, London, but the bulbs exploded, showering the table and players with glass. Roberts, despite being cut and burned, went on to win regardless. But he never trusted electricity again and always insisted on gaslight. It was Roberts who set the sartorial standards for the game, wearing a dinner jacket and high collar in the evening.

Like many entrepreneurs after him, Roberts tried to export the game to the United States and France, playing at the Central Music Hall in Chicago and Madison Square Garden in New York and arranging for W. J. Peall, 'the Mighty Atom', to play at the Folies Bergères in Paris. Like all later attempts to evangelize the US and the French, he was unsuccessful. The Americans preferred to stick to pool and the French to *their* favourite indoor sport. In all, Roberts made eleven visits to India, three to Australia, two to New Zealand, two to America and one to South Africa – a remarkable log for a Victorian traveller.

Peall was one of Roberts's main rivals, a tiny man barely five feet in height who was nonetheless a stupendous potter. An enthusiastic motorcyclist and motorist when these pursuits were just beginning, Peall was once summonsed in Reigate for exceeding the 12 mph speed limit. When ordered to stand up in court, he was able to reply in all innocence: 'I *am* standing up, sir.' Peall was playing William Mitchell at the Black Horse Hotel, off Oxford Street, in 1883, when Mitchell recorded the first-ever thousand break at billiards. Three years later, Peall himself scored the first two thousand break, for which he won £50, and then the first three thousand break in 1888, potting a thousand reds on the way, watched by the future King George V, then Duke of York, at the London Aquarium. A cheery little man, he lived on to be 97 and often appeared at post-war matches to watch Joe Davis.

By the turn of the century Roberts was suffering badly from the effects of pneumonia and fading eyesight. Despite this he won a challenge match in 1899 against the rising star, Charles Dawson, for £100 and gate receipts of over £2000. For his last match soon after this, he arrived in Manchester one cold night in a brougham, smothered in blankets, to play William Mitchell when he was scarcely able to walk round the table. It was his last great victory.

Mitchell was to vie with Dawson, Edward Diggle, H. W. Stevenson, George Gray, Tom Reece and Melbourne Inman for the top spot in billiards between the retirement of Roberts and the First World War. For all that, he was a prodigious drinker. Once, when he turned up late for an exhibition, he couldn't hit the object ball. 'There will now be a short interval,' declared the harassed promoter, bringing down the curtain on the shortest session on record.

George Gray, an Australian, looked set to dominate the game with his model two-eyed stance and his mastery at in-off the red. But his confidence was curiously shattered when he lost a tournament everyone expected him to win after the other pros substituted ivory for the composition balls he was used to. He had an overpowering father, who constantly tapped his elbow with a walking stick in practice to keep his cue arm straight. The effect was to destroy his natural rhythm and make his cue arm uncontrollably unsteady when he played in competition. He finally gave up and went to live in Singapore.

Edward Diggle, a Manchester marker with an ungainly stance, was obsessed by the fear that someone was following him, and always kept a gun by his bed. One night, when he was sharing a room with Willie Smith, he suddenly woke up, shouted 'They're here, Willie, they're here', fired two shots through the bedroom door and went back to sleep. In later life Diggle was asked to address an important function after dinner. He rose to his feet and said: 'I have been asked to make a speech about billiards. Billiards is a funny game' – then sat down again.

By 1907, Tom Reece had so mastered the art of the anchor cannon, trapping the balls in the jaw of the pocket, that he compiled a ludicrous break of 499,135 in Soho Square over a period of five weeks. The path of the cue ball became so worn in the cloth that it just rolled along the track. At one point he turned derisively to his opponent, who hadn't played a shot for weeks, and said: 'What chalk do you use?' The anchor stroke was then banned.

The tedium endured by the old-style billiard player is illustrated in this description by 'Hurricane' Higgins, for whom the tempo would have been unbearable:

I've never understood what motivates billiard players. Can you imagine that – you get dressed up in your lounge suit in the afternoon, you go on, you break off and then you sit there for the rest of the afternoon. You don't get a shot. Then you go back to the hotel and change from your lounge suit into your evening suit, and you go back and still don't get a shot. And the next morning you get up and shave and go back in the hall and the guy's still at the table. That would drive me to distraction.

Joe Davis used to joke about his trousers getting shiny as he waited for Walter Lindrum to finish a massive break.

The personal rivalry of Tom Reece and Melbourne Inman, both on and off the table, became an amusing feature of the game. Reece was a swimmer and had come to billiards only by accident, through having to walk past the tables on his way to the swimming pool. He was a buttoned-up man of artistic temperament who found Inman's taunting aggression too much to handle. Inman, in turn, enjoyed roughing him up. It wasn't just the Twickenham Terrier's manner that irritated the more fastidious Reece – especially the rattling of his cue – but his play, which was wilder than Reece's sense of artistry could take (though Joe Davis, who played both, rated Inman the better player, saying Reece had a very floppy action). Once, when Inman fluked a shot with some characteristically forceful play, Reece flared: 'How did you do that?' 'I believe you know my terms for tuition, Mr Reece,' Inman replied.

On another occasion they were playing in a provincial hall when two scruffy lads put their heads round the door.

'Put it across him, Tommy,' yelled one of them.

'Would you mind telling your friends to be quiet, Mr Reece,' said Inman.

It is perhaps no surprise that when, in 1919, the President of the Billiards Association, Lord Alverston, the judge who had sentenced Crippen to death, was presenting a trophy to Inman, Reece was heard to cry out: 'Excuse me, my lord. But if you knew as much about Inman as I do, you would have given Crippen the cup and sentenced Inman to death!'

Their double act had begun with a challenge match for £100 in 1903, which Inman, ever the fighter, just managed to win. As late as 1921, when Reece had narrowly beaten Inman in Sydney, he told a local paper: 'Inman has always been on my shoulders. He has unnerved me, made me anxious and fretful and haunted me like a nightmare. Now I have thrown him off.' This was just wishful thinking, for the rivals were to stay on each other's backs for many years to come. 'They genuinely disliked each other,' Joe Davis said, 'but to some extent they played to the gallery with their theatrical rudeness and cross talk.'

They couldn't start a match without complaining about the condition of the balls, the cloth or the carpet. For one match Inman demanded that the red be dyed the colour of a tomato.

'Look, we're not running a greengrocer's shop,' said Reece. When Reece was accumulating a huge pendulum break (a variation of the anchor cannon, where the balls were rocked rather than trapped in the pocket) and Inman was glumly sitting it out, Reece turned to the referee and said: 'This man ought to pay to come in. He's just a spectator.'

The banter went on after their competitive days were over. In 1940, when Thurston's, the pre-war temple of snooker near Leicester Square, was destroyed by a German land mine, old Reece appeared the next morning to survey the devastation. Standing amid the smoking rubble he stroked his chin and said thoughtfully: 'It looks as if Inman was playing here last night.'

Reece was clearly a very odd man. When Joe Davis was about to beat him after a week-long match, he left before the end, walked out into Piccadilly, lifted his hat on the end of his umbrella and shouted, 'Hurray, Davis has beaten old Reece!' On another occasion, in Harrogate, when it was again clear he was going to lose, he suddenly jumped to his feet, swept the balls off the table into his pockets and went off home, bidding the crowd – but not his opponent – goodnight.

Inman was a cooler customer. Once, after a jolly evening at a club, he drove off in his car and knocked down a row of red lamps by some road works. As the startled night watchman came out of his hut, Inman roared: 'I've taken all the reds, damn you. Where are the bloody colours?' Increasingly annoyed at an exhibition match by a referee who kept following him around with the rest, he finally yelled: 'For God's sake, man, put that thing away. You look like bloody Neptune standing there.'

In 1920 Inman challenged Willie Smith – a linotype operator from Middlesbrough who was always refusing to play in the official championship for complex contractual reasons or rows over the rules – to an acrimonious grudge game, which turned out to be the biggest money match of the age. Smith was an anti-establishment rebel who played a fast adventurous game and preferred working-class audiences to the black-tied gentility of Thurston's. This reluctant genius was to emerge from a period of bitter rivalry with Joe Davis in the 1930s to become a friend in later life. He once told Joe rather disarmingly 'I don't agree with your advice, Joe. In fact, I've never agreed with anybody.'

Smith, Clark McConachy (the man who gave his cue away) and Tom Newman became the leading trio, though the irrepressible Inman was never far behind, winning his first world title in 1908 and his last in 1927. Even ten years later, when he was nearly 60, Inman was still causing a stir. In a snooker match against Newman he amazed everyone with what the *Daily Express* called 'a most remarkable shot' for the yellow when he was stuck behind the pink. 'A *massé* or swerve would have been useless, and Inman successfully played to the left-hand cushion and hit the yellow so thinly that he cut it into the right lower pocket.' In another frame he potted two colours in succession without pausing for a red in between and had to be penalized. Then, in another incident, having addressed the cue ball, he suddenly straightened up and confessed to a foul so negligible that nobody – not even Charlie Chambers, the referee – had noticed. Somehow I doubt if he would have owned up so readily if his opponent had been Tom Reece.

McConachy had an even wider span, losing the finals of 1924 and 1934, winning in 1951 and losing to Rex Williams in 1968 at the age of 73 while suffering from Parkinson's disease. To beat the shakes he played with a giant 36-ounce cue. It was a tribute to this eccentric man's lifelong mania for physical fitness.

'How are you?' people would say.

'Fit as a buck rat,' McConachy would reply, chest out, shoulders back, eyes ablaze. He was a strange character, a painfully slow player, and as strong as a horse. He could lift Walter Lindrum up in a chair without trouble and would sometimes walk round the table on his hands before a match.

He was once outwitted in a game with Tom Reece at the Marlborough Club in 1921 in front of King George V. Reece told him in a confidential whisper that the King didn't like red ball play, which was McConachy's speciality. So he cut it out, only to see Reece pot the red ball repeatedly to win the match.

McConachy, a deeply honest man, was shocked. 'You told me,' he said to Reece afterwards, 'that the King hated red ball play'.

'Yes, I did,' said Reece, 'and it's true.'

'But you played it yourself,' McConachy protested.

'I know,' said Reece, shaking his head sadly. 'And did you see the way the King was scowling at me?'

One of the most remarkable sights on the post-war billiards circuit was the one-armed player and referee, Arthur Goundrill, who had lost his left arm up to the elbow at the battle of Ypres. Despite this handicap, he could play exhibitions at which his handsome looks and lively personality made him a popular attraction. He was good enough, using his stump as a makeshift bridge, to play with Joe Davis and perfected a long screw-back which Davis much admired. He made breaks of 235 at billiards and 66 at snooker. He specialized in trick shots and once gave a command performance of them before King George V and Queen Mary on the private table at Buckingham Palace. Walter Lindrum was the only other player ever to be granted this honour. They both received a set of gold and enamel cuff links.

This table has now gone from Buckingham Palace, as I discovered when I attended a meeting of editors there in what used to be the billiards room. King George V used to play snooker frequently after dinner at York Cottage, Sandringham, but when he was at 'the big house' as he puts it in his diary, he played billiards. At Osborne House on the Isle of Wight the table has an elaborate painted decoration designed by Prince Albert. The table is in an L-shaped room, one end of which is a drawing room and the other the billiard room. This enabled the gentlemen of the Household to sit on raised leather seats to watch the game while still theoretically in the Queen's presence – she being round the corner in the drawing room.

Before it was destroyed in the war, Thurston's was to snooker what Lord's is to cricket and Wimbledon to tennis. The match room was like a miniature House of Commons or the smoking room of a London club, with leather seats and oak panelling. J. B. Priestley once said of it: 'Beyond the voices of Leicester Square, there is peace. It is in Thurston's Billiard Hall, which I visited for the first time the other afternoon to see the final in the Professional Championship.' (Joe Davis was beating Tom Newman, as he beat him in the UK final every year from 1934–39.) Priestley went on:

> Let me record that for one hour and a half that afternoon I was happy. If Mr Thurston ever wants a testimonial for his Billiard Hall, he can have one from me. The moment I entered the place I felt I was about to enjoy myself. It is small, snug, companionable. Four or five rows of plush chairs look down on the great table, above which is a noble shaded light, the shade itself being russet-coloured, Autumn to the cloth's bright Spring. Most of the chairs were filled with comfortable men, smoking pipes. I noticed a couple of women among the spectators, but they looked entirely out of place among the fat leather chairs of a West End club. I had just time to settle down in my seat, fill and light a pipe myself, before the match began.

Priestley concluded his article in memorable style:

> When the world is wrong, hardly to be endured, I shall return to Thurston's Hall and there smoke a pipe among the connoisseurs of top and side. It is as near to the Isle of Innisfree as we can get within a hundred leagues of Leicester Square.

Fred Davis has another, less poetic explanation for this characteristic calm of Thurston's. 'People often went to sleep,' he says. 'Businessmen would go out and have a heavy lunch with a few drinks, then slip in to watch the play and with the silence being broken only by the rhythmic clicking of the balls, they would slide off into a snooze. They seemed to reckon they got their money's worth that way.'

Tom Newman, a gentle, lantern-jawed man, had been discovered as a teenage prodigy by old John Roberts, making his
first century at the age of 11 and his first 500 break at 15. Though
both his temperament and his cue action were suspect – his arm
was somehow twisted round his back so that his potting was
suspect – Newman took the title six times in the 1920s until first
Joe Davis and then the Australian, Walter Lindrum, got the
measure of him, just as they were to get the measure of everybody else.

The unhappy truth is that Walter Lindrum became so pro-
ficient at billiards that he completely destroyed the game as a
public entertainment. There can be no other sport which died
because its leading players were too good. The game as practised
by the leading professionals became so different from the one
played by amateurs that few people were interested in paying to
see it. This was a new, more demanding clientele, many of whom
had served in the war. The deferential Victorian age was over.
The results and the pattern of play, particularly the repetitious
methods of scoring, became too predictable to watch for long
hours.

Walter Lindrum was born at Kalgoorlie in 1898 into a billiards
family. His father, brother and nephew were all champions.
They had a family billiard saloon where miners bet for hundreds
of pounds. At the age of three Walter lost the top of his right
forefinger in a mangle, so his father taught him to become
left-handed. When he was four he miraculously escaped injury
when a tree fell on the bedroom he was sleeping in. At five he
was swept away in a river and given up for dead, but held on to a
tuft of grass until he was rescued. He made a century break at the
age of twelve. His father locked him in the practice room for four
hours a day, later put up to seven – two in the morning, three in
the afternoon, two at night – and even more when he was older.
It is perhaps no wonder he grew up to be a strange, aloof man,
given to bouts of total indifference to anything outside the game.

After that nightmare challenge match in Sydney with Willie
Smith in 1929, during which his wife had died, Lindrum agreed
to visit Britain at last. Until then he had always demurred, partly
for fear of the climate (he had a bronchial condition) and partly

because he wasn't used to the ivory championship balls. He also had a paranoid fear that the Brits would always do down a colonial, just as George Gray had been done down twenty years before, and as Don Bradman, the cricketer, was done down by Jardine in the bodyline series at that time. In 1930 he asserted his superiority in a classic four-way match (sponsored by Janus, 'the new wonder cloth') that was billed as 'the greatest tournament ever seen'. He finished level with Davis and Newman and ahead of McConachy after giving them all 7000 points start. Lindrum's close cannon play, nursing the balls slowly along the cushion, was unbeatable. In his first ten months in Britain he made 110 breaks of over a thousand. In 1932 he made the world record break of 4137, which has never been beaten. He scored a century in 29 seconds and a thousand in 26 minutes.

Apart from being in a class of his own, Lindrum increasingly seemed to inhabit a world of his own. He was thoroughly unreliable over appointments, money and women. Joe Davis went to fetch him from the Strand Palace Hotel one day to resume an unfinished break and found him slumped and unshaven, badly hung over, with no interest at all in going on. After pressing him to shave and dress and pushing him into a taxi, Davis then watched with mixed feelings as he scored a thousand break against him, playing as if on autopilot. His lethargy was often noticeable, even in the billiard hall, but it never seemed to affect his play. Sydney Lee walked back with Lindrum to his hotel after a session in which the tip of his cue had nearly come off. Instead of mending it, Lindrum insisted on having a cup of tea and 'watching the girls go by'. He went back finally without securing the tip and scored yet another thousand break.

By this time Lindrum had shown himself to be the greatest billiards player the world had ever seen, beating Joe Davis in the championship finals of 1933 and 1934 and making five breaks of over a thousand. In doing so, however, he had taken the game to its ultimate – and thereby destroyed it as a public spectacle. He had perfected his art more thoroughly than any sportsman in history. In 1934 he returned to Australia and never came back. He refused to return the trophy and made impossible conditions for defending it. The championship had to be suspended for sixteen years. When revived in 1951 (without him) it was for only one year. In 1968 it was revived again for a challenge match between Rex Williams and the septuagenarian McConachy, which had more curiosity than sporting value. Since then, despite several attempts to breathe new life into the game, billiards has never recaptured the magic that fired the giants of the golden age.

Lindrum withdrew more and more into himself, protecting his invincibility by appearing only for exhibitions and eschewing competitive play. He seemed to become trapped behind an emotional wall of his own making, isolated by his own genius. But the genius never deserted him. When, in later life, Sir Robert Menzies, the post-war Australian prime minister, threw the balls haphazardly on to a table and invited him to show everyone how to make a thousand break, he did it at the first attempt.

From the moment he left England, however, billiards as a spectator sport was, in Joe Davis's words, 'dead as mutton'. Significantly, the *Daily Mail* switched its sponsorship from billiards to snooker in 1936. Although responsible for its final manic phase of popularity, Lindrum also helped to strangle it. He was capable of playing an attractive all-round game, but he was obsessed by the need to compile massive breaks which only he had the technique, the concentration and the sheer force of will to achieve. As Joe Davis put it: 'I knew and appreciated that they were almost miraculous, but the public became blasé about them. And as more players leapt on to the bandwagon, producing a large number of points but very few thrills, the easier we made it appear. Barring any truly radical change in the rules we had more or less mastered what, in my opinion, is the most scientific game in the world. It was our own fault. In 1933 Walter, Mac, Tom Newman, Willie Smith and I had undoubtedly produced some of the finest billiards the world has ever seen; but we bored the public.'

There was only one way forward now for the professional game. It was called Snooker.

## Chapter Four

# MR SNOOKER

It was Tom Webster, the *Daily Mail* cartoonist, who first called Joe Davis 'Mr Snooker'. Later, as his eminence rose, the sobriquets were elevated too: 'the Sultan of Snooker' and 'the Emperor of Pot' were two that caught on. There can be no doubt he deserved them all, for it was he, more than anyone else, who saw that in snooker they had an ideal and ready replacement when professional billiards suffered its sudden thrombosis in the 1930s. He also had the organizing genius and force of character to make things happen in that moribund world.

I was present when he made what must have been his last public speech before he died in 1978. It was at a dinner of the Saints and Sinners Club at the Dorchester Hotel in London's Park Lane. Although he was frail, he was as neat and smartly turned out as ever, a worthy heir to John Roberts, the man who set the standards for the modern game. I can't remember exactly what he said, but I do remember the respectful silence in which he was heard and the sustained and warm applause when he sat down. There was a strong sense, shared by everyone in the room, of saying goodbye to a legend – as indeed we were.

The scale of Joe Davis's problem in gaining official recognition for snooker can be gauged from the response of the governing body, the Billiards Association and Control Council, when a snooker championship was proposed in 1924. The Secretary, A. Stanley Thorn, wrote back: 'The suggestion will receive consideration at an early date, but it seems a little doubtful whether snooker as a spectacular game is sufficiently popular to warrant the successful promotion of such a competition.' (The prickly Thorn must be spinning in his grave at the thought of the 18

million people who watched the 'spectacular game' between
Steve Davis and Dennis Taylor in the 1985 world championship
final.)

This official attitude reflected the disdain that billiards professionals then felt for snooker, which they regarded as a less
skilled, more knockabout game for amateurs and gamblers. Joe
Davis was once entering the Midland Hotel in Manchester to
play a snooker exhibition when he bumped into the old billiards
pro Tom Reece in the foyer. Reece, a great friend of jockeys,
happened to be with Gordon Richards at the time. He called out
to Davis: 'Where's your ruddy corduroys and clogs, then?' He
despised the 'tomato game', as he called it.

Davis knew better, however. He knew from his own billiard
halls around Chesterfield and from the experience of colleagues –
George Nelson in Leeds, Tom Dennis in Nottingham and Bill
Camkin in Birmingham – that snooker was rapidly replacing
billiards as the people's game. 'I had a feeling in my bones that
snooker was the game of the future,' he said later. Up to that
point snooker had been used as a 'filler' to keep the crowd
amused when billiards tournaments finished too early, rather as
exhibition matches are played now. But Davis sensed that the
crowd were willing him to get through the billiards so that they
would have a frame of snooker to watch, or even two.

The rules of billiards had grown so complicated and the play
so repetitive that it was easy to see why snooker should become
more popular. Its rules were basically simpler and there was a
great deal more going on. Even the colours made for more visual
stimulation and variety. There was more uncertainty and much
more excitement – a vital ingredient if people were to feel they
were getting value for money during the Depression. Billiards
did not, of course, die overnight. It still had many supporters and
probably commanded more club time than snooker until the
Second World War; the arrival of billiards' ultimate genius in
Walter Lindrum gave it a big boost in the press. But the writing
was on the wall – and Joe Davis was the first to read it there.

He himself finally wrote to the Association, proposing the
financial conditions for a snooker tournament, while Camkin
drafted the rules. In 1927 the BA & CC were forced to concede,

but did so with a bad grace. Having demanded that they and the winners should each take 50 per cent of the entry fees, they then spent the winners' half on paying for the trophy. When the gate receipts were divided among the players, all that was left for the winner was six pounds ten shillings (compared to the £60,000 collected by Dennis Taylor in 1985). The man who pocketed the six pounds ten shillings was, needless to say, Joe Davis, who went on to win every world snooker championship until he retired undefeated from tournament play in 1946.

Joe Davis has always had critics who have been quick to point out that what was good for snooker was also good for Joe Davis. And there can be no doubt that he was more alive than most to the commercial possibilities of the game. But in the early years of the snooker championship he was acting out of faith rather than self-interest or greed – and it needed superhuman faith at that time to move the mountain of official disapproval and see beyond the grotty venues and the poor cash rewards to the exciting future that still lay some years ahead for the game. When he won the world's first snooker championship in 1927 for that measly purse of six pounds ten shillings, it wasn't in the palatial surroundings of Thurston Hall near Leicester Square, but in Bill Camkin's billiard hall in John Bright Street, Birmingham (Camkin was the referee). The following year he defended the title against Tom Dennis in the back room of his opponent's pub in Shakespeare Street, Nottingham. The world's first snooker final merited only four paragraphs in *The Billiard Player* and hardly any mention in the papers at all.

Yet when Joe went on to beat Tom Newman at Thurston's for the world billiards championship in 1928 – holding both titles at the same time – it was not only a press sensation, but brought the whole of his home town out to greet him at Chesterfield station. He was engulfed in a sea of singing, chanting supporters and swept up on to a charabanc to be greeted by the deputy mayor, then led by police and a brass band round the town square and through streets that had been closed to traffic for the first time since the end of the war. The game had found its first superstar.

Joe Davis had been born the son of a miner at Whitwell in Derbyshire in 1901, but by the time he was two his parents had taken over the Travellers' Rest at Whittington Moor, near

Chesterfield. He was then, as often happened to eldest children in those days, farmed out for several years to live with his grandparents at Newbold and returned to find that his father was now landlord of the nearby Queens Hotel, which boasted three attractions denied to the Travellers' Rest: a licence for spirits, a crown bowling green – and a full-size billiard table. A common feature in the lives of all great snooker players is access to a table at a tender age, which helps to explain why so many come from backgrounds in the drinking and gambling fraternities, where such things were more readily available. Such backgrounds also tend to breed a strong competitive urge to succeed.

Many players come from the racing or boxing worlds: Joe Davis came from both. His father, clearly an enterprising fellow, took trainee boxers into his pub, ran a football team, and was also the starter at Chesterfield races. He later branched out into cinemas and billiard halls and became an alderman. Joe made his first century break at the age of 12 and was lucky enough to be taken up by a local entrepreneur, Ernest Rudge, who had a table in a room at the bottom of his garden and invited top players like Tom Reece, George Gray and Willie Smith to the town for matches. All of these were asked in time for their comments on young Joe's performance and style.

Here they hit a snag, for Joe's stance was quite unusual in that he sighted the balls along his cue with his left eye like a marksman, instead of adopting the standard two-eyed stance. Gray, who had a model two-eyed stance himself, commented: 'The boy will never be a good player until he alters his sighting.' Willie Smith, twice world champion and doyen of British billiards before Joe reached his peak, was asked for a second opinion. He studied Joe's play for half an hour before concluding: 'The kid's all right. Let him play his own road.'

What none of them knew then, including Joe himself, was that the boy who was to become arguably the greatest snooker player of all time, and the second greatest billiards player after Lindrum, had only one eye to play with. His right eye was later found to be effectively dead, quite useless for focusing. Specialists have since maintained that this might actually have helped his play, since he got a direct sighting of the balls, whereas focusing with two eyes can be slightly inaccurate if, as usual, one lens is stronger than the other. It still seems a strange disability for a games player to have, especially in a sport where eyesight was to cause such problems for the likes of John Spencer, Dennis Taylor and, latterly, Ray Reardon, and where the lighting wasn't as good as it is now. Willie Smith used to joke in later years, when Davis became a champion: 'It's a good job for the rest of us that Joe doesn't have *two* good eyes!'

Another physical attribute he shared with Dennis Taylor was the ability to play awkward shots left-handed rather than use the rest. Davis learned to play left-handed when Chesterfield miners refused to take him on right-handed at gambling games of Pink Pool. His brother Fred was probably the best two-handed player in the history of the game, certainly in Joe's estimation. It's curious how professionals hate playing with the rest. I often find that I can pot a ball more surely with the rest, but that's probably because my bridge hand isn't as steady as it should be and because using the rest forces one to concentrate a little harder than usual on the shot. The pros, of course, find it harder with the rest to impose 'side' on the cue ball with the required sureness of touch – a sophisticated problem that most of us find rather less pressing than hitting the ball at all.

Joe Davis's early experience of Pink Pool, essentially a potting game, was a great help in developing his snooker. He always maintained that the old pros were wrong to denigrate the skills required of snooker and that billiards, even at championship level, was actually an easier game. So much of it consisted of cannons, which did not require the same precision or the same concentration as potting a ball; there was nearly always some recovery stroke to be made if you were marginally off line, which was not the case in snooker.

Whatever skills snooker required, Joe Davis was to refine them by unrelenting practice. He actually invented, on his own practice table, most of the technical ploys that are now a standard part of a modern player's repertoire. He experimented with 'stun', for example – stopping the cue ball by hitting it low – because he found it was less hazardous than the usual practice of sending the ball up the length of the table at an angle and thereby putting it at the mercy of the nap, the cushion and the state of the cloth. He discovered that potting the ball harder with 'stun' or 'screw' on the cue ball gave him more control than the old-fashioned trickle shot towards the pocket.

During an unscheduled lull in the 1985 world championship, when Steve Davis had seen off Ray Reardon 16–5 in the semifinal, the BBC got out from the archives an historic old black-and-white film of Joe Davis making a century break. While it was being shown there was a sudden, reverential hush in the sponsors' room. I happened to be sitting between Rex Williams, the former world billiards champion, now Chairman of the World Professional Billiards and Snooker Association, and Sydney Lee, one of the great jobbing pros and a world amateur champion between the wars, who later forged a new career as referee on TV's *Pot Black*. It was a fortunate conjunction, because Sydney, now 75, had the spectacle of Joe in front of him as a starting point for reminiscences about the old days and a reference point for present-day comparisons.

'Joe had you beaten before you started,' he said, 'because of his presence. He exuded such authority in his person. I averaged 50 points a break against him once for a whole week and still lost by 8000 points. He was a giant, a king.' Then he added, rather to my surprise: 'But I'd rate Steve Davis to beat him all the same. His positional play is so precise. He's the best I've seen.' I asked Rex Williams and John Pulman, who was champion for a decade from the mid-1950s, if they agreed with Sydney Lee's verdict. 'No,' they said in unison. Rex went on: 'Joe was the greatest. He dominated. His artistry among the balls was a joy.' Pulman nodded in agreement. 'Steve's safety play makes him very hard to beat, but he's essentially a manufactured player. Joe was an artist, a natural. He flowed.'

It was uncanny to look up and see him flowing on the screen more than twenty years before. What struck me most was that the game seemed exactly the same as it is now – the same stuns, screws and power shots – and the same speed around the table. Joe moved as fast as Jimmy White or Alex Higgins, sizing up a pot at a glance then potting it. I had somehow expected it all to be rather more sedate and stately. The balls were clearly less manoeuvrable and the pockets tighter in those days, and you therefore needed to be closer to a ball to pot it.

It is probably pointless to speculate on whether Joe would have beaten Steve, or vice versa – as pointless as comparing Grace, Bradman and Viv Richards as batsmen in cricket. They would probably have beaten each other time and again. Joe never had to play so many tournaments in such quick succession as players do today, and he didn't have so many opponents to face of roughly equal calibre. There was also less pressure in those leisurely matches: you had a whole week to catch up. Joe would not have relished playing Jimmy White best of nine frames. Nor did he come under the same commercial pressures. Against that, nobody yet knows how soon modern tournament players will burn themselves out under these pressures, in the way that most young golf pros fade in their late twenties, leaving the field to a handful of brilliant stayers. My own guess, for what it's worth, is that Joe Davis, with his steady temperament, his gift for technical innovation and his eye for a penny, would have relished the challenges of the modern game which owes so much to his example. We can be fairly sure, if we can be sure of anything in this unpredictable game, that no champion will ever again remain unbeaten, as he did, for two decades.

When it comes down to it, what *is* the decisive factor that marks out the genius: is it temperament or technique? The champion must have both, of course, in unusual measure, but Joe Davis himself had no doubts. He once overheard an exchange between two spectators leaving a hall where he had won one of his great victories.

'Joe can make those balls do everything but talk,' said one.

'Yes,' said his neighbour. 'It's a gift, something a person is born with – like Caruso's voice.'

He smiled wryly to himself at the thought of all those hours on the practice table, the self-discipline and the determination to win. There is a tenacious jut to Joe Davis's jaw in those old pictures and cartoons that probably holds the key. Late at night in the bar of the Grosvenor House Hotel in Sheffield, during the world championship, one of the country's leading snooker coaches (some would say the best), Frank Callan of Blackpool, explained to me the three

main requirements in a champion: talent, dedication – and 'bottle',
a use of the word that would have puzzled Joe Davis in his
lifetime. But he clearly had plenty of it, as he showed when he
came so close to beating the legendary Walter Lindrum at
billiards.

He also had a style, a stance and a physique that suited the
potting game. He was stocky, not very tall – and one recalls that
the greatest billiards potter of all time, the red ball specialist, was
W. J. Peall, the 'Mighty Atom', who stood five feet nothing, less
than twice the height of the table; Jimmy White, in our day, is
another case in point. Dennis Taylor, at five feet nine, is the same
height as Joe Davis, and has the same stocky build. Joe Davis's cue
was likewise short and heavy and his cue action correspondingly
short, sharp and straight, targeted by that marksman's left-eyed
stance. Billiards requires a mastery of angles, snooker an ability to
hit one ball into another and then into the hole, which means
pinpoint precision in the striking of both balls. Joe Davis's short
back movement and his level action, even in the follow through,
meant that he was always dead in line and (a key phrase in his
book) 'in control'. Control of the cue ball and control of the self
are the essence of the game.

Joe Davis was in control of his own career more completely and
more efficiently than any player since John Roberts. As in so
much else, he set the pattern for other professionals to follow.
Apart from tournaments, many of which he arranged himself, he
played a constant round of exhibition matches, sometimes five in a
single day. He wrote a regular column for years in the *News of the
World*, and produced a number of classic instruction manuals
(from one of which Steve Davis learned to play). He had no
manager to look after him and wrote dozens of letters every week
in search of engagements, endorsements and promotional deals.
'If there were not any sponsorships going, it was not for want of
trying on my part,' he said later. 'I thought of every product that
might conceivably – and sometimes inconceivably – have any
bearing on billiards and snooker and then offered my services in
endorsing them. I tried eye lotions and hair lotions, shirt makers
and shoe makers without eliciting the slightest flicker of interest.
The only contract for endorsing a product that I obtained in those

days was for Churchman's Top Score cigarettes, which I then used to smoke.' As ever, it was the tobacco industry that came to snooker's rescue.

He had a long link with Kay Sports, who produced miniature tables, and with Peradon and Co., the oldest cue manufacturer in the country. Apart from the billiard halls around Derbyshire which he shared with his father, he had an interest at various times in halls at Manchester, Cambridge, Blackpool and Kilburn in London (though he disposed of this one when the clientele got too rough).

It is fair to say that Joe Davis frequently had to live off his wits, especially in the Depression of the 1930s, when professional billiards suddenly went out of fashion. Fortunately, wits were a commodity he never lacked. When Walter Lindrum withdrew to Australia clutching the world billiards trophy, defying everyone to 'come and get it', Joe set off for the Antipodes in the vain hope of bringing him back to the championship table. It wasn't to be, for Lindrum proved an impossible man to deal with, failing to answer letters or keep appointments or changing the terms of an agreement in mid-discussion. Joe found himself stranded on the far side of the world with no visible means of support except for his cue. It turned out to be enough, helped by wild wagers in Wagga Wagga and a fat roll of banknotes for making a bizarre trip through the night to play in a barn for an old sheep farmer in the outback on the oldest table he had ever seen.

On another occasion, when he had just taken a pile off a stranger who challenged him (without recognizing the British champion) in a hotel, the Australian turned to him and said: 'You're some player. I reckon you must have slept with Joe Davis.'

'No,' said Joe, 'but I've often slept with his wife.'

He never took money to lose a match, though he was offered plenty to do so by the gamblers who have always thrived on the fringe of the professional game. The public have ever been suspicious of last-frame deciders, believing them too good to be true and that the result has somehow been fixed or contrived in advance. In Joe's time the players sometimes ensured that there was play on the final day, to avoid killing the gate, but they denied ever fixing the result. Diggle, one of the old billiard pros, was

asked about this at the turn of the century and replied enig-
matically: 'There's tricks in every trade but ours.' One gets the
same answer today.

When the Second World War came, Joe Davis applied his skills
at improvisation to a new challenge: show business. He created an
act on stage in which his trick shots were magnified and reflected
to the audience by means of a huge angled mirror. As always, he
worked hard to perfect his act and ended up at the London
Palladium. He met his second wife, June Malo, while she was
playing Dandini to Noele Gordon's Prince Charming, and
became friends with people like Tommy Trinder, Sid Field,
Arthur Askey and Tessie O'Shea, personalities with whom he
obviously felt at ease. He also raised a great deal of money for
charity. By such methods he managed to keep the image of
snooker – and, of course, his own – well before the public for the
duration of the war.

In 1946 he took a share in Leicester Square Hall, which was built
on the site of the bombed-out Thurston's, and replaced it as the
showcase of tournament snooker (he appointed a young man
called Ted Lowe as manager). Joe deserves the credit, not only for
keeping snooker alive in the war, but for restoring the professional
game after it. He retained his snooker title in 1946, beating Horace
Lindrum, Walter's nephew, then immediately announced his
retirement from tournament play. He was at the height of his
powers but felt, as he put it, that 'it was not good for the game,
indeed for any game, to be dominated by one man'.

The fact is, though, that he continued to dominate the game
more than ever from exile, just as John Roberts and, for a time,
Willie Smith had done before him. As the best player, the game's
biggest personality, chairman of the players' body, part owner of
Leicester Square Hall, he was Mr Snooker indeed. He was a
formidable man of affairs. When the BBC wanted to negotiate for
the right to show snooker or billiards on television, it was Joe they
had to talk to – and Joe who appeared. He had a virtual veto on all
new professionals; if he didn't like somebody, or thought they
didn't fit his image of the game, they were liable to be frozen out.
Clive Everton sums up the situation at this point in the game's
history in his classic *Story of Billiards and Snooker*:

That Joe had the interests of the game at heart there is no doubt. With professional players squabbling and an ineffectual governing body there was a desperate need for a strong man to take charge as he did. Neither did anyone begrudge him his legitimate commercial pickings. But his retirement from Championship play was soon to devalue the Championship itself – just as Roberts' withdrawal had devalued it. In less than ten years, professional Snooker was to decline from that peak of the 1946 final almost to the point of extinction.

It was widely believed in the game that King Joe had abdicated to make way for the accession of his brother Fred, who was twelve years his junior. He had narrowly beaten Fred in the final of 1940 (known as the Davis Cup) scoring a century to clinch the final frame 37–36, which must have been a real nail biter, especially as it was between two brothers. Only the Doherty brothers in the early days of Wimbledon – and maybe the Compton and Charlton brothers at soccer and the Chappell brothers in Australian Test cricket – have come anywhere near matching this feat. But Fred was surprisingly beaten in the 1947 final by Walter Donaldson, a dour Scot who had returned from the Army and locked himself away for weeks on end to practise in a friend's loft. Even though Fred went on to win the world title eight times out of ten, this was undoubtedly a great disappointment to Joe, who, some observers felt, was sometimes less than supportive of his younger brother, putting him down in public and denigrating his talent. ('Wipe that smile off your face,' he was heard to bark at Fred at a practice session and said dismissively to him about an easy shot: 'Even you should get that one.') But this bad period between the brothers, if there ever really was one, cannot have lasted for long. What must have irritated Joe was Fred's ability to play well without laborious hours of practice, which suggests that his was probably the more natural talent.

Fred, whose warm personality and twinkling sense of fun were to charm TV audiences in the 1960s and 1970s in *Pot Black*, was one of the first players to succeed with glasses, his eyesight having been found to be truly dreadful. A specialist said he was lucky to see the other end of the table. There was also a question mark against his dedication to the game, especially when measured against his brother. As a wearer of spectacles and a nonsmoker and nondrinker, he found the atmosphere on the club circuit sometimes hard to bear. He also spent a long period out of the game, helping his wife run a hotel in Llandudno.

Even so, he has the distinction of being the only player to have beaten Joe on level terms at snooker, a feat he achieved three times. There was a period around 1950 when he may have had the edge on his brother, though over their careers as a whole Joe was the undisputed master. The first time he beat Joe was by 36 frames to 35 in an *Empire News* tournament at Leicester Square Hall in 1948. Even then, he had victory snatched from his grasp when the sealed handicaps were opened at the end. Harold Mayes, the sports editor of the *Empire News* (for which Fred wrote a column), had actually given Joe (a rival snooker columnist in the *News of the World*) a two-frame start, an insulting piece of one-upmanship towards the unbeaten world champion. His intention was to boost his own man and humble Joe, but it had the unintended effect of giving Joe the match and depriving Fred of the first prize of £450. The full historic significance of Fred's 'victory' over his brother was lost in all the fuss. It was sometimes said that crafty Joe preferred to give his opponents a start, so that in the event of his being beaten he could still say they hadn't beaten him off level terms, thus preserving his precious record intact.

Joe's own official verdict on Fred at the end of his life was a generous one: 'His cue action and stance were near perfect and when in form he never batted an eyelid or moved his head or body so much as a millimetre. This made him very hard to beat when he took it into his head to do battle. But if he had a flaw in his make-up it was a tendency to be temperamental, at times giving the impression that he could not care less.' At the 1978 world snooker championships the BBC played the Beatle song, 'When I'm 64', to mark Fred's appearance on the screen. His amazing achievements in reaching the semifinal that year – after two heart attacks (ironically, Joe himself collapsed with a heart attack while watching this match and died a few months later) and actually winning the world billiards title at 67 – surely disposed of any doubts about the capacity of both brothers to compete with today's top players.

Joe's last great triumph had been to make the first maximum break at snooker, 147, in public. This meant potting all 15 reds, each followed by a black, then all the colours in succession. From the end of the war this had begun to seem a possible target – snooker's equivalent of the four-minute mile, which was actually to be achieved by Roger Bannister a year before Joe's feat. In 1946 Fred Davis had made a break of 133 and Joe 134 in consecutive frames. Peter Mans, from South Africa, made 137 in the same year (it was his son, Perrie Mans, a left-hander famed for his long potting, who beat Fred to reach the 1978 final). Joe took the record to 140 in 1947, the Canadian George Chenier made 144 in 1950, only to be overtaken by Joe a month later with 146, just one off the elusive maximum. But it was to take another six years before that single-point barrier was finally broken down in public (a number of players had scored 147 in witnessed practice frames, the first being E. J. 'Murt' O'Donoghue, a New Zealander, who is still alive at the age of 85.) It became something of a private obsession for Joe.

Eventually it happened at Leicester Square Hall on 22 January, 1955 – just a week before it closed for the last time – in a game against the veteran Willie Smith. It was Joe's 564th century break. Ted Lowe, the manager, who was there, describes the great moment:

> The maestro was more than likely to clear the table but on this occasion every priority was aimed at breaking his own record and becoming the first man to make a 147 break under championship conditions. All went well for him until he had scored 104, when he left himself on the wrong side of the fourteenth red. The cue ball was tucked between the red and a top pocket. Both balls were on the side cushion with only an inch or so between them. His only hope was to drive the red almost the length of the side cushion more than ten feet into the 'blind' baulk pocket against the nap of the cloth. I reckon any bookmaker would have offered 100 to 1 against Davis succeeding. Joe literally sweated and fretted over the position he had left

himself in, longer than for any shot played in his life. You could have heard a pin drop and I felt my own fingers shaking with the tension. But he played it and as the red dropped into the pocket, a relieved Joe, playing faster than even Hurricane Higgins, scrambled the remaining balls into the pockets as though he believed that the slightest hesitation could cause him to fluff a shot. As the last ball went down, even the seventy-year-old dour Northerner Willie Smith flung his arms round Joe's neck, and the crowd stamped their feet for the first and last time at Leicester Square.

This was the only time in all the years I had known Joe that he revealed nerves. When the cheering had died and we began to move from the table to my office, he gasped: 'Ted! For God's sake pour me a large brandy.' After sinking it even faster than the last black in his 147 break, he phoned his wife June, who knew how much that maximum break meant to him, and told her the good news. Understandably enough, she burst into tears.

Apart from Joe and June, I was the only other person who knew just how much that 147 effort had taken out of him and when the tension had completely gone some hours later over a celebration dinner, he summed it up:

'I played some terrible positional shots as the chance of achieving this record became more possible. I cannot ever remember having been in such a state of nervousness and near panic in all my career. After putting two long pots into the baulk pockets at 32 and 80 and each time screwing back for the black, I lost position hopelessly at 104. With thirteen reds and blacks potted, I found the cue ball between a red and the top pocket on the side cushion with only an inch or so between them. I heard the spectators sigh with dismay. The break looked all over. I had only one chance. It meant I had to drive the red straight down the side cushion more than ten feet into the blind baulk pocket. My heart was beating fast and I found it almost unbearable as I hesitated, taking more time than for any other shot in my life. Yet as the red passed the centre pocket, I knew it was in. I was now excited and sank the last few balls as fast as I could. But how I suffered before it was all over!'

Many players have since made at least a dozen maximum breaks. Willie Thorne has scored more than anyone in practice – but not, as he puts it, 'under the cosh'. Yet Dennis Taylor and Terry Griffiths, both world champions, haven't scored any, even on the practice table.

Joe Davis was given the OBE in 1963, ostensibly for his charity work. Bannister, the first four-minute miler, was later knighted, as were Stanley Matthews the soccer star, several cricketers, including Jack Hobbs, Don Bradman, Len Hutton, Frank Worrell and Gary Sobers, and Gordon Richards the jockey. It can only have been a residue of the old social snobbery against snooker that stopped Joe Davis being knighted too. Two or even one decade later, he surely would have been.

Joe's 147 was to prove the last great flourish of a dying sport, for professional snooker soon went into a decline as sudden and as unexpected as billiards had suffered twenty years before. Just as Lindrum had honed billiards to perfection and thereby killed the game, so had Joe Davis, it seemed, finally achieved the ultimate in snooker and left nothing for his successors. It wasn't quite like that, for the causes went deeper, but the closed shop in professional snooker did have the effect of driving customers away and Joe must take some of the blame for that.

The amateur game had continued to flourish and was bursting with talent, but Joe and his colleagues ruthlessly excluded newcomers from the professional ranks. Incredibly, Rex Williams was the only new professional admitted to the club between 1950 and 1967, with the result that the public wearied of the same old faces. And with Joe himself out of contention, the handful of pros were like the tribe that lost its head. Many amateurs were at least as good as the pros at this time and made a living out of betting in the clubs. Since 1972 they have been allowed to keep prize money and some amateurs can pick up several thousand pounds in prize money in a season. An amateur called Dickie Flicker, from Hackney, beat an extraordinary record (originally set by John Roberts, senior) by playing non-stop at Leicester Square Hall for 45 hours and 7 minutes, during which he played 137 frames, potted 1668 balls and walked over 24 miles.

Some brilliant amateurs in the 1960s, like Patsy Houlihan,

were refused admittance because of their 'connections', which were thought to be too close to the gambling world for the highly polished professional image that Joe was trying to foster. 'It was very hard to turn pro,' Houlihan says. 'Joe Davis was the kingpin. His word was law. When he said yes or no, that was it.' Patsy was a self-confessed hustler in the early days. A very popular character and later a pro, he had the unnerving experience of being backed for high stakes by the Kray twins. But there was less and less money coming into the professional game, which made the existing pros even more reluctant to admit any new mouths to feed. It was a self-destructive cycle leading nowhere. By 1957, there were only four entries for the professional championship, which was won by the mercurial John Pulman. The tournament was then suspended until it was revived on a challenge basis in 1964, an indication of just how low the game had sunk.

Rex Williams attributes the crisis mainly to the advent of commercial television and the massive increase in the number of sets that it brought, keeping people at home round the family hearth, so that many clubs and cinemas went to the wall. It is ironic to reflect that television, which was to seize the game of snooker and boost it into a world of untold riches in the next twenty-year cycle, had first reduced it to the depths. So much so that when Joe Davis was asked on his retirement in 1964 what future he saw for professional snooker, the game's greatest evangelist replied: 'What future? Snooker has no future.'

## Chapter Five

# SPORTING THEATRE

Joe Davis became so strongly associated with snooker in the public mind – an association he cultivated assiduously over the years – that it is surprising to discover that he was not, in fact, the first player to appear on television. That honour went instead to Willie Smith and Horace Lindrum at Alexandra Palace in April 1937. (Nor was Joe the first to make a century break in front of the cameras: that was done by Mark Wildman while still an amateur in 1962.) Joe made his TV début a month after the others, in May 1937, in a ten-minute demonstration of billiards with Tom Newman. Sydney Lee also recalls being televised before the war when he challenged for the UK billiards title. None of these films (all black-and-white, of course) survives, though there are some remarkable archive shots of Walter Lindrum demonstrating nursery cannons, prodding the balls nimbly along the cushion to amass a prodigious break. In one film the table has been taken out of doors into bright Australian sunshine, presumably because of the light. One shudders to think what it did to the cloth, which must have become too hot to touch.

Lighting has always been the bugbear of televised snooker and the technical problems involved were not conquered by BBC engineers until the late 1970s. There were a number of disasters before that. In one televised match the heat from the lights was so intense that it caused the formica on the cushion rails of the table to curl up; the rails grew so hot that the players burnt their hands on them. In another tournament an exploding light burnt a hole in the cloth. In another, while Alex Higgins was playing, a bulb fell and burnt the carpet. It is surprising to recall that Higgins's dramatic breakthrough to the world title at his first attempt in

1972 – a landmark that changed the whole history of snooker – was not witnessed by television cameras at all. The first world final to be televised (and then only in parts) was the match between Ray Reardon and Eddie Charlton in 1973. On that occasion new floodlights for colour TV caused such problems of glare and dazzle that the players had to stop until two of the lamps were switched off. There was also a row over lighting at the 1976 final – a disastrous occasion in every way – when the players threatened to walk out. After that Nick Hunter, the BBC producer who was covering his first world championship, set out to find a permanent solution, which he duly did over the next two years with the help of a BBC lighting specialist called John Crowther. Hunter has been in charge of BBC snooker coverage ever since.

'We didn't realize in those days,' he says, 'that shining lights on a snooker table could make so much difference to the players.' A main problem was the many reflections from the lights off each of the shiny balls, making it difficult to judge distance or direction. This was solved by a sort of skirt which hid the offending lamps from the table while still providing enough light for the cameras. Strip lights solved the problem of bursting bulbs, but they also have a gauze-like filter underneath, just in case. The new lighting rig also reduces the heat on the table, which previously dried out both the cloth, which was like a skating rink, and the players, some of whom used to lose several pounds in weight in the course of a game. The old snooker table shade had to go, with the result that the players' facial expressions, previously hidden, were now visible to the cameras and to the crowd – and the crowd, of course, were now visible to the players, some of whom found it all too distracting and suffered from stage fright at crucial moments. The private world of the snooker player was thus made public, which accounts for much of its success on television. There is no hiding place. David Vine, the BBC commentator, describes it as 'pure sporting theatre'. You can also see more of the game. At cricket, even with close-ups, you cannot really see the ball moving off Botham's bat through the air into the pavilion, but at snooker all the subtleties are laid bare just as they occur. You do not even need slow motion replays, as in soccer, to see what really happened in the goal-mouth scramble.

There are normally four cameras focused on the table, two at ground level and two overhead, all of them at the black spot end. Camera one, on the left, looks across the table and also picks up the sitting-out player in his chair on the other side; camera two does the same from the right. Some of the most revealing shots are of the waiting player composing his facial expression while his opponent humiliates him. This is the most frustrating aspect of the game for the player: while your opponent is at the table, there is absolutely nothing you can do but wait for him to make a mistake. At least in golf you can keep on going round the course, and no matter how well your opponent plays you always have the chance to do better. Camera three covers the whole table from twenty feet above, and camera four zooms down for close-ups of the balls. At home now, watching play from an armchair, I sometimes find myself muttering 'camera one' or 'camera four' as the picture changes. They keep experimenting with the colour of the balls and both BBC and ITV have had their own sets specially made for the cameras. They have developed a new red that shows up brighter on the screen and a new brown to distinguish it more clearly from the reds.

The cameramen are connected to the director through head-phones and watch the match through a viewfinder above their heads. I was interested to note that the viewfinders are in black and white, which must make it harder to spot the colour of the balls; this probably explains why they keep peeping out from behind the camera to look at the table itself. Coloured viewfin-ders are evidently scarce and expensive. The cameramen's job is so tiring – ricking their necks to look into the viewfinder, fol-lowing every angle, making out the colour of the balls, guessing the next shot, listening to instructions, heaving the camera around – that they have to change over fairly frequently, usually in mid-frame. The new man creeps up behind on soft soles and takes over the headphones while the other one creeps out as quietly as he can under the baleful glare of the referee.

The director sits in a scanner, a cramped caravan or Porta-kabin, outside or (at Wembley and some other venues) deep underground in the car park. At Sheffield there are about a dozen BBC vans and caravans parked all over the pavements around the Crucible, hiding the theatre itself from public view. Inside his scanner, the director is surrounded by screens and chooses which of the pictures to transmit, depending on the state of the game. He talks into the cameraman's headphones throughout, telling him when to close in on a shot or a player's face or even to focus on an incident away from the table, such as a pretty girl in the crowd. This requires not only fierce concentration ('it feels like jet lag after a tournament', one of them told me), but knowledge of the game, for nothing can annoy a viewer more than finding that the picture isn't showing him what he wants to see. Both Nick Hunter and Trevor East, his ITV counterpart, are fully aware that fancy camera shots can sometimes interfere with the viewer's pleasure in the game. East takes pride in allowing journalists, rather than technicians, to make the key decisions over what viewers should see.

I wandered in and out of these TV scanners at various venues on the snooker circuit. At Wembley, where the BBC were showing the Benson and Hedges Masters, there was a flap on about advertising symbols on the players' clothes. Kirk Stevens, the Canadian, was wearing a snooker suit designed by the Savile Row tailor Tommy Nutter, said to cost £1000. The fuss was about Auntie showing the maker's name on camera. 'There it is,' said a triumphant BBC man, staring into a screen close-up of Stevens leaning over the table: 'It's on his trouser pocket!' The solemn order went out from director to cameramen: 'At all costs avoid the wording on Kirk's backside.' I was reminded of Chaucer's 'Miller's Tale':

> Kirk was branded on the bum
> God send us all to Kingdom Come.

Then down to the nitty-gritty of TV coverage as Stevens plays Tony Meo:
  'Go in tight on the cue ball. See how tight the black is.'
  'Pull out, number one, wider, wider, show me the bottom pocket.'

'Number one, show me the red across the table into the corner.'

'Number two, pan out to show his whole leg on the table.' Great excitement as a girl fan rises from the audience and presents Kirk Stevens with a drawing of himself. 'Get in on that card,' the director orders the cameraman urgently, 'and don't lose track of that girl.' This is matched by an Indian lady in a red sari seeking Meo's autograph – all good grist for the cameras. Stevens reaches for a consoling cigarette after leaving a black on the edge of the pocket – doubtless to much rejoicing in the Benson and Hedges room upstairs.

Then, suddenly, the unmistakable tones of Margaret Thatcher come ringing through the door. She can't – surely – be here? No, it's just a monitor of the BBC news in the caravan next door. By this time I find that I am stiff, legs numb, head tight with concentration – and I am only watching them at work. The director then makes a joke, addressed to Ted Lowe in the commentary box, which is perched above the cameras in the hall. 'Did you hear the one about the radio commentator who said "Bobby Robson has just pissed a fatness test?" ' Then: 'Talk about the picture, Ted.' Ted duly obliges: 'I think the red will go past the black into the corner pocket.' A moment later: 'Great pot that. Meo is having a lot of thinking time. He's making absolutely sure he gets this.' The director roars with laughter as Meo misses by a mile. My pretentious joke about the Thoughts of Meo is greeted with the groans it deserves.

'Whispering' Ted Lowe, the best-known voice in snooker and one of its most engaging characters, acquired his throaty stage-whisper at Leicester Square Hall in the early days of television, when he sat behind the commentator, the late Raymond Glendenning, passing on expert tips which were not meant to be picked up by the microphone. This was before there was a separate commentary box and they had to sit in the front row of the crowd, as in boxing. In boxing, though, the roar of the crowd ensures that the broadcast comments don't reach the ears of the men in the ring. In snooker they had to operate in total silence – hence the whisper, in case they were heard by the players. Once, when John Pulman was at the table, Lowe said confidently into his microphone: 'He is now about to take the red and will come off the cushion to position himself on the black'. Pulman duly obliged. Lowe continued: 'Following this red, Pulman will go down the table for the red just at the top of the pack and will be well placed for the black again.' Again Pulman did exactly as forecast. This went on for several shots until finally Pulman turned to Lowe and said: 'Ted, do you mind if I play my own bloody game now!'

On one occasion the opposite happened: there was no whisper from Ted Lowe. He had been taken ill and slumped over the microphone. Rex Williams made frantic signals to the director for a replacement. Jack Karnehm had to step over the unfortunate Ted, who was carried out on a stretcher (happily he recovered and was back next day). While this drama was being played out, there was no commentary for eight minutes – and nobody noticed.

The director's quip about Bobby Robson was an in-joke to remind Ted of his own famous boobs in the commentary box, which have made him a regular contributor to *Private Eye*'s 'Colemanballs' column over the years, as he himself recounts with relish. He once said innocently, in hushed tones: 'Fred Davis, the doyen of snooker, now sixty-seven years of age and too old to get his leg over, prefers to use his left hand.' While I was in the scanner myself I heard Ted say: 'Dennis Taylor is one of the best left-handed players in the game – except, of course, for left-handers.' In the early days of colour TV he once said: 'And for those of you watching this in black and white, the pink sits behind the yellow.' Or, at a moment of high excitement: 'The audience are literally electrified and glued to their seats.'

At the Jameson tournament in Newcastle – this one covered by ITV – I looked in on the commentary box, which is well situated above and behind the table. The commentators, two at a time, can watch on monitors or sit up straight and look at the table itself through a glass panel. They are connected by earphones to the director in the basement scanner who prompts them from time to time. The thing is knowing when to come in to assist the viewer's understanding and when to shut up and let the picture speak for itself. They tend to say less now than they used to in the early days, on the assumption that viewers have become more sophisticated. There is tension in the box when they are going out live. It is a source of annoyance to commentators that some of their pithiest remarks are never heard by viewers because that particular frame is among those recorded but not shown. When they want to say something they pick up a hand microphone and speak into it. There is also a 'lazy' microphone (unheard by the audience) into which they can talk back to the director. As we look in, they are about to go on the air and Rex Williams appears to be troubled. 'There's a buzzing in the ears,' he mutters into the 'lazy' microphone. 'You shouldn't have drunk so much last night,' says East unsympathetically as he closes the door. They are good friends. Commentating is not as easy as it sounds. When asked to try it, one well-known player sat speechless in his chair, quite unable to utter a word. They are paid about £160 a day for sitting in a confined space that gets as hot as a sauna. Iced or spiced drinks are essential.

Meanwhile, Dickie Davies, the presenter, is waiting to interview Steve Davis and Alex Higgins on an improvised studio set with armchairs. There is a snooker table at one side where Willie Thorne is practising. Dickie is having his hair curled with a brush by a make-up girl. Steve is waiting patiently with stereo plugged into his ears, probably soul music. He is wearing jeans and sneakers. ITV wanted to interview Tony Knowles about his alleged cancer scare, a sensation in that morning's tabloids, but he has already sold the story exclusively to one of the Sundays. 'Thank God they don't insist on being paid for interviews,' says East. 'It's a breath of fresh air after soccer. It's probably a hangover from the old days – "Christ, I'm on the telly!" '

No Alex. 'Where's 'orrible 'Iggins?' shouts a studio man. 'We'll have to interview him tonight,' says another. 'If he's in a fit state,' says a third. They all swap Higgins stories. One man says: 'Last night we were talking about lateral thinking. "What's the use of that?" Higgins sneered. "Where's the reality in it?" I told him it was like the sense of achievement you get when you complete a crossword. Alex replied: "The only achievement I want is making money. Anybody for cards?" ' The technicians shake their heads sorrowfully at such shameless lack of spiritual grace. Finally, the Hurricane sweeps into the studio. He is in a good mood, unaggressive, even friendly – and sober. The interview goes well.

Problems in the scanner, though, where a match is dragging on longer than expected. They have to juggle times with precision, for some games are to go out live and highlights from others are recorded for the evening roundup. Every shot is logged with its own time code for future reference. Stopwatches and clipboards everywhere. Then there are commercial breaks to be allowed for. It is a mind-boggling operation with much shop talk about 'live crossovers' (which means, I gather, switching from one video tape to another while transmitting), and a great deal of mental arithmetic and split-second judgements on how long a match is going to take. This one, between Dennis Taylor and Joe Johnson, is problematical. 'This isn't going to fall right for us, I can feel it in my water,' says East glumly as Johnson misses a yellow. He turns out to be right, but they very nearly pull it off by some fast talking to the video recordists outside – and would have done it with thirty seconds to spare if someone had not switched over to the wrong video machine in the confusion. With all that computerized technology on hand, a human error has bungled it. East sits back and lights a cigarette. A single, incandescent swear word fills the room, evidently addressed to all and sundry, including me for putting a jinx on them all, then gently down the microphone to Dickie Davies: 'Sorry about that, old bean.'

Before *Pot Black* began in 1969, snooker on television had consisted mainly of fillers between the races or when the cricket was rained off – trick shots, phoney games where the players were instructed to ensure that the result depended on the final frame, and lifeless challenge matches between Joe Davis and a revolving set of opponents chosen by himself. They even tried to introduce numbered balls to make the game more comprehensible to viewers in black and white. Soon after Joe Davis retired in 1964 snooker disappeared from the television screen altogether. As Clive Everton sternly observes: 'In such travestied or corrupt forms as the game had come to be seen, this was the best thing that could have happened, for when a new opportunity presented itself a fresh start could be made.'

The man who reinvented snooker for colour television – and thereby saved the game from extinction by creating a rich new sporting élite – was Philip Lewis, then a BBC producer in Birmingham, now head of events and entertainment in London, supervising things like Royal weddings and *Come Dancing*. Nick Hunter was his personal assistant in the early days. In the late 1960s he was one of the first people in Birmingham to have a colour TV set and this got him thinking professionally about the new opportunities opening up for the medium. Memos had been winging their way around the Corporation about colour TV and what the BBC could come up with to exploit it. 'I remember waking up one morning and thinking, "Yes, it must be snooker," ' Lewis recalls. 'It was as simple as that, chiefly because of the colour of the balls.' He rang Robin Scott, then his Controller at BBC2, who was enthusiastic. Then he rang Ted Lowe, who had been knocking on the doors of the BBC for years in an attempt to persuade them to show some snooker again. He told Ted that two conditions had to be met: the table shade had to go to allow for a lighting nest, and the pros had to agree to a single-frame 'sudden death' format. He was amazed when Lowe rang back in an hour to agree to both conditions. Sydney Lee was brought out of retirement as the referee.

What they had concocted together was *Pot Black*. The title came from Lewis, who had seen billiards and snooker played in South Wales as a boy. 'What always struck me,' he says, 'is that the game was popular with the upper classes and with the workers. Only the middle class despised it.' 'Pot Black' was the name of a game he had played with his chums when they went to a billiards arcade after school. They would put sixpence in the meter for thirty mintues' play; before the meter ran out they would use up any time left to respot the black. In the early days of *Pot Black* there was so little public interest that they had to send for the barmaids, canteen ladies and cleaners from upstairs to fill the spectators' seats in Birmingham's Gosta Green cinema. The playback from the TV critics was immediately encouraging – Philip Purser of the *Sunday Telegraph* compared the snooker players favourably with the 'hysterical pooves of the football field'. One elderly woman wrote in to say: 'The programme is full of nice-mannered people with smart bow ties.' The audience figures were a revelation as the public responded to the quiet delicacy and precision of the game. Soon the audience began to clamour for seats and started arriving by the coach load. It was clear that dozens of people were crowding round each programme in pubs and clubs, making a total that did not register on the graphs of audience measurement. No one, including Ted Lowe, had expected such an overwhelming popular response. Suddenly, the BBC had a success on its hands and snooker was back in business. How does Phil Lewis feel now about making so many other people very rich? 'It doesn't bother me really,' he says modestly. 'Just occasionally, when I'm parking my little car among their Rolls-Royces at Sheffield, I begin to wonder, but not for long.'

Reg Perrin, producer of the programme for twelve years, says: 'Pot Black is now internationally acclaimed as the biggest shop window ever in professional snooker.' As it happened, snooker had some new goods to put in the shop window, for the start of Pot Black coincided with the arrival of new faces on the professional scene, notably those of John Spencer and Ray Reardon, whose appearance and general demeanour went down well with viewers. Reardon won the three-frame final in the first series, beating Spencer, who reversed the order in 1970. The two went on to share the world championship throughout most of the 1970s, replacing John Pulman and Fred Davis as the leading players in the game. They brought a new style, with greater emphasis on potting and cue power, rather than safety play, and prodigious use of screw and side. In the world final of 1970 Spencer amazed and delighted an Australian audience with his ability to bring the cue ball ten feet back down the table for position. Curiously, he had given up the game for a whole decade in snooker's lean years after making a century break as a fifteen-year-old, and it was only a fluke invitation from the National Spastics Society that brought him back to the table. Even then he nearly gave the game up in the 1960s because he was fed up with the governing body. He must have been glad that he hung on.

For the world snooker championship at Sheffield the BBC now mounts its longest operation of the year: 300 hours

recorded, 120 hours on screen, reaching a staggering peak audience of 18.5 million people – 45 per cent of all homes in the land –
not counting those who watch the special programmes prepared
for overseas or the best-selling video which is put on the market
afterwards. It has cost the Corporation over £4 million to secure
exclusive television rights to the world championship until 1990,
plus the cost of actually covering it. This last item was estimated at
£1.3 million in 1985 by the *News of the World*, which described it
as a scandalous waste of public money (the 'British Bonkers
Corporation'). In line with the standard anti-BBC bias of the
Murdoch papers, it highlighted the one-hundred and forty staff
required to cover the event, some of them on generous overtime
rates (it would be instructive to compare the rates and the manning
in the *News of the World*'s own machine room). The BBC says
snooker is still relatively cheap television when the cost is divided
into the number of hours shown on screen, and that the personnel
are genuinely needed over the seventeen days that have to be
covered by staff working away from home. This sounds fair
enough to me. The *News of the World* campaign looked curiously
ill judged and élitist by the end of the championship, when its own
readers must have joined nearly everyone else in enjoying live
coverage of the most gripping sports event of the year. If it's any
consolation to the taxpayer, ITV were prepared to pay much more
money for the rights.

When I went into the BBC transmission scanner it was on one
of their blank afternoons, the producer's nightmare, when a
semi-final had finished inconveniently early. They were padding
out with an exhibition match, interviews and feature items like
'shot of the championship', for which 200,000 viewers had sent in
entries; we had to step over the piles of letters, mounting higher
with every post. Relations backstage are always more tense on
these occasions because the items in the programme are
unfamiliar, the running order keeps on changing, and things are
suddenly cut out because one subject is over-length, and the poor
presenter doesn't know where he is with his script. The link man
has to know which bits have been dropped in case he inadvertently
introduces them and then looks a twerp. David Vine, normally
crisp and competent, is registering a mild degree of impatience.

'Can we have some decision on shot of the championship please? I can't go on waffling.'

'We need to hear from the post office if there are any more entries.'

'Have you remembered the caption for Junior *Pot Black*?'

Suddenly, a warning voice in the scanner: 'We're losing colour – it's bloody VT3 again. Do you want a "do not adjust your set" caption?'

'Is it bad tape or just the machine?'

'There's a scratch on the tape – hell, the label on the box says, "Don't use".'

David Icke, the other presenter, suddenly appears on a screen in the scanner munching a plate of sandwiches. He looks up unperturbed and winks at the camera's intrusive eye. 'You can't fool me,' he says cheerily. 'You're not coming on to me for a while. No panic. Keep life in proportion. When the black box comes to take you away, these little things won't matter.' And munches on philosophically.

Nick Hunter, a tall spare man, rather reserved, first met the snooker people in 1966 when he was a sports producer in Manchester. 'We put a table in the studio and used snooker frames as fillers between the racing on *Grandstand*. We'd say to players like John Pulman, Rex Williams and Fred Davis, "You've got seventeen minutes" – and they'd knock off a frame to any length we wanted. While I applauded their professionalism and the way they could play a frame against the clock, the greys and blacks didn't seem to me to herald a TV sport with much of a future.' After the launch of BBC2 he drifted out of sport into light entertainment, producing The Spinners and Olivia Newton-John. In 1976 he was suddenly landed with the world snooker championship because it happened to be on his home patch in Manchester. It was a disaster, he says, 'a real eye-opener'. There were problems with the promoter (who disappeared with some of the bills unpaid), with the lighting, and with the hall at Wythenshawe, which had beer floating all over the floor and a roof that seemed about to cave in. Even so, he saw the possibilities. 'All those crinklies in waistcoats, they were marvellous, and you could actually see that Alex Higgins's fingers were red raw with biting them. I had never realized that snooker could be like that, people cheering and clapping and sitting on the edge of their seats hardly daring to breathe.' It was Nick Hunter's achievement to extend to snooker tournaments the daily coverage given to sporting events like Wimbledon and to conquer all the technical problems involved in doing so. Instead of a glimpse of the final, or edited highlights, he created a portrait of the whole event, building up slowly to a climax as viewers became more involved, selecting their own heroes and villains as they went along.

After the 1976 experience, Hunter went to Aubrey Singer, then his Controller, and put an ambitious plan for wider coverage – 'he took very little persuading'. The crucial difference was moving to the Crucible Theatre in Sheffield in 1977. This had the right dramatic ambience and was just, but only just, the right size for the cameras to cover two tables in the early rounds. The venue was suggested by the wife of Mike Watterson, then the promoter of the tournament and later chairman of Derby County Football Club, after she had seen a play performed at the Crucible. 'The theatrical atmosphere was perfect,' says Hunter, 'better than some studio with lashed-up scaffolding.'

The viewing figures for the 1978 finals were incredible – 'we opened champagne every time we got them'. An unexpected and enthusiastic part of the new audience were housewives during the day, who rapidly picked up the expertise. The nation stayed up late and went to bed red-eyed. Fan mail, flowers and telegrams poured in; queues of autograph hunters formed outside the stage door. The BBC trembled with excitement at its rave success. 'Those were halcyon days,' Hunter recalls. 'We used to say to ourselves, "It'll never be like this again" – and in a sense it can't be, though we've had even bigger audience figures since. It was like having a new baby.'

'Backstage at the Crucible,' wrote Peter Fiddick in the *Guardian*, 'there is a sense that the result hardly matters, that something new is happening. The top professionals are very conscious of their new audience and its implications. For them, the game is at last being shown properly, at length, with all its tactics, and the fact that it could prove even more popular that way opens a whole new future even to men said to be potting £30,000 a year.' Fred Davis, making a remarkable comeback at 64 in a game he thought had died years before, explained: 'What the public are getting here is the feel of what it is like playing under pressure hour after hour for days on end.'

At the BBC Brian Wenham (now Director of TV Programmes) and Cliff Morgan (now Head of Outside Broadcasting) were influential supporters. 'We worked out the key questions,' says Hunter: 'Does it televise well? Are the British any good at it? Is it easy for the public to understand? The answers were all strongly in the affirmative.' The production problems had become more manageable with the development of new video recording techniques which permitted more precise editing of highlights (i.e. cutting out the really boring bits). He accepts that there is probably enough snooker on television now, but the viewing figures do not support the argument that the game is already over-exposed. The WPBSA has had to step in more than once to stop matches it regarded as TV 'overkill' or just gimmicks. In one of these proposed TV spectaculars Steve Davis and Terry Griffiths were due to play two American pool champions. Meanwhile Mrs Muriel Wall told the British Migraine Association that watching too much snooker could give you a headache. 'It's a major source of migraine,' she warned.

'If ever a game was made for TV,' says Hunter, 'it was snooker. I well remember an amazing frame four years ago, when the last red got stuck behind the pink with the black on the edge of the pocket, and Willie Thorne and Bill Werbeniuk played for twenty-five minutes without potting a single ball. Technically it was brilliant play, but I was worried it might make dull TV. Well, we got a bigger response to that than anything we'd done. We made it "Frame of the Day" and we still get requests to show it. The amazing thing about snooker is that the more we transmit the bigger the viewing audience gets. People get hooked.'

The viewing figures and the emergence of new working-class heroes – Ray Reardon on *The Parkinson Show*, Terry Griffiths on *This is Your Life* – prompted ITV to make stronger efforts to get in on the act. Thames televised three days of a tournament in 1979, but ran into trouble with overtime rates for their crews, with the result that they economized on their recording and thereby missed the chance of showing the first televised maximum break of 147 by John Spencer. It was in one of the three semifinal frames they chose not to record. It was another four years before Steve Davis made the first maximum break on television in his *annus mirabilis*, 1981; ironically, it was against Spencer. Two years later, Cliff Thorburn made the first 147 to be shown in the world championship, after fluking the first red.

The independent companies were always at a disadvantage against the BBC because their federal structure encouraged internecine arguments (like the recent one over *Dallas*) and made decision-making more cumbersome, especially where large sums of money were involved. 'We underestimated it,' admits John Bromley, head of sport at London Weekend Television, 'especially its huge appeal to women viewers. It has everything going for it – it rarely overruns, like tennis you know where the ball is going to go, you can get more revealing close-ups of the players' faces than in any other sport. Above all, of course, it's gladiatorial.'

When Channel 4 arrived it doubled ITV's scheduling options, making it easier to create room for snooker. Since then Trevor East has been brought down from Central Television in Birmingham to coordinate all ITV snooker coverage, working out of Thames TV in London. He worked hard behind the scenes to secure exclusive TV rights in the world championship from 1985–90, and actually offered more money than the BBC, but not enough to break the old ties of loyalty between the Corporation and the WPBSA, who are still very conscious that it was the BBC's *Pot Black* which helped to save the professional game from extinction in the 1960s. 'It was that loyalty clause that beat us in the end,' says East. 'I have to admire that.' He had calculated that an offer of £7 million would be needed to wrest the tournament from the BBC, but the ITV network committee, thinking they knew better, authorized him to go no higher than £5 million – which, though higher than the BBC offer, was not enough to do the trick. East, a former football writer whose cheery outgoing nature is in sharp contrast with Hunter's more reserved approach, intends to give the BBC a good run for their money. The Independent Broadcasting Authority, however, to judge by a brief party conversation I had with its Director General, is surprisingly snooty about peak-time snooker, which comes oddly from the so-called 'people's channel'.

I found Trevor East greatly troubled about the Dulux tournament in Derby. He explained that he had been obliged to ask the professional body to agree to reduce the number of frames for each match from eleven to nine because of the slow play. Unless the committee agreed, the matches might not be finished in time for the viewers to see the result. He did not like the idea of television interfering in the sport – 'the tail wagging the dog' – but he could see no alternative. The players were two frames an hour slower this season, he reckoned. They were being more cautious; the difference between going out in the first or the second round could mean as much as £4000 to a player. He knew his request would not be fair on those eliminated in eleven-frame preliminaries who might have been leading after nine, but it could not be helped. 'If snooker is for television, it must learn to adapt to television's needs, which are the viewer's needs,' he added defensively. His request was granted. In fact, East need not have been so conscience-stricken about it. One of the effects of television has always been to reduce the length of matches: the BBC and sponsors required that from the start. *Pot Black*, of course, is a single frame until the final. Fred Davis once scratched from a tournament in the 1950s because he did not regard 37 frames as a fair test of skill. Challenge matches in the old days usually took a week and sometimes a fortnight; the world championship itself took up the best part of a year, moving around the country from round to round. Television put a stop to that too. Most of Joe Davis's fifteen world championship finals lasted more than 70 frames, whereas today they play only half that number in the final – just enough, Nick Hunter hopes, to get a definitive result.

Television has not only given snooker the kiss of life, but poured manifold blessings on its head. Mainly, of course, it has brought money into the professional game – in amounts Joe Davis could never have dreamed of. More young players have come along to refine their art in pursuit of the massive prizes, thereby refreshing the game. Those weary hours on the practice table, which deterred many young hopefuls in the 1960s, now have some point and incentive. Television has changed snooker in a few breathless years, as Alexander Clyde of the London *Standard* put it, 'from a cosy little travelling circus to a multi-million-pound industry'. The television exposure has attracted commercial sponsors who want to see the name of their product up in lights before the admiring millions in this glamorous company – especially those, like tobacco firms, who are otherwise forbidden to advertise on TV. The players themselves are in great demand for exhibitions on the club circuit, attracting a new audience brought to the game by television. The best of them have become showbiz personalities, much sought after for opening supermarkets or appearing on quiz shows. Sales of snooker tables have grown beyond all records – either for people's homes or to furnish the new clubs that have been springing up all over Mrs Thatcher's Britain, despite (or maybe because of) the level of unemployment. None of this success would have been attained, however, unless the game had been ready and equal to the challenge that television brought to it. Fortunately, the new breed of players have the right qualities for the modern age – none more so than the game's first media superstar, the Hurricane that blew in from Belfast.

## Chapter Six

# THE HURRICANE

---

The Jampot, a Belfast billiard hall, has become notorious as the place where Alex 'Hurricane' Higgins misspent his youth. His teachers at nearby Kelvin School called it the Gluepot because they could never prise him away. He seems to have been almost permanently there from the age of ten to fourteen, learning how to play snooker in a hard school. 'I was in the Jampot morning, noon and night,' he says, 'trying to hustle grown men.' He used to hide his satchel under the table, away from the prying eyes of school inspectors, and backed himself to win with his dinner money. When this ran out he would mark for the other players at threepence a time until he had enough money to play again.

'You might be boiling over wanting to play and there you'd be, scribbling on the back of a cigarette packet,' he says. 'Still, it was a good way to learn. I was watching their mistakes. I was taking it all in.' He lived on Coca-Cola and Mars bars. His sister Anne says: 'He had 36 days at school in his last year: the rest of the time he was in the Jampot.' His sisters would be knocked back by the smoke when they were sent to look for him in the dingy room, illuminated only by the lighting over the tables. He still plays as if the lights might run out at any moment and as if he is still paying for them.

Danny Blanchflower, the ex-soccer star who sometimes partners Higgins at golf, recalls the Belfast of those days: 'There were boys kicking footballs round the streets and a lot of people out of work. Men drifted into the billiard halls who had very little money, and they were playing for all they had. The only light would be the one over the table, and you could see the strain on these characters' faces. It was like a theatre.'

I found the Jampot – or what remains of it – down a side-cut filled with builders' rubble, behind the offices of Taskprint Security Services on the Donegal Road. It is a desolate place, a tumbledown warehouse with a green roof, now divided into a pool hall, containing four tables and about twenty fruit machines, and a bingo hall. It looks across the sunken railway culvert to Eastwoods Car Flattener Service. The walls are covered in obscene slogans that could hardly be dignified as graffiti: 'Billy Fuck the Jampot', 'Victor UVF', 'Fuck the IRA' – a reminder that this is the heartland of the Protestant working class. It is virtually the last building still intact on a seedy brick-strewn site that would make a Fagin's paradise or a setting for the last killing scene in *Odd Man Out*. Even the name has not survived. 'It's a hundred years since it was called the Jampot,' I was informed by a toothless old lady in one of the Victorian back-to-backs that surround it. Among many other indignities, the building had since been used as a sewing factory and a warehouse for timber and hardware.

Higgins was brought up in nearby Abingdon Street, now vacated and boarded up ready for demolition with a sign that the structures are dangerous. His parents have moved to a new house in the Sandy Row area. It is all part of the Department of the Environment (Northern Ireland) Comprehensive Development Area 21 – 'Site acquired for redevelopment including housing, commercial, industrial, educational and amenity projects'. It is hard to believe that any modern 'amenity project' could match the service offered by the Jampot to the Higgins generation – or, for that matter, the services offered by the crumbling Eleanor's Pie Shop on the Donegal Road. It was eerie walking down the empty street, past the deserted houses, rather like being on the deserted set of a Western film. Here and there, like the last tooth in an old man's mouth, a house was still occupied, with a brightly polished door and a defiant display of flowers in the front window. There was an old fly-poster celebrating 'Jesus – the champion of champions'. One boarded-up house had a faded Union Jack still flying from a pole – an apt symbol, perhaps, for the troubled province itself.

Later, as I was leaving the heavily guarded *Belfast Telegraph* building, I saw a big white church across the road and remembered that I'd once been given the improbable information that the Trelford family were commemorated in Belfast's Protestant Cathedral. This must be it, the Cathedral Church of St Anne, so I ventured inside. I soon found the window, close to a plaque honouring Carson, the leader of breakaway Ulster. It showed King David playing psalms on a lute and also being anointed by Saul. The inscription read: 'This window, a bequest of James Trelford, commemorates many members of a family who worshipped in Belfast Parish Church continuously for over 200 years, especially James Trelford (1854–1928), honorary secretary of the Cathedral Board, 1920–28, and Robert Trelford (1858–1947), Vestry Man 1902–46'. There was also a Trelford Street in Belfast.

It turned out that this branch of the family had gone to Northern Ireland from England with William of Orange's army in 1720. Two brothers stayed on to become successful farmers. Other members of the family went south, where there is a graveyard at Galway stuffed with Trelford remains, and some went on to the United States. Meanwhile, the parent branch had stayed in England oblivious of their Ulster connection. My mother's mother was a Dublin Catholic. So, having gone to Belfast in search of Alex Higgins's roots, I had stumbled on some surprising roots of my own.

Eddie Swaffield recalls meeting Higgins for the first time as a tiny ten-year-old in 1959. 'He'd got hold of sixpence from somewhere. Half of it was to pay for a game of snooker in the Jampot, but he wanted me, as an older boy, to put the other threepence on a horse in the betting shop. He hasn't changed much since, only the stakes have got much bigger – he bets in hundreds now.' (Higgins is rumoured to have wagered £2000 on himself to win the 1985 Benson and Hedges tournament, which he lost.) Swaffield remembers how the boy Alex taught himself to play difficult shots. 'He picked up "side" so that he could pot a long ball along the cushion. He worked it all out for himself that the "side" could be imparted to the object ball and this would make it hug the cushion.'

Higgins says: 'I never had any formal instruction. I never learned by words, but by watching.' He gradually moved up the

Jampot's eighteen tables as his game improved until he found himself face to face with Damon Runyon characters like Georgie 'The Bug' McClatchey, and then graduated to the Shaftesbury Club and the YMCA to play in local leagues. He claims that he acquired his legendary speed round the table by playing with a bully called Jim Taylor, who used to smack him around the head unless he moved away quickly enough. He was soon scoring century breaks inside four minutes. Experts are still amazed that Higgins has survived so long at the top – over fifteen years now – with what many of them regard as basic 'faults' in his technique. The main problem is the way he lifts his head as he makes the shot. Every part of the body should be perfectly still when you pot, yet Alex seems to be moving before his cue action is finished. Some people say this must be an illusion, that he must be still for an instant as he actually plays the shot. Willie Thorne has said: 'Technically, he is just a phenomenon. He does every-thing wrong: his stance is square, he lifts his head, his arm's bent, he snatches at some of his shots. Of all the pros, Alex would be about the last one you'd want to copy technically.'

There is no denying his talent. Fred Davis says he has 'one of the sharpest brains in the game'. John Pulman goes further and describes it as 'the quickest brain the game has ever seen'. Steve Davis stresses the importance of the crowd to Alex – 'it makes him feel like God'. He adds that 'when Alex is playing at his best, he's the best player in the world'. Terry Griffiths says: 'I love watching him play. He's so exciting. But his patience tends to run out a shot or two before other players.' Doug Mountjoy: 'Sometimes he will do something just for the crowd. He might have an easy positional shot on, but he'll do the outrageous.' Ray Reardon: 'It's not all bang, crash, all that business. He knows where the ball's going. He's a top-class professional and he reads the table as quick as a flash.' Jimmy White: 'He's the only player that other snooker players will actually go and watch – including me.'

The impact of Alex Higgins on the snooker scene of the early 1970s was phenomenal. 'Before Alex, snooker was dead,' says Swaffield. It would be hard to imagine anyone less like the Joe Davis prototype of the professional player. His idol was George

Best – like him an Ulster Protestant and (also like him) given to moodiness, drink and girls. But first he tried something else: he went to be a jockey at Eddie Reavey's stables near Wantage in Berkshire. It did not work out – he was constantly in fights with the other stable lads and soon tired of the mucking out. He also had a weight problem. He drifted to London and took a job in a paper mill, venturing out at night to play till dawn in Soho clubs. One of his regular opponents was a musician in one of the London orchestras. Eventually, after Alex had scored centuries in successive frames, the musician gave up. Says Higgins: 'He looked at me in a meaningful way. For a minute I thought he was going to say, "Don't shoot me, I'm only the piano player", but all he said was "Take this, I've had enough". And then he gave me his cue. After that I presume he stuck to Mozart.' Before long he was homesick and went back to hustling in Belfast. He won the Irish amateur title in 1968 at the age of nineteen. Eddie Swaffield maintains that at this time Alex had the most gifted natural talent the game has ever seen. 'He played shots that should have been impossible, that *were* impossible for anyone else.' Television, he claims, never saw Alex when he was at his very best, even though he has since played some memorable snooker for the cameras.

   The breakthrough came when he played for Belfast YMCA in the final of the British amateur championship at Penycraig Labour Club in Bolton. He won the title virtually singlehanded. He was spotted by a local promoter and matched against John Spencer, who was then at his peak. He stayed on in Lancashire, a hot spot for snooker, playing at the Old Post Office Club in Blackburn, the Elite in Accrington, and at nearby Oswaldtwistle, where he had a flat. He may have been influenced by the fact that his fellow countryman, Dennis Taylor, had gone to live in Blackburn. He strongly denies the legend that he suddenly turned up with his cue case in the North of England like a gunslinger for hire, throwing out the challenge: 'I'm a snooker player. I play for money.' The reality, Alex maintains, was more prosaic and more workmanlike – hour after hour of practice on the Old Post Office Club table and three-handed games (known as 'sticks') with Dennis Taylor and Jim Meadowcroft for half-a-crown a go.

Not all players believe in the value of practice, on the grounds that you can leave your best shots on the practice table. Fred Davis sometimes went straight into a match without even a warm up. Dennis Taylor has rarely done more than an hour a day. But Higgins finds he needs it to loosen up and regrets that his punishing schedule – trains, boats and aeroplanes (he has not driven a car since he hit a lorry while he was a learner) – does not give him as much time as he would like. 'By the time I've travelled all day and played all night, and crawled into bed in the small hours, I want to sleep late in the mornings. I know I've burnt the candle at both ends in the past, but I've learned the value of sleep.'

The Year of the Hurricane was 1972, when he won the world professional title at the first attempt. '1972 was my year, my property, my personal piece of the calendar. It was the year when everything changed, not only for me, but for snooker.' It started to go right in January when he beat Jack Rea for the Irish professional title, a crown he had worn for twenty years. Rea recalled afterwards: 'He was a pure attacking player, willing to gamble on position. That Friday night in Limerick, when he Hurricaned me 9–0, he had the crowd behind him right from the start. He broke me really.'

In the world event he met former champion John Pulman, whom he respectfully addressed as 'Mr Pulman', in a long-drawn-out quarter final. Higgins eventually won the match, picking up a great deal about safety play, a part of the game he knew little about. His next opponent, Rex Williams, then the world billiards champion, says: 'Had he not played Pulman in the previous round, he wouldn't have beaten me. He has a very good brain for snooker, and in that long match against Pulman he learned enough about safety to beat me 31–30 in the semifinal.' Higgins was helped by a fatal miss on the blue in the final frame which Williams still remembers vividly: 'That blue could have changed the direction of both our careers. I knew I'd lost the match *then*.'

In the final Higgins came up against the formidable figure of Spencer. It was staged in the concert room of the Selly Park British Legion in Birmingham, a far cry from Thurston's,

Leicester Square Hall or the Crucible. There were no television cameras and only three or four journalists, who had access to a single pay phone with no light in it. In fact, the only light in the room was the one over the table, which made it virtually impossible to write or to see. Even this was plagued by power cuts (it was the time of the first of the Scargill miners' strikes) during one of which Spencer and his wife were stuck between floors in a lift for half an hour. The spectators were perched precariously on planks and beer crates. Higgins recalls: 'It was bedlam in there, with chairs being shoved about, pint pots crashing, and people passing the time of day and strolling round the table while you were lining up your shots.' Clive Everton wrote in *Snooker Scene* at the time: 'Higgins opened up as if he was playing a light-hearted knockabout as pots flew in from every conceivable angle.' He missed only two pots all week that he might have been expected to get and won by 37 frames to 32. The prize was £480 – 'these days they fine me more than that', says Higgins ruefully. He had, however, taken the precaution of backing himself over several weeks at 10–1, 4–1, 2–1 and 6–4. It was the biggest upset for years.

'Snooker was never the same again,' says Everton simply. The image so carefully fostered by Joe Davis was transformed utterly. This thin, pale, hollow-cheeked ex-jockey was something new to the professional game, cutting through its genteel pretensions like a swordsman. Apart from George Best, Higgins's idols were Muhammad Ali and Lester Piggott, men who went their own way and, in the fashionable argot of the time, did their own thing. 'Suddenly,' as one paper put it, 'snooker is trendy.' Higgins styled himself 'the people's champion', wisely abandoning an earlier promotional idea that he be billed as Alexander the Great. He had Che Guevara posters on his walls. He carried around with him the air of the pool-room shark, the hustler (a world made familiar to people at that time by the Paul Newman film), the matador or the lone silent gunslinger of the Old Wild West. He was moody and mercurial, a buccaneer. The snooker establishment looked down their noses, but the public loved it. Not only sports editors, but news editors and television producers, began to take notice. He became a headliner, snooker's very own pop star, moving the game for the first time in its history off the back page and on to the front page of the tabloid press. Snooker, which only shortly before had seemed to be a moribund sport for middle-aged men in bow ties, had found a man with modern media magic. He was the subject of a successful TV documentary, showing him standing on abandoned railway platforms in the middle of the night. It was made by John Morgan, who recalls having to rescue Higgins from late-night escapades while the film was being made. On more than one occasion he removed Higgins from the clutches of the law in exchange for a promise that he would play an exhibition at the police club – when he had sobered up. His off-table exploits were spread across the popular Sundays. His propensity for getting involved in scrapes, usually while the worse for drink, coupled with his dash, skill and bravado, made him a popular anti-hero. He clearly did not give a damn for anyone.

This was the start of the stream of hell-raising stories that go on to this day. Dennis Broderick, one of his early managers, recalls a typical incident:

We wondered what we'd taken on. One Christmas we gave him his wages, his presents and his flight ticket to Belfast. About three in the morning the phone rang. It was Alex.

'Hello,' he said, 'I'm at the Ace of Spades.' (About three miles away.)

'What are you doing there, Alex?'

'I'm skint. I lost it all at roulette. Can you pick me up?'

He still had his flight ticket. No money. Cleared the lot.

But he's not a bad lad, really.

In the old military classification, he drinks 'regularly and unwisely'. As a former would-be jockey, he knows the horses but, according to one of his friends, 'he is the world's worst card player'. Over the years his wild conduct has brought him fines, fights, bannings, appearances in court, a marriage break-up, a health breakdown, arguments with referees, and any number of late-night brawls in clubs and hotels. Headlines like 'Higgins Blow-up', 'The Hurricane and the Back-Scratching Spitfire Girl', 'Drunk and Naked – Alex dragged his Wife round the Floor by her Hair', 'Hurricane is Cleared of Hitting Bedroom Blonde', etc., are part of the legend. Some of his behaviour, especially when he abuses fans seeking autographs, is plainly tiresome and inexcusable. He once threw a pile of fan letters out of his car window in the Peak District.

Many of his troubles appear to stem from the exhaustion suffered by his thin frame from his late nights and long cross-country journeyings, and by frustration at sudden losses of form. And, of course, the drink. A friend said: 'Living with Alex was like living on the edge of a volcano. One minute he'd be calm, happy – two glasses later it was like World War Three.' He went through a bad patch in the early 1970s when a hotel porter stood on his favourite cue and broke it. He was in a terrible state in 1981 and had to have medical tests in a nursing home, where a *Mirror* writer, Noreen Taylor, found him:

> He was lying on his bed crying and swearing he would never look at another vodka. From now on it was to be fruit juice only because he would shortly be teaching Steve Davis a few lessons on snooker.
>
> When that crying session ended, Alex reached under the bed and pulled out a bag filled with vodka miniatures and beer cans. The tears soon changed to giggles and the following night he was entertaining friends.
>
> He is like so many people who have groomed themselves brilliantly for one thing, and one thing alone. They fail to get to grips with all other human aspects that contribute towards making a rounded personality. To put it at its most simple, he is a genius with a snooker cue but a novice at relationships.

Yet he is genuinely liked by people who know him well. Eddie Swaffield says he is basically lonely, always in need of company. Until his marriage, which steadied him for a while, he was drawn to a series of father figures, some of whom let him down. Del Simmons, one of the game's top administrators, doubles as his manager now – because, it is whispered, nobody else will take the job on. To his credit, it has to be said, he is devoted to his family, to children, to animals and to the many pals he picks up easily wherever he goes. He also does a great deal of unsung work for charity. He once sat up all night composing a poem to his wife for her birthday.

He is a natural focus of controversy and has been in trouble with the authorities for playing in braces, in a green suit, in a Fedora hat, in an eye-patch, and for playing without a tie (he now has a medical dispensation for this, on the grounds that ties give him a rash). He has walked out of matches and been frog-marched out of them. He has fought with the crowd, sworn at them, even thrown his cue at them. He left India in a hurry after offending people by taking his shirt off because of the heat. A recurring theme in Higgins stories are his fits of repentance, scrawling notes of apology, offering to come back the next night to make amends, even proffering cash in compensation. How long can he go on at this pace? 'Indefinitely,' he says. 'I'm a whizz kid and flamboyance will never die.' But in 1972 he gave himself only a decade at the top. 'I can't go on for ever,' he said. 'When I've got enough money, say in ten years, I'll get out and go into business.'

He has certainly stayed at the top longer than anyone could have foreseen, having been prematurely written off on more than one occasion. He lost in the final of the world championship to Reardon in 1976 and to Thorburn in 1980, but came back glori-ously in 1982, against all predictions, to seize his chance after Steve Davis and Terry Griffiths had both gone out surprisingly in the first round. He came through a desperate 13–12 finish against Doug Mountjoy and a 16–15 semifinal against Jimmy White, taking the last two frames in death-or-glory style by sheer guts. He won a closely-fought final against Reardon by 18 frames to 15, finishing with the brilliant flourish of a total clearance of 135. This was followed by tearful scenes of joy as he called up his wife Lynn and baby daughter Lauren to share their moment of triumph with millions of television viewers. Nobody could begrudge him a taste of the fortune he had brought to the game.

For it was undoubtedly Higgins who first brought the money into snooker after his dramatic victory in 1972 and all the attendant publicity. After that the promoters, the commercial sponsors and the BBC got together to run tournaments in a more businesslike way. 'I was a major force in bringing snooker out of the shadows,' he says with characteristic humility. 'I was the one that made it a spectator sport, an entertainment. If I hadn't started the ball rolling like that, I doubt that you'd have the young boys in the game that there are now, because most of them were inspired by Alex Higgins. I have created an audience of millions who have never even played the game.'

He is still, after all these years and all the damaging publicity, number one at the box office. A tournament director told me that the next most popular draw is Jimmy White, with Steve Davis and Dennis Taylor some way back at third and fourth. There is an intensity about Higgins's style – pacing round edgily in the pool of harsh light that separates the table from the semi-darkness of the main arena – that is compulsive to watch. I find I am oddly disappointed when he is eliminated from a tournament. 'Our interest's on the dangerous edge of things,' as Browning put it. Higgins himself is baffled by the source of his exceptional crowd appeal. 'I don't know what it is I have for them. I know that I excite them. When I walk into a hall packed with two thousand people I can feel it wash over me. I turn people on like no one else does.' The effect is to turn himself on as well, rather as cricketer Ian Botham is sometimes inspired by the crowd. 'It's as though a racing driver has suddenly found an extra gear, like overdrive. Some force takes me over and I know I can't miss the balls. I feel wonderfully alive – unconquerable, invincible.'

Writer Jean Rafferty, observed this process in her book:

It's as if at some point during a match he moves from being Alex Higgins to being the Hurricane. He's rolling, the crowds are with him, he carries them with him. But it's not the demonstration of power that his sobriquet would suggest. If he resembles any natural phenomenon it really isn't the Hurricane sweeping everything before it by force. It's an electrical storm, incandescent, erratic, ripping the air apart in unpredictable bursts. Other players channel their desire to win into will, but the Hurricane goes beyond that. His desire becomes will in the heat of inspiration. Any player who chooses inspiration as his protection, the quality he relies on most when he is threatened, is a gambler, a real high-roller, and of course that's why the public love him.

1   Kirk Stevens – 'a lost soul on the snooker circuit'. An opponent claimed he was 'as high as a kite on dope'. (Eamonn McCabe)

2 Alex 'Hurricane' Higgins: At his best when the crowd is behind him – 'It makes him feel like God.'

3  The tearaways: Kirk Stevens – 'battles of the mind' – with Jimmy White, the most fluent natural talent in the game. (Eamonn McCabe)

4　Del Simmons, 'the Sheriff presiding over Snookertown's gold rush. His face is one of the most impressive landmarks in the game.' (Eamonn McCabe)

5 Referee Len Ganley, 'the Jolly Green Giant': 'To use my hand on a ball would be desecration.' (Eamonn McCabe)

6  Steve Davis with Barry Hearn, 'his manager, partner, promoter, Svengali and friend'. Their partnership revolutionized snooker's rewards.

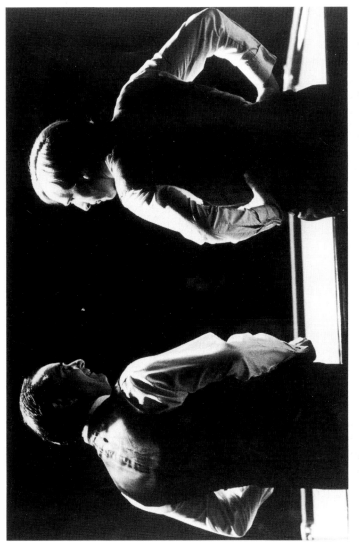

7 The Welsh mafia: Ray Reardon, ex-miner, ex-policeman, six times world champion, 'the man of many masks', with Terry Griffiths, who finds release in martial arts and a motor-bike.

8 The Romford mafia on the move. Steve Davis, manager Barry Hearn, Robbo the 'minder', and the rest of the gang all tread the same path to the Crucible.

9 Dennis Taylor – 'the man who put the smile back into snooker' – peers through the glasses that helped him to the top of the world. (World of Sports Photos)

10   Jimmy White, the 'Tooting tearaway': the most fluent natural talent in the
     game. (Eamonn McCabe)

11 Alex 'Hurricane' Higgins – 'he cut through the game's genteel pretensions like a swordsman. Snooker was never the same again.'

12　Steve Davis lines up a shot, with referee John Williams in the background. 'Opponents have the look of sailors who can hear the crack of the iceberg.' (Eamonn McCabe)

13  Cliff Thorburn – a man 'attuned to life's little ironies, with the air of a
riverboat gambler settling down for the heat of the night'.

14  Tony Knowles – the fruits of success include a house in Tenerife, a disco and a chip-shop, and still he doesn't smile. (Eamonn McCabe)

15 Big Bill Werbeniuk: 'A big soft thing like a teddy bear – 30 pints a day on doctor's orders.' (Sporting Pictures (UK) Ltd)

16    Steve Davis, the highest paid sportsman in Britain: 'I've tried to be flash, but I'm afraid I'm not very good at it.' (Roy Peters)

John Roberts philosophized in the *Daily Mail*: 'Perhaps this haunted man embodies for people the neuroses of modern life.' Hugh McIlvanney of the *Observer* explained it thus:

'You need more than the agitated vulnerability of Higgins's face, the impression that beneath the fancy open-necked shirt sharp teeth are gnawing away at his entrails, to explain his appeal to the modern game's mass public. Another part of it may be the raw sense of the streets that he brings with him into a world where the dress and manners of the pros have always sought to put distance between them and the image of snooker halls as repositories of the coarse and the dubious.'

Unfortunately, the coarse and the dubious have recently been flocking back. This is the darker side of his popularity as 'the people's champion', drawing an unwelcome clientele of raucous yobbos into the game, playing up to them with his McEnroe–type tantrums when he dislikes a referee's decision. It would be unfair to suggest, however, that all Higgins's fans are of this type. His air of a little boy lost widens his appeal to an altogether different group of people.

Angela Patmore, who wrote a book with Higgins and another on sporting stress, dedicated a poem to him that conveys something of the emotional charge he generates:

> I've seen my game grow weary all these years,
> learning the hard way – safety first and last:
> you can't allow a pro an opening –
> he'll kill you if he can, as you would him –
> we clench each other with an iron grasp –
> our jaws are set tight like the tables grim –
> for every ball there's a fierce bargaining.
> And through it all, I've learned to play the part
> as clinically and cold as any man:
> to grit my teeth and hide away my heart
> and all the flair that made me what I am.
> But sometimes when the house is full, sometimes
> I hear a sound like the wind, and through my mind

there sails the magic of the coloured balls
and long reds like a matador's rich blood –
it takes me like a river in full flood
and bursts the banks of all these petty rules.
And then I hear my song without a name
and go back to the crowd from whence I came.

It is clearly a most unusual man who can appeal to such a widely disparate range of human feelings – and Higgins is nothing if not unusual, as he admits himself. 'Listen,' he says, 'when I came into this world they threw the blueprint away.' Some people might say that was providential. Certainly the game's administrators would. Rex Williams, the WPBSA chairman, put it this way: 'Snooker can afford only one Alex Higgins. Any more and the game would risk destroying itself.'

When Higgins was fined £1500 for stirring up the crowd and swearing at Wembley, women fans were divided over his treatment. Ann Wilton of Egham wrote to *Snooker Scene*: 'To blame Alex for his followers' behaviour is so illogical as to be ludicrous. If there was any justice in the world, he ought to be awarded at least an OBE for his services to snooker instead of being knocked like this.' Mrs I. E. Diffley of South Croydon disagreed: 'Higgins' dress (or lack of it), his behaviour when he is losing, his general demeanour, all bring the game into disrepute. It is awful for him to be called the people's champion. We too are people: he is not *our* champion.'

The final verdict will probably be that Alex 'Hurricane' Higgins did more good to snooker than he did to himself.

*Chapter Seven*

# BARRY AND STEVE

Down an alley just off Romford's shopping precinct, wedged between the station and a multi-storey car park, stands the headquarters of the highest-paid sportsman in Britain. Steve Davis, the snooker champion, is lying full length on a sofa reading his horoscope in a tabloid newspaper, perhaps seeking reassurance that the omens are right for his next tournament. The smart modern furnishings and décor around him are clearly part of snooker's prosperous new image, rather than the smoky down-at-heel atmosphere I was expecting – and even vaguely hoping for. Outside the front door, however, there is another entrance: this one leads up some steps into a cavernous, green-painted snooker hall straight out of *The Hustler*, where working-class males of all ages from early teens upwards, some of them unemployed, are potting balls with an enviable sureness of touch.

It was up here, over table 13 in this dingy smoke-filled room – once (but not now, I am assured) the haunt of gamblers and villains – that Steve Davis, then eighteen and just out of school, first met Barry Hearn, the man destined to be his manager, partner, promoter, Svengali and friend. That was in 1976, the year Davis won the British junior amateur billiards title. Not only did the meeting change both their lives: it revolutionized the whole game of snooker. Two years later, Steve turned professional and signed a contract with Barry at a bus stop in Blackpool. In another three years he was world champion, and he and Hearn (the 'H' is silent, they say in the game) were well on their way to becoming snooker's first millionaires. Their historic meeting came only two years after Hearn, an East End chartered accountant with interests in property and the clothing trade, had come into the game as chairman of Lucania Snooker Clubs. 'I thought I'd bought a chain of toilets,' he says. Davis, who had been taught snooker by his father at Plumstead Common Working Men's Club, had gone north of the river to Romford in search of competition. When he asked to enter the Lucania tournament, which he had seen advertised in a snooker magazine, Hearn was called up from his office to see what the youngster could do.

Neither man recalls the meeting as an earth-shattering moment. 'There's no way I thought he was a champion,' says Hearn, who cringes at the memory of the untrendy clothes Davis was wearing. Nor was he encouraged by the sight of his red hair. Davis, typically, can remember that he was playing a four-cushion shot to get out of a tricky snooker when Hearn appeared. 'As soon as he walked through the door, Providence smiled on me,' Davis says simply, with genuine gratitude. The feeling is mutual. Their success has been due largely, of course, to Davis's remarkable skill with a snooker cue, but also to Hearn's remarkable skill with money, which has helped to widen the commercial opportunities available to all professionals in the game. They had the luck to be young (Hearn is ten years older than Davis) and to be teaming up just as the snooker boom – triggered by its huge popularity on colour TV – was taking off.

Hearn is an exuberant, fresh-faced, outgoing man whose directness, especially over money, is either brash or engaging, according to taste. I find him clever, quick and very funny, with a deadly gift of repartee which Steve gamely struggles to match. He has done much, one suspects, to help Davis overcome a natural diffidence. 'He didn't say a word to me for two years,' says Hearn. 'He didn't say a word to anybody. He was among East Enders who aren't exactly delicate about how they treat you. He couldn't defend himself physically. If that's the case and you can't do the job verbally, you'll get eaten alive. They used to verbal him to death up there.' Hearn has been a guide in that rough world and a trusted friend in moments of crisis and self-doubt. When Davis was going through a bad patch during the world championship of 1981, Hearn took him up to his hotel bedroom and played Space Invaders with him for hours on end on a video machine, which apparently did the trick. On other occasions he has been tougher, forcing Davis to show more confidence in himself. 'Be the guv'nor' is his favourite piece of advice. He exudes a rare and enviable sense of personal fulfilment, and once said to me: 'I can't add anything to my life.' In a game where self-control under pressure can be as vital as technique, having a man like Barry Hearn in your corner is an asset not to be underrated.

Their greatest year was 1981, when Steve won five major titles, including the world championship, at the age of twenty-three. It was to set the pattern for the professional game in the 1980s just as surely as Higgins's first victory had shaped it in the 1970s. Jean Rafferty, who followed the snooker circuit that season, wrote in her book:

One image is left of the 1980–81 season – Steve Davis holding up the winner's trophy, flashlights exploding all around him like champagne, gleaming silver cups flashing bright as fireworks under the television lights, Steve Davis winning and winning and winning. The image of him holding his trophy up in triumph has been burned into the brain of every other snooker player in the country. It follows them, haunts them, torments them. Some it has almost destroyed.

Steve's own memory of first winning the world title is equally vivid:

I potted the green and a glance at the scoreboard told me I needed the brown along the bottom cushion to be safe. It went in like a dream, and all of a sudden it hit me that I had done it. From the moment I potted the blue and scrambled in the pink, I felt the tears welling up inside me. The whole place erupted. I was so overcome by emotion that I shut my eyes in disbelief. Then I saw Barry charging towards me, teeth clenched, fist clenched. I knew just how he felt. We had dreamt of this moment for so long. He hit me like a tank, grabbing me hard around the shoulders and almost knocking me to the ground. By now tears were flowing down my cheeks, and I was really glad when Susan, Barry's wife, came along and gave me an excuse for a proper hug. There I was at the top of the world and I couldn't laugh for crying. The whole thing is on video and I play it time and time again. I never tire of watching it.

Hearn says:

The reason we get on is that while we're diametrically opposed on so many things, we join in the middle in the things we share – an enjoyment of life, doing our own thing as well as we can possibly do it, giving 100 per cent, scrubbing the personal when there's a job to do, not taking any liberties – but without crossing over into each other's hallowed territory. I don't influence Steve on the playing side, though I like to talk to him about it. He doesn't involve himself in the business much, though I sit down with him from time to time and he asks questions about where we're going. But he will not talk to me about tax or take a set of his accounts home and study them.

Like all good partnerships, theirs is based on self-interest and mutual respect. Hearn fills an empty place in Davis's life. 'It's almost as if he's the public Steve Davis, the one Steve's too shy or too reserved to act out himself,' says Jean Rafferty. 'Where Steve has to be seen as cool, unemotional, dedicated, Barry is loud, extravagant, ebullient, galvanizing others with the electricity of his own enthusiasm. Where Steve is restrained, correct in his demeanour, Barry is flash. Where Steve is cautious, Barry is a gambler, an adventurer, a swaggering, marauding, ruthless busi-nessman who's built up an empire just for the fun of it.' It is a convenient arrangement. Hearn can drive a hard bargain without Davis seeming to be difficult. He can be identified with all the ruthless things that might otherwise tarnish Steve's image. Steve can reserve his own ruthlessness for the snooker table – and earn them both a fortune.

Davis says: 'We're both very good at what we do and they are so different we need each other. It started as an older brother/ younger brother thing between us, but now we've become friends, though I'm obviously still guided in certain ways because he's a clever bastard.'

Hearn: 'I've been guided in some things by the relationship too – I now know several rock groups I didn't know before! I'm still not in love with the game in the aesthetic sense that Steve and his dad are, because they really love it. The old story about Boycott is true of Steve as well: given the last hour of the world, Davis would go out and practise. Me, I'd go out to the bank for the last banking.'

He clearly relishes his reputation as a money maker – 'the all-powerful warlord among the snooker barons', as the *Sun* called him. His Romford HQ, the paper said, 'is to snooker what Threadneedle Street is to banking'. In the club, originally built by Millicent Martin's grandfather, Hearn has created an immaculate matchroom with red leather banquettes. 'I'm a specialist at making money,' he says. 'I'm not good at anything else.' He also manages Terry Griffiths and Tony Meo and (more recently) the new world champion Dennis Taylor in a company called Matchroom Professionals. 'We're a fully-fledged blue-chip company now,' says Hearn. 'We're not as big as ICI, but we run our show just the same as a big company like that.' There is also Steve Davis Ltd, Steve Davis Properties and Steve Davis Pro- motions, for which he may seek a quotation on the unlisted securities market.

Asked in a lighter moment how he would describe his relation- ship with his players, Hearn replied: 'It's easy. They give me the prize money and I give them their cues back!' When one of the players gently quibbled about being made to attend a race meeting with a potential sponsor, Hearn said briskly: 'It's not your mind I need, just your body, thank you very much.' Asked if he had insured Tony Meo's hands, he replied (in my hearing and Meo's): 'No, I've insured his brain – much smaller pre- mium.' He also said of Meo, who has sometimes lost matches he should have won: 'If only I could persuade Tony not to concede before the referee has tossed the coin, he'd be all right.' The other players understand and accept that Davis will always be the number one client for Hearn. Meo's progress was held back by serious illnesses of his two children, and he missed his first tournament victory in the LADA Classic when he was distracted by a shout in the crowd and missed a vital yellow for a final clearance against Steve Davis. Winning the Winfield Masters in Australia will send him into the new season with more confidence.

Meo, whose Sicilian father died when he was 13, was brought up by his mother in the family restaurant in London. He was a champion table tennis player at the Ernest Bevin Comprehensive in Tooting, but was soon attracted to playing snooker with Jimmy White, a younger pupil at the same school. For day after day they played truant at the Zans billiard hall and learned to back themselves in money matches all over London. This was about all Jimmy did learn, however, and he still has trouble with reading and writing (but not, I suspect, with arithmetic). Tony Meo made a maximum break of 147 at the age of 17, the youngest ever recorded. Jimmy White must have acquired his habitual air of the artful dodger around this time. Steve Davis remembers seeing White for the first time at a Neasden club at the age of 12: 'He had broken his leg and was playing with his walking stick.' Jimmy's father recalls him arriving at his workplace one day to borrow £3. He fobbed him off with half that amount – and was astonished to find that he had converted it into £1000 by the evening. White has had managers who have tried to shape his career, who have curled his hair and straightened his teeth. But it seems unlikely that they have earned as much money for him as Hearn has done for the less naturally talented Meo – or that White has held on to as much.

Hearn has secured three massive sponsorship contracts for his players. One is with Courage, who organize all their exhibitions; one (said to be worth £1 million over five years) with Riley Leisure to endorse snooker tables; and one with Goya, who have launched a Matchroom range of toiletries, including an aftershave that may have the sweet smell of success. (Hearn has signed contracts for fifteen other countries to promote it.) Then, of course, there is the prize money. Embassy, who sponsor the world championship, have guaranteed more than £4 million until 1990. In Sheffield alone the players compete for £300,000, including £60,000 for the winner. When Steve Davis turned professional in 1978, his fee for an evening's exhibition match was £50: the rate now can be at least £4000. This helps to explain how his earnings, forgetting investments and other sources of income, are around £750,000 a year. The investments are said to include Mayfair property and forests in Scotland. Hearn's own mansion, says Davis, 'has so many bedrooms he hasn't been in them all'.

To see Barry Hearn at Romford is to realize just how important personal, even physical contact is to him. He trustingly hands out wads of notes to the staff. These are his people. 'Years ago we built a little wall round us and we've kept the same people inside. We've let in very few blokes from the outside. It's a wonderful form of independence to be able to say who we're going to deal with and who we're not. We said to ourselves years ago: "Right, we're going for it, we're going to give it everything we can, and we don't want anybody around we can't get on with." ' Which makes the author feel all the more honoured to have been invited to become an honorary member of the Matchroom.

Hearn promises value for money and demands the highest standards from his players. At an exhibition they are expected to turn up on time and to be properly groomed, not to drink, to mix with the clientele and to put on a polished evening's entertainment, including jokes. For this reason he wouldn't manage Higgins or White, because of their unreliability. I attended the first exhibition evening the whole team had given since Dennis Taylor joined them. Earlier in the day they had lunched with the board of Lloyds Bank. The exhibition was for a small group of staff and clients of Cathay Pacific, presumably in return for airline tickets. The setting, the Connaught Club in London, was a far cry from the Crucible, with the sounds of the bar and the fruit machines breaking in on the play. 'It's nice to be in a snooker club again,' said referee Len Ganley, himself part of the cabaret act, gently sending up his usual TV performance. When Griffiths fluked a shot, he cried 'Jammy sod', instead of giving the score. It was a fun evening, won by Terry Griffiths, who turned disarmingly to the crowd in mid-break and said, 'Good, aren't I?'

All four players showed off their trick shots, accompanied by a patter of jokes. Taylor had the best jokes (many of them Irish), Griffiths the best trick shots. Davis has developed a cockney comedian's routine which is surprisingly relaxed, given the tensions coiled within him. He can even make jokes now about his last-ball defeat by Taylor in the world championship. He claims that he stopped for petrol at a service station on the way home from Sheffield, still feeling sore and sensitive about losing the title. When he had paid, the assistant called after him: 'Don't you want glasses?' He turned crossly, not realizing she meant a free gift, thinking she was joking about his miss on the black or about Taylor's huge glasses, or both, and chided her: 'Now don't you be cheeky!'

Hearn takes care of his players, providing cars, including a magnificent Cadillac with a TV set in the back, and staff to arrange all their appointments and filter their telephone calls – in addition, of course, to handling their money. The psychology seems to be to build up his players' sense of their own importance, so that they are not distracted from the contemplation of victory by the minor admin of life – and also, one suspects, to make their opponents feel slightly overawed. Hearn knows that half the battle is in the mind. Big Bill Werbeniuk, the Canadian, put it shrewdly: 'Some people went out of their way to make Steve unpopular. They wanted a Muhammad Ali situation, with a huge publicity machine behind Steve setting him up as invincible. They wanted to frighten the rest of us and give Steve a head start. And it worked. The pros got to believe the propaganda and were afraid of Steve. What's more, Steve believed the ballyhoo that he was the greatest. And that made Steve play even better.' The best case for Hearn is that practically every other player in the game would like him to be their manager. On call are the famous Romford 'mafia', led by Ron and Robbo, the 'minders', who act as drivers, batmen, bodyguards, cheerleaders and someone for Steve to have a quiet drink with during tournaments before he goes to bed. They are so full of snooker lore, and their personal loyalty so far beyond question, that he finds their company more relaxing than anything else.

Apart from driving a Porsche with a telephone (SD 147), Davis's only luxury appears to be buying dozens of soul music records. ('I've tried to be flash, but I'm afraid I'm not very good at it,' he was once disarmingly quoted as saying.) He also plays chess, a harmonica and an electric grand piano. Unlike most snooker pros (and unlike his manager), Davis rarely indulges in the side-stakes which are a lively feature of the game. Nor does he drink much, apart from the occasional lager or white wine, and never when a match is in the offing. He is pale, carrot-haired, over six feet ('too tall for a snooker player,' he says), with rangy arms (the left one now two inches longer), double-jointed knuckles (which helps his bridging action), and as thin as Fred Astaire. It is his steely self-discipline, which shows also in his devotion to practice, that makes him such a formidable opponent. Clive Everton says, 'Steve has a playing method that is as mechanically perfect as you can get it.' In addition, he plays 'as if he had been injected with a massive dose of mind-focusing, body-enhancing adrenalin. To put it another way, the knowledge, the technique, the hours of practice, the attention to detail in his preparation, his regulated lifestyle, all strike sparks against the basic "him or me" urge to survive so that the flame of winning inspiration is lit.'

The same awed tone is detectable in a remark by Kirk Stevens after a match against him: 'I have never seen anyone more intense than Steve was that day. He was scary even to be sitting ten feet away from. He had eyes like a shark. I felt like Little Bo Peep surrounded by wolves.' Hugh McIlvanney wrote: 'His talent is so frighteningly substantial that it tends to pervade the table even when he is seated, quiet and ostensibly unhostile, a dozen feet away.' Opponents, he says, 'have the look of sailors who can hear the creak of the iceberg.' Davis himself explains his success in more prosaic terms: 'No one has my consistency and I enjoy it more than anybody else. When I start doing something wrong I can trace the fault and get out of it quickly.' He has a perfectly straight, gun-barrel cueing action and a level of concentration that is matched only by Cliff Thorburn's. To keep himself on his toes he has a check list in his waistcoat pocket, containing reminders like 'bridge hand', 'breathing' and 'stance'. Hearn says: 'What I want to see in Steve's eyes is something suggesting anaesthesia. If they look dead, that's good. It means he's into it.' Angela Levin in the *Mail on Sunday* detected a monastic quality in that look: 'There's an innocence and enthusiasm about him that could make him the newest recruit to a seminary.' Although the Romford crowd would doubtless roar with laughter at that, Hearn himself admits: 'Sometimes I wonder if he's for real.'

His mother Jean, a teacher from whom Steve has clearly inherited his mental sharpness, says: 'He always had tremendous powers of concentration once he was really interested in something. By the age of three he had learned all the moves of chess and by five he was playing simple games with his dad.' He began snooker even earlier, before he can remember, at the age of two on a miniature table with balls like little beads. His father, Bill, a driver for London Transport, introduced him to Joe Davis's snooker manual and encouraged his interest in the game. He is still, according to Steve, 'my teacher, my biggest supporter and my sternest critic, all rolled into one'. Their son's talent came as a surprise to them both.

There was no forewarning of all this in our family [Jean told *TV Times.*]. Everyone just grew up and went into offices or worked with their hands. We expected our children to go along the same way. Because Steve was quiet and school work came fairly easy to him, I pictured him in a branch of local government.

He was always very fond of ball games, but he soon opted out of football once he was at secondary school and it turned into a rough contact sport. Anyway, he never really pulled his weight as part of a team. He preferred table tennis, where he could play solo. He was only about seven when my husband, Bill, a keen snooker player, rigged up a board on the table top and Steve spent hours patiently practising his shots.

By the time he got to the sixth form, he didn't have a thought for anything but snooker. He was perfectly capable of passing his 'A' levels if he had needed them for what he wanted to do, but by then he was playing so much snooker he didn't have any time or interest left for maths and English.

We never put any pressure on him to stick to his schooling – we just weren't the sort of parents who could lean on our children – but I'm glad he had the extra years in the sixth form. I think it gave him an orderly mind and ability to express himself, which have stood him in good stead.

I'd never dreamed you could make any money from playing at snooker, but then, when everyone started telling me that he had the makings of a champion in a sport that was really taking off, I was as pleased as punch for his sake.

For all his enjoyment of the game, Davis has had to cope with extraordinary mental pressures from quite an early age. 'When you're in a match your very soul is out there for everybody to see. It's a kind of nightmare,' he says. Towards the end of his final against Dennis Taylor, and for some time afterwards, he was stumbling through such a nightmare, the robot turned zombie, gulping for air like a stranded goldfish out of water. After the match most of the press went on to the victor's party, but I went back with the Romford crowd to the 'wake' at the Grosvenor House Hotel. I remember trying to console Davis with the thought that Muhammad Ali was no less of a legend because he'd lost a few fights. 'Got it,' said Steve, tapping his head and rocking about (but not with drink), holding hands desperately with Susan, Barry's wife. He hadn't 'got it' though – or not then. Hearn looked equally devastated, and close to tears. It was he who had taught Davis to be a winner, to settle for nothing less than the best. But his pupil was so willing that there came a point where his own ambition took over.

I asked Barry how Davis would cope with defeat. 'We've gone for perfection. When we fail it hurts – it hurts me, it hurts Steve especially. He's given up wife, children – what *for*, if he isn't world champion. I've tried to say to him: "Look we have all the money we'll ever want, just relax." But he can't. He only knows who he is because I've told him that he's number one. Now he isn't and it's hard to take. Tonight he doesn't know who he is. Tomorrow we'll bounce back again.' For the next week the Romford telephone never stopped ringing with messages from 'well-wishers and weeping women', as Hearn called them. 'I told them all: "Don't worry, love, we've cut him down and the crows have stopped pecking."'

Curiously, though, this harrowing experience – witnessed by millions on television – may have removed one of the pressures which he and Hearn must have both deeply resented in the past, though they say little about it: the fact that crowds have always seemed to want Davis to lose and have given their support more

readily to his opponent, especially to swashbuckling figures like
Higgins or White. By losing, Steve Davis may actually have
gathered more fans than he ever did by winning, as the public
finally accepted him as a fully paid-up member of the human
race. 'It could only happen in this country,' he says. 'All of a
sudden everybody loves me because I'm a loser.' To which
Hearn responds with spirit: 'They'll have to learn to hate you
again, then, because next year you're going to be a winner.' Davis
says he understands the crowd's attitude to him, even if he
doesn't always like it. 'You get only one winner at anything, so
by necessity the majority of people are losers. They associate
with them and love them – and shy away from the likes of me.'
One sensed the mind of Barry Hearn behind that rationalization.
Jean Rafferty wrote of this phenomenon of people wanting Davis
to lose:

> His lack of doubt has made him a champion but it has often
> needled his opponents, who think he's arrogant, and it appears
> to alienate part of his audience, the part that writes him off as a
> snooker machine. It's perhaps a symptom of the times that
> people can find perfection boring. We're so used to looking in
> sport for the stress points. We wait for McEnroe to throw a
> tantrum. We like it when the human machine breaks down.
> Steve Davis comes as close to perfection probably as any
> sportsman has ever done, is cool, competitive, patient, accur-
> ate, courageous, skilful, intelligent. And it is still not enough.
> People want the machine to break down.

The TV satire programme *Spitting Image* tried, in its usual
unsubtle style, to convey him as a dimwit. The dialogue between
Davis and Hearn goes like this:

> 'Why can't I have a nickname, Barry? There's Hurricane Hig-
> gins and Whirlwind White.'
>     'Oh, what about "Windy". No? OK, "Very Windy". Steve
> "Very Windy" Davis.'
>     'I've got it, Barry . . . Steve "Very Interesting" Davis. Yes,
> that's it.'

'I'm glad we've got that settled. Now I'm going up for my glass of milk and a nap.'

Surprisingly, it brings a roar of delight from Davis. 'It's me to a T,' he says. 'Barry and I do it as a double act at parties.'

He can exhibit a sharp cockney wit on occasions. Once, when he was guest at a celebrity lunch at the Old Bailey, he was amused by the sight of a brand-new judge peacocking around in a bright red gown. 'He can't be for real,' he said to his neighbour. 'I'll have you know,' came the reply, 'that he's a High Court judge and very important indeed, much more than we ordinary circuit judges in black.' Davis replied: 'Never mind. Where I come from he's only worth one point and you're worth seven!'

It has been said that Davis could destroy the game as an entertaining spectacle if he goes on winning everything, just as Walter Lindrum destroyed professional billiards in the 1930s. Some people fear that the game might then lose some of the excitement and unpredictability that make it so successful on television, with a consequent drop in revenue if the ratings fall. Hearn does not accept that. 'I don't believe people can get so bored with a game like snooker even when one person is always on, because it's an interesting game and all the matches are different because you're playing different personalities all the time. We are aiming for Steve to become a legend in his sport.' Davis is undaunted by that prospect. He says simply: 'I want to dominate the game, win the world championship every year, and get to a stage where people say I'm unbeatable.'

The world championship keeps recurring in their conversation. I saw them in Romford shortly before the 1985 tournament in Sheffield, and my notes make interesting reading in the light of what was to happen there.

*Hearn*: The world championship is vitally important for us to win this year . . .
*Davis*: . . . and always will be.
*Hearn*: And next year it is going to be even more important.
*Davis*: Every year. You've got to be world champion.
*Trelford*: What's so special about it?

*Davis*: I shall be the winner, the world champion. I shall go to the Far East as the world champion and I'll be introduced as the world champion all through the year.

*Hearn*: You can win every other tournament in a season and the season is not a success if you're not the world champion. On the other hand, you can fail at everything else and then win the world championship, and that's the only thing that matters. It's like a drug. You've got to be world champion.

*Davis*: And it's a failure if you're not, and you've got to work on it for next year if you're beaten.

In this context the degree of anguish he showed after Sheffield becomes more understandable. His very identity and sense of personal worth were on the line. 'Snooker is my fulfilment, my justification,' he says. 'If I flop at after-dinner speaking, or in any other area of my life, I can always say to myself, "It's OK, you're world champion at snooker!"' But not, of course, when he's not. Unlike the rest of us, Steve Davis awards himself no consolation prizes. 'He's so hard,' says Barry Hearn, 'he brings tears to your eyes' – or so he would have us believe. 'Terry Griffiths once told me there's a savage beauty is losing,' says Davis. 'I didn't know what he meant. But I do now. And I can't pretend I like it.'

## Chapter Eight

# ON THE CIRCUIT

Snooker has always followed the football season, running from early September to the first week of May, with the world championship providing the same sort of climax, crown and culmination as the Cup Final. In the old days, so Sydney Lee told me, the professionals would lock up their cues for the summer and only take them out again in the autumn. Now, however – as with soccer – the snooker season is being stretched at both ends. Overseas tours and holiday camp engagements make demands on the top players, with hardly any remission, throughout the whole year.

The 1984–5 season broke off, appropriately enough, with a black-tie dinner and golfing weekend at the plush Redwood Lodge Hotel and Country Club at Bristol, organized by the Association of Snooker Writers. It had everything but snooker itself. Nearly all the stars were there (no Alex Higgins, no Jimmy White, but the whole of the Romford team), plus the game's top administrators, Del Simmons and Paul Hatherell of the WPBSA (whose headquarters are in an immaculately restored Georgian house in neighbouring Clifton). The sponsors were out in force (Embassy and Rothmans cigarettes, Lang and Jameson whiskies, Courage beers, Goya aftershave). The equipment manufacturers were also there. There were awards to Steve Davis (Player of the Year), Dennis Taylor (Personality of the Year) and Clive Everton (Services to Snooker). It is a mark of the public's insatiable appetite for anything to do with snooker that the proceedings should be recorded for ITV's *World of Sport* even though there was neither a cue nor a table in sight. Instead, they heard jokes from Taylor and Willie Thorne, who are clearly cast as the game's comedians; speeches of bawdy brilliance (parts of which were presumably not judged suitable for their viewers) by Dickie Davies and John Bromley, Controller of Sport at LWT; and a statesmanlike address by Steve Davis, who said it was most important that all players conduct themselves as professionally off the table as on it. 'Keeping *out* of the news – that's important for snooker players,' he said. Nobody needed reminding of the previous season's highly publicized off-table exploits of absent friends like Higgins, who had been fined by the WPBSA for urinating in a flower pot, or Tony Knowles, who was pictured in the *Sun* with a bevy of topless beauties.

I talked to Davis afterwards and found him coolly controlled, with a sharp understanding of what the game needs. He advised me against trying to write about snooker technique – 'nobody wants to know about that, I can see their eyes glazing over. Let's keep some mystique and mystery in the game.' He had had an average season for him the year before: that is to say, he had won nearly everything. He was clearly the man to beat in the season ahead, and nobody here was placing any bets against him. 'It's Davis number one,' Ted Lowe whispered to me, 'and there's no number two in sight. It could be Knowles if he had the character.' *Snooker Scene* concurred: 'It is difficult to see where a player able to beat him consistently is going to come from.' There was a prophetic note, however, in the pre-season comments of Alexander Clyde, of the London *Standard*. 'Call me naive if you like, but I have one fervent wish as the young millionaires set off on another chase for that pot of gold in the 1984–5 season – to see a few of the also-rans depositing some egg on those illustrious faces from time to time.' Who, in particular, did he favour? 'The hilariously funny Dennis Taylor, whose presence in a press room is like a breath of fresh air.'

There had clearly been no shortage of fresh air for the game's personalities over the summer months. Their normally white faces were healthily bronzed after visits to snooker's outlying colonies in Australia, Hong Kong, Singapore, Thailand, Malaysia, Sri Lanka and the new Costa del Sol classic, the first major tournament in Spain (won by Dennis Taylor). Davis had been bitten painfully on the leg by an insect in Bangkok. There were

Porsches, Jaguars and Mercedes in the car park outside and at least one Rolls Royce. The wives were strikingly gilded and bejewelled and obviously enjoying themselves: being a snooker widow can often be a lonely and anxious existence. But this was a time of hope for them all. 'This is a unique occasion,' said Bromley. 'Players, sponsors, officials, press and TV all in one room, all having a good time. Can you imagine the Football League laying on a do like this? Or the Test and County Cricket Board? Or the British Boxing Board of Control? Or the Jockey Club? Never. Snooker is the only sport where everyone is this friendly.' Barrie Gill, who has helped to promote this game as well as motor racing, agreed: 'This is still a community and few sports can say that.' Clive Everton was a little more cautious: 'Yes, there is a community, and it's just holding itself intact.'

Del Simmons, the man who negotiates all the game's contracts with sponsors and television companies – and gets £60,000 a year for himself – was puffing contentedly on a cigar that was almost the length of a snooker cue. 'This game has reached a pinnacle,' he said, 'and I don't want to see it fall flat on its face.' Del's own face is one of snooker's most impressive landmarks and needs Raymond Chandler or even Damon Runyon to do it full justice. Anthony Holden called him 'an elegantly rough diamond who is snooker's behind-the-scenes Mr Big'. He brought the same breezy language out of Janice Hale: 'Big and bearded like a heavy in a spaghetti western, Del Simmons rode into Snookertown nearly ten years ago looking for cuemen to hire. He stayed to become Sheriff, presiding over Snookertown's gold rush.' Apart from his other duties, Simmons also rides shotgun over Alex Higgins in a little-envied role as the Hurricane's sorely-tried manager. He has had profitable arrangements with BCE, the table firm, and took 20 per cent on various cue contracts with players. He is undoubtedly, as *Snooker Scene* put it, 'a commercial animal of some ferocity'. But he also, as the magazine conceded, 'helped take the game forward at a lively pace'.

The pace at which the game has changed was shown in a retirement speech by the WPBSA secretary, Mike Green, who recorded a gross annual turnover of £23·50 in his first season in the job in 1970. It rose to £24·75 the following year – and is now over £4 million. It's no wonder that some of the older players like John Spencer still feel rather dazed by it all. In 1970 he was one of only six professional players in the game: now there are 116. He looked round the crowded room in amazement: 'Ten years ago I wouldn't have envisaged this. None of us would.' There was to be £2 million at stake in the season ahead – and that was just the prize money.

The season proper began four days later in the less opulent surroundings of the Skean Dhu Hotel in Glasgow. It had old-fashioned scaffold-type tiered seating in a ballroom made even less prepossessing by the off-white dustsheets draped carelessly over it. This tournament, the Langs Scottish Masters, was won with ominous smoothness by Steve Davis. He beat Jimmy White 9–4 in the final, almost before the Londoner had woken up from a tough and bad-tempered 6–5 semi final against Tony Knowles, who had, in his own words, 'got all upset and aggressive' at a refereeing decision.

There was more controversy over the table, supplied on this occasion by E. J. Riley (tables at major events are usually supplied by BCE). Players complained on the first day that the cushions were dead and it was found on inspection that cushion bolts were missing. The cushions were also thought to be marginally high, leaving very little of the cue ball to hit. Higgins described the table as 'diabolical'. *Snooker Scene* said the cloth was not of championship standard and must have been used before as there was evidence of more than one baulk line.

Knowles's conduct over the refereeing decision added to his reputation as a graceless know-all, and White added to his reputation for speechlessness, though he was dressed more smartly than usual and there were some signs that he had been coached by his new manager in a series of new clichés for the press. ('It was a great match. It was a shame there had to be a loser', etc.) The loser in his case consoled himself with £6000 against Davis's £10,000, while Higgins and Knowles got £3000 each.

The first of the big money tournaments (£150,000 in prizes) followed on immediately in the Eldon Square Leisure Centre, Newcastle-upon-Tyne. This was too soon for Dennis Taylor and Willie Thorne – last seen as circuit comedians at the Bristol dinner – who were unamused to find themselves stranded on the Shetland Islands after an exhibition. The regular airline refused to fly, so they had to hire a four-seater private plane to Aberdeen, then took a taxi for the two-hundred and eighty miles to Tyneside from the granite city. This cost over £800, but fortunately both of them earned rather more than that in the tournament – £4300 as losing quarter finalists. Taylor might well have gone further – he felt in cracking form – but he had to scratch from his game against Silvino Francisco because of his mother's sudden death at Coalisland, County Tyrone, an event that affected him deeply and cast a pall over everyone else. Another death was to sadden this usually happy tournament when Jimmy Dilkes, the itinerant programme seller who travelled wherever the game was played – 'one of snooker's good guys', according to Janice Hale – collapsed in his hotel room. The circuit was still homely enough for the players – the older ones anyway – to show a genuine sense of loss for this little old man with his scones, tea and cider and his 10p maximum stake at cards.

The Leisure Centre was far from an ideal venue. Attendances were poor and were made all the more obvious by the cavernous ceilings and bare walls of the room in which the games were played. It was chastening to see spectators ordering gravy and chips for lunch in the restaurant. But there were few other signs of the North-East's economic depression as one elbowed one's way through the crowds in the shopping arcade to the snooker tournament upstairs. Nor in the discos and nightclubs where the players went to let off steam after hours. All except Higgins, that is, who, rumour has it, was banned from one for abusing a manager who had warned him to take his feet off the table. It wasn't a good week for Alex, who went out easily to Davis, as he had done at Glasgow a few days before. This time he was reported to have behaved badly in the arena, too, signalling his frustration by shooting the cue ball off the table and sounding off angrily to the press about his wretched luck. A correspondent to *Snooker Scene* complained about his 'loutish behaviour' and 'immature outbursts'. Eugene Hughes, a fellow-Irishman, had better luck, picking up £10,000 as a beaten semi-finalist – his best performance on the circuit and enough to pay not only for furnishing his new house in time for a second child, but for a startling red suit he had ordered. He was so pleased with himself in the red suit that he had 3000 posters printed.

Knowles had another refereeing row, this time on an abstruse technical point, with Len Ganley, a bearlike Irishman known to some of the players as the Jolly Green Giant or 'the Ball-Crusher', after his lager adverts on television. 'We're not saying Len Ganley inspires fear and trembling, but you'd definitely get permission in writing before you nicked chips off his plate,' Julie Welch once wrote of him. He is the most visible, because he is the biggest, of the tournament referees. He gives the impression of being in charge of the whole building, not just the table, as his policeman's eye fixes on a squeaking camera or a latecomer or someone rattling a crisp packet in the audience. The referees take special pride in their turn-out. At one tournament Ganley's dressing room was found to contain twenty-six shirts, five tuxedos, eight pairs of identical black size 11 shoes, several smart suits and thirty-six pairs of white gloves at £7 each. Asked why he needed the gloves, Ganley looked shocked: 'To use my hand on a ball would be desecration.' (Higgins has been known to lick the cue ball between frames to keep it clean, but not while Ganley is around.) He mixes with the players in the bar and discos, but he does not drink alcohol any more; several times I've nearly knocked over the limeade he balances on the edge of the press bench, out of view of the cameras. The concentration required of a referee is formidable, just to keep out of a player's way. 'I've come in after eight and a half hours and had to have a swill down with cold water to invigorate my mind again. You have to play the break with a player all the time, know which ball he's going to play, and the five or six after that. You have to flow with him, be with his mood, not be slow putting a ball back. You must keep up his momentum for him.' Alex Higgins once moved so fast round the table that he knocked a referee's crutch out of his hand and under the table, leaving the poor man hopping on his one leg. Any mistakes leave deep scars on a referee's memory. Once, in a match between Tony Meo and Doug Mountjoy, Ganley called Tony Knowles's name because he spotted him sitting nearby. That one ended in laughter all round.

But Knowles was not laughing over the refereeing incident in his semifinal, even though he went on to win it. But then Knowles does not seem to laugh much at all. He does not even raise a smile in the pictures of his so-called sexy romps that he posed for the *Sun*. One showed him with a girl spreadeagled topless in her suspenders across the green baize: it was this final sacrilege that cost him a £5000 fine for bringing the game into disrepute – a modest tax on the £25,000 fee he is said to have been paid by the paper. He once managed to read out a solemn press statement, without a flicker of a smile, denying that he had 'at any time sought sexual pleasure through wearing women's underwear or lingerie'. What do the girls see in him? 'I never buy them a drink. I never buy them a meal. I never dance with them. The only thing I offer them – apart from myself – is a lift home. And it works – every night of the week and sometimes several times a night.' Or so his ghost writer claims. Less transient rewards of his fame are a house in Tenerife, a cottage and a converted schoolhouse in Lancashire, a snooker club, a chip-shop and a disco called 'T.K.'s'. And still he doesn't smile.

He is conventionally tall, dark and handsome and dresses as sharply as John Travolta, appearing backstage in a black leather jacket for the first of the nightly conquests. He is so tall that he can sit on the table and put one foot on the floor. He is a contrast to one of his early opponents, Steve Newbury, who is serious and bespectacled, with a father, mother and sister in the snooker world. When Newbury drops his chalk, the camera catches him scrabbling on the floor beneath his chair. He had the game virtually won, but let Knowles come back from the dead. Knowles explains the match afterwards, shot by shot, in a droning monotone, revealing an obsession with the tactics of the game that makes some pressmen go a long way to avoid his conversation. An exception is Alasdair Ross of the *Sun*, a big brooding man who gives the impression that he is closer to Knowles than his agent. Janice Hale spoofed Ross's punchy, pacy style as follows: 'Ally Ross stormed into The Sun public house tonight, smashed back nine pints of lager, crashed his glass back on the counter and then went spinning out of the door. Then Ross slammed world champion Steve Davis for not waiting until he had rushed back before blasting into his third round match against Manchester's Silver Fox, etc., etc.' Back at the table, Knowles lives up to his number two world ranking by reaching the final, but goes down 9–2 to another impeccable performance by Steve Davis. He collects £18,000, Davis £30,000: but only Davis smiles, all the way to the bank.

More money than ever (about £250,000, including £45,000 for the winner) is at stake at the finals of the Rothmans Grand Prix at the Hexagon, Reading, one of the best venues in snooker. More money, too, for Steve Davis, whose new contract with John Courage is announced – and a row when the news breaks prematurely in the *Daily Mail*. The audience is disappointing, but they include three female visitors from Holland who were sufficiently hooked by snooker on television to book a holiday here. They had come across it by accident by twiddling the knobs on their set late at night. Two young players, Neal Foulds and Dean Reynolds, made the early news. Foulds beat Willie Thorne, which came as a surprise to both, especially after Foulds had changed the tip of his cue four or five times until his father, also a pro, loaned him one of his own. He then beat Knowles to reach the semifinal – 'it's surprising how badly you can play and still win sometimes', he said modestly. Reynolds caused some controversy in beating Silvino Francisco because TV replays showed that he had twice fouled the ball without being called by the referee. Should he have declared them himself, like a batsman 'walking' after a catch in cricket? Opinion is divided. Reynolds says he hadn't noticed the fouls and anyway it was the referee's job to blow the whistle. He gets his comeuppance in the next round when he is whitewashed 5–0 by Davis with what a commentator calls 'intimidating all-round competence'.

Also in impressive form are Dennis Taylor, in his first tournament since the death of his mother, and Cliff Thorburn, known as the 'Grinder'. In the semifinals Taylor dispatches Foulds, and Thorburn, living up to his nickname, shows that Davis is human after all. Experts say that Thorburn's relative lack of cue power gives him a narrow range of shots, but his control and concentration ('he thinks before every shot, as I try to do', says Davis) and his mastery of the geometry of the game make him a formidable opponent. 'I'm a rejuvenated man,' he said after beating Davis. 'It's good that after twenty years I can still improve. I wake up in the mornings looking forward to playing snooker.'

Nonetheless, he was comprehensively beaten 10–2 in the final by Taylor, who played like a man possessed. It was a popular victory, Taylor's first championship after thirteen years as a professional. The press room and his fellow pros were willing him to win, mainly because of his bereavement. There were tears in the press room that night. 'It was hard not to feel that here was a man who had triumphed over so much: grief, bad eyesight, long runs of poor form,' said Janice Hale. 'Nice Guy Comes First' was the headline in *Snooker Scene*, which described the final as 'one of the most memorable emotional evenings' in snooker history. Taylor acknowledged the transformation in his attitude to the game since his mother's death: 'I don't think I'll ever feel the pressure I did in the past. When something like this happens, you realize that snooker comes a poor second to your family.' It struck me that these words chimed oddly with an interview Steve Davis gave to *Woman* that same week: 'If I had to choose between snooker and sex, then I'd say snooker – because it's my life. It's what I've striven for, to become the best in the world.' Here were two contrasting philosophies: one saying that top snooker required the sacrifice of wife and family; the other that only when you realized that family came first in life could you play at your best. Which philosophy would prove to be the stronger under fire if they ever clashed *in extremis*? We had to wait a few more months to find out.

But Davis bounced back immediately at Preston Guild Hall to win the Coral UK trophy over Alex Higgins, who had beaten him dramatically the year before. On that occasion Higgins had come back from 0–7 down to win 16–15, leaving Davis with just a faint lingering doubt over his capacity to hold a commanding lead under pressure – a doubt that was to remain deep inside him. This time Higgins came back from 5–9 to 8–9, but Davis held on for the £20,000 first prize. Taylor had gone out 9–2 to Knowles in an emotionally numb performance in the second round – like, as one writer put it, 'the dustcart after the Lord Mayor's Show'.

Two Canadians, Stevens and Thorburn, went out in the semifinal – Kirk, as ever, having courted disaster by flying in from home just before the start (he once missed a tournament altogether by leaving it too late). Part way through the week Thorburn was hit by bad news from home: his manager and friend, Darryl McKarrow, had been found frozen to death after a heart attack on a hunting expedition in Manitoba. No wonder he was not amused at a tough decision in his match against Higgins when referee John Smyth failed to hear him nominate the green and declared a foul – even though most of the crowd and millions of TV viewers had clearly heard him. Appealed to by Thorburn, Higgins said nothing, which caused Cliff to leave the arena to cool off, muttering: 'There is a code. I've played by it all my life.'

Kirk also had his problems. He discovered that – unbeknown to him – somebody had set up a Kirk Stevens fan club, inviting people to send in £3 for membership. He quickly disowned it. Bill Werbeniuk, the giant Canadian who has to drink thirty pints of lager a day to steady his hands and his nerves, was so distressed by British press coverage of the Queen's visit to Canada that he refused to allow the *Daily Star* to attend the press conference after his first round defeat – a deprivation borne stoically by the *Star*'s man, Graham Nickless. The *Mirror* man, Terry Smith, a large, ungainly figure famed for his clumsiness, managed to knock somebody over, break a trouser press, collapse some scaffolding and lose a shoe while walking downstairs. He once fell over some cables in the ITV studio and had to lie silently with his face in a plate of sandwiches because Dickie Davies was on the air. He engages in the following deadpan dialogue with Jimmy White, whose speed around the table is not matched by his speed of language or thought away from it:

'I've put two inches on my cue.'

'What does that mean, Jimmy?'

'It's longer.'

Compared with this, there is a touch of class in an overheard remark to Steve Davis by one of the scorers, John Bramwell: 'Do you get your Perrier water from Lourdes?' Meanwhile, old Fred Davis is reported to have been surprised to find a chimpanzee, escaped from a circus, taking refuge on his practice table. 'Is this my opponent?' Fred is quoted as saying. 'I don't know all these new professionals.'

The end of the year brings a break for doubles in the Hofmeister world championship at the Derngate Centre, Northampton. This is won – surprisingly to some, because they are such similar players – by Higgins and White, who beat Davis and Meo in a classic semifinal and then Thorburn and Thorne for the £34,500 first prize. 'Alex played out of his head,' said Jimmy appreciatively. It is an interesting reflection on Higgins that he always seems to play well in events where he has a partner. It would be good, though unlikely, to see him paired with Steve Davis. Tony Meo announced that he has bought a greyhound. Davis, his Romford colleague, already owns two racehorses, Golden Triangle and Action Time.

Racing and snooker, never far apart, came together again as the circuit rolled on to the Mercantile Credit Classic (formerly the Lada Classic – sponsors kept changing confusingly all year) at the Spectrum Arena, Warrington. For this was Willie Thorne's long-awaited breakthrough to the big time, and with Willie came a whole stable of hangers-on, led by the legendary 'Racing Raymond' Winterton, a ticktack man given to loud checked jackets who follows him everywhere. Willie's devoted family own the Snooker Centre in Leicester, having graduated from the Shoulder of Mutton at Braunstone. Willie's followers, who always put their money where their mouths are, include Runyonesque figures like Creamcake Smith, Handbags Barry, Carton Ken, Robert the Rat, Billy the Dip and the Red-faced Man from Braunstone. His practice partner is Gary Lineker, the England soccer player. 'My closest friends like Racing Raymond, Gary and Creamcake have stood by me through thick and thin – and it's mostly been thin and thin,' he said. Thorne, a tall, bald man with a droopy walrus moustache, has scored forty-three maximum breaks on the practice table but never, as he puts it, 'under the cosh'. He has been accused of 'choking' and lacking 'bottle' when it mattered, failing to clinch matches from winning positions. He is an easygoing character, with a rather lazy air, and an incurable gambler.

At Warrington, however, he surprised everyone by the ease of his victory. Kirk Stevens left his arrival even later than usual, flying in from Toronto at 7 a.m. on the morning of his match. He need hardly have bothered, for Thorne saw him back on the plane 5–1 before beating Virgo, Davis and Thorburn to claim his first championship title and £40,000 – much of this, he claimed, already owed to the bookies. The key moment came in the deciding frame of the semifinal when Davis, uncharacteristically, went for an ambitious, hard-hit green to the centre pocket – and, even more uncharacteristically, missed – when he might have played up safe behind it. Thorne cruised from 8–8 to 13–8 against Thorburn with an unstoppable rhythm he had previously shown only in practice.

A darker side of the snooker culture emerged at this time when Mark Thompson, the British junior champion, killed himself at home in Derby at the age of 19. The pressures on a young snooker player on the edge of professional ranks were thought to be a contributory factor. He had an obsession that something might happen to his cue, which has prompted Freudian interpretations of his fate. *Snooker Scene* philosophized thus on the predicament of young men like Mark Thompson:

In boyhood and adolescence, snooker is just a game. It is exciting to compete and disappointing to lose but the future stretches out to infinity and if you lose one match, so what? You'll win the next or the one after. Natural coordination is at its keenest and if natural ability is there it is easy to expect that, if you practise, improvement will continue steadily.

As a player approaches manhood, it begins to dawn that there is more to it than that. The upward trend of improvement is no longer automatic and is certainly slower, even with practice; the next generation is already challenging; it becomes necessary – for pride as well as practicality – to earn a living rather than wait to be supported wholly or in part by family; it is realized that there is more to life than snooker; girls appear on the scene; life becomes more complex. The awful question forms in the mind: what else can I do apart from snooker if I don't make it?

What can be learnt from this tragic case? Only that the

unprecedented opportunities which the snooker boom has created for young players have brought with them pressures which are insufficiently understood. It is not enough for a player to have the ability. He needs the right advice, the right support, the right friends and, above all, the adaptability within himself to make the transition from promising junior with nothing to lose to full-time player with adult responsibilities and expectations to fulfil.

After being runner-up three times already this season, Cliff Thorburn finally went one better at the Benson and Hedges Masters at Wembley, taking £37,500. Had he won all four finals, we would be treating him like Steve Davis. His final with Mountjoy was a deeply boring affair, characterized in the press room as 'Cliff Grinder versus Doug Brownsuit'. It went on so long, with so many misses and so much defensive play, that the journalists had their stories written and ready to send before the final frame was over. I glanced at one prepared intro in a typewriter: ' "I'm fed up with being a bridesmaid," Cliff told our reporter after the match.' What he did, in fact, say after the match was, as usual, more interesting than any invented quotes. He kissed the trophy and said quietly, choking on the words: 'This one's for you, baby.' Everybody knew he meant his late manager, who had died in that gruesome hunting episode in Canada.

Thorburn gives the impression of being one of the most adult and most private members of the snooker circuit, a man of great natural dignity. He also has a wry and attractive sense of humour. Jean Rafferty saw 'the elegance of an Edwardian gentleman dressed for the theatre, the seducer's moustache and air of ruthlessness of a man inspecting the chorus line for his next mistress, or deciding which method of removal to choose for his last one'. He was once called 'the Rhett Butler of the green baize'. The air of a riverboat gambler is not far out, though he denies he was ever a hustler. He began in the local pool hall at Victoria, British Columbia, then entered the big time at Seattle, working as a dishwasher on the Victoria-Seattle shuttle boat. He was brought up in a heavily male environment and his father forced him into all sports (Cliff thought his mother was dead until he found out, when he was already grown up, that she was still alive). He worked for a time as a cotton picker, converting his 16 dollar earnings into 300 dollars at night on the tables. He was once chased round the table by a Japanese fisherman who had gone berserk with a knife.

He hopped on a freight train to Toronto to watch the veteran Canadian champion George Chenier, who had played with Joe Davis, and developed his famous concentration by playing long night sessions for cash. He played all the snooker towns – Oklahoma City, Phoenix, Detroit, Jacksonville, Los Angeles, San Francisco. 'Just one or two nights and I was gone. Normally you just cleaned them out and left town.' He once played continuously for 54 hours to take $1000 off a man called Canadian Dick in San Francisco. 'He came in with a jar of speed pills to stay awake,' Thorburn recalls. 'But I really knew he had come to play when he laid out three pairs of socks.' By the end, he says, 'we were like two hard-hitting heavyweights in the last round of a title fight. Punch drunk, swaying on our feet.'

The audience felt a bit like that at Wembley. Watching Thorburn and Mountjoy sparring like fighters unwilling to hit each other, one yearned for the speed and the threat of the unexpected that Higgins, White and even Davis can provide. I found myself thinking: why does one prefer the Canadian to the Welshman? Perhaps it's because Thorburn, with his deadpan Walter Matthau look, gives off the sense that he is a more subtle person, better attuned to life's little ironies. (The only time he has behaved badly was against Davis in the 1981 world semifinal when – rattled by an apparent breach of snooker etiquette – he called him 'an arrogant bastard'.) Mountjoy is built like a dark pit pony, all thighs and shoulders – a miner's build, except that the real miner, Ray Reardon, has a whippet's frame. This is a crinklies' final, both over 35, and one reflects that their athleticism in getting a leg on the table is not to be underrated, especially for anyone carrying a decent lunch. There is a sleepy air about the play, a lack of adrenalin. Older players know when to stop when they're ahead, carefully eschewing risks to keep a frame going in case they let the other man in. But it can be dreary to watch.

Wembley is different from the other snooker venues. It is much bigger for a start, which means that the theatrical atmosphere is lost, and people cannot see the table as clearly. The crowd are not so well informed. They applaud indifferent safety shots because they do not know any better. There is a great deal of drinking and betting, which you can place with an 8 per cent tax inside the hall, 2 per cent cheaper than outside. My wife was subjected to a further barrage when she objected to the foul language behind her. Willie Thorne was put off his shot when somebody shouted: 'Why don't you go home, Willie?' Stevens was likewise distracted by a woman, evidently drunk, who kept shouting 'Come on Kirk', and had to be escorted from the arena. The referees were said to be under instructions from the sponsors not to discipline the crowd. Nick Hill, the master of ceremonies, said: 'Our tournament is above referees having slanging matches with the crowd. It is just crude. Our system has worked for ten years.' It wasn't working now, with up to a thousand spectators in the hall shuffling in and out as they felt like it and barracking the players, especially Davis, whom they seemed to regard as some kind of social renegade or working-class Tory.

For a pastime bred on hush, [wrote Hugh McIlvanney in the *Observer*] snooker has shown a disconcerting tendency to include among its audience a minority boozed and boorish enough to feel and sound at home on a football train. No doubt the sense of outrage over a few tiresome incidents at the Benson and Hedges Masters was exaggerated in places. But the suggestions from within the sport that what millions saw and heard on television represented nothing more than a healthy heightening of atmosphere, that the sour, malevolently timed barracking should be regarded as a helpful release mechanism for adrenalin, may have a hint of mercenary rationalization about them. Nobody is anxious to take a swing at the goose that lays the golden eggs, even when it is dropping something smellier on the floor.

Practically all sports now suffer from having minorities among their followers who feel a compulsion to be participants, a cheap urge to join in the theatre the games create, whether it be by invading a football pitch or catcalling at the Conference Centre.

The villain of the piece, as ever, was Alex Higgins, who signalled his delight at beating Davis 5–4 in the first round with a war dance towards his supporters in the crowd, in the course of which the words 'I'm fucking back' were clearly seen, if not heard, on television. 'Millions of viewers were upset,' raged the *Sun*. That may or may not be so, but only three complained to the BBC. Higgins's fine of £1500 for 'bringing the game into disrepute' provoked the scrupulously fair Clive Everton to comment: 'The fine is certainly extremely severe in the light of the offences alleged and it is difficult to escape the conclusion that he has been punished, at least in part, for the excesses of a section of his supporters and for the dislike which, rightly or wrongly, he has attracted in certain quarters.' I recalled seeing Higgins the night before this match staggering across the deserted, ticket-strewn hall of the Wembley Conference Centre, balancing a pint of beer, and thinking: he's not taking the Davis contest seriously. As so often with Alex, nothing can be taken for granted.

All this turned out to be as nothing compared with what was to follow the Dulux tournament at Derby, where the awful spectre of drugs (Kirk Stevens) was to succeed girls (Tony Knowles), drink (Alex Higgins), bad language (Higgins and others) and laying waste to hotel rooms (Jimmy White) as the game's most evil scourge.

But first there was an interlude for the English professional championship (for which the Irish, Welsh and Canadians didn't qualify) sponsored by Tolly Cobbold at Ipswich. Davis beat Knowles comfortably 9–2 to collect £17,500. The only excitement all week was when a coach load of spectators, due to fill the front rows of the audience, turned up late for the final. People further back had just clambered over the seats when the latecomers arrived, causing a long delay and a scene like the Charge of the Light Brigade, as those behind cried 'forward' and those in front cried 'back'.

The Dulux (formerly the Yamaha) at Derby started with a row over slow play between Tony Meo and Tony Knowles, who walked out in protest. 'The game was taking so long that I decided if Meo could take a rest so could I,' he explained. Janice Hale said this only showed 'just how pompous and opinionated Knowles has become'. Meo, who won the match, has an odd habit of tapping one finger up and down in his bridging hand as he plays a shot, his wide gold wedding band glinting in the lights.

A bigger curiosity at Derby was a young pro called Dene O'Kane, a former magician, who went into Guru Maharishi meditation between frames. But that was not enough to make Steve Davis disappear from the tournament, a trick that is rarely performed – though Kirk Stevens managed it on this occasion. Kirk went into a form of meditation of his own – 'it was like the sort of trance that Davis and Thorburn get into and which I have sometimes felt when I play them. I was so lost in the game that it was the most enjoyment I've experienced in years.' In the final, when Stevens lost 12–9 to Silvino Francisco, he was accused of being in a different sort of trance – Francisco was later quoted as saying he was 'as high as a kite on dope'. There was some unseemly jostling as Silvino, angered by Kirk's unscheduled pit stops between frames, tried to follow him into his dressing room to see what he was up to.

When all this emerged a month later at the world championship in Sheffield, Francisco was fined £6000 by the WPBSA for a variety of offences, including telling the *Daily Star* of his suspicions. But Stevens had already admitted taking drugs in the past, and by the time the season was over and he was safely back in Toronto, he had confessed: 'I am a cocaine addict.' Even his manager admitted: 'He is stoned all the time.' Kirk said: 'I spend about 300 dollars a day on my habit and I once got through 30,000 dollars in just three weeks on cocaine. I think I've probably wasted about £250,000, possibly more, on this drug over the past six years' – the whole period in which he has been a professional snooker player. Whether Francisco was right to suspect that Kirk was snorting cocaine during their final at Derby may never be known, because drug tests were not introduced until a month later. Stevens passed the test on that occasion – but also went out in the second round.

For all his white suits and his Bucks Fizz glamour, Kirk

Stevens has always looked a lost soul on the snooker circuit, which has heightened his appeal to expiring young females in the audience. He often smiles for no obvious reason. Clive James wrote of him: 'You can tell when Kirk is thinking. When he is not thinking he looks like an Easter Island statue with a sinus problem. When he is thinking, he still looks like that, but licks his lips.'

He started on the road in his teens, playing cue games for money all over Canada and North America. 'When I was fifteen, I looked twelve, so when this little wimp went up to somebody and said: "Like to play for 500 dollars?" they thought they couldn't lose.' Although he never had his thumbs broken like Paul Newman in *The Hustler*, he was beaten up a few times. His car was once chased out of town by a hail of bullets from irate losers at Dayton, Ohio: he decided not to hang around to collect his 10,000 dollar winnings. When he was nineteen his mother was murdered in a house blaze by a man who had sent her a warning by telephone and then doused the place in petrol. Not surprisingly, Kirk says that day 'will haunt me for the rest of my life', and it seems safe to assume that his troubles date from the trauma of that event.

The life of an itinerant overseas snooker player did not make things any easier for him. 'There's not much family continuity or stuff like that,' he says. He also lost a girl friend: 'I took snooker over her. That's what it came to. I didn't get over this in five minutes.' For a time the Canadian players shared a house in Chesterfield known as the Canadian embassy, and Kirk developed a younger brother/older brother relationship with Cliff Thorburn. 'It used to be important to me to have the approval of older players,' he says. 'Then I realized that they would never give it to me. You have to take total responsibility for winning. It's never fate, it's always you.' He has experimented with his technique, shortening his cue, standing like Steve Davis, sighting the ball more consciously. But it is the battles of the mind, rather than the table, that sort out the champions from the nearly men of snooker, and that is where Kirk Stevens's problems clearly lie.

Silvino Francisco, who netted £50,000 at Derby, is the son of a

Portuguese fisherman who sold his boat to buy a restaurant in Cape Town. The restaurant had two snooker tables. The pressure of anti-apartheid forces in sport and the need for stronger competition have forced him to Britain, where he lives in Chesterfield with his English wife. His elder brother Mannie, himself a fine player, runs the family snooker table and accessories business in South Africa. Mannie's son, Peter, is also a pro. Silvino, who has the dark romantic eyes and Latin looks of a pre-war matinée idol, beat Stevens by managing to keep his head over the final frames, but he also had a good deal of luck, including three outrageous flukes which must have made Kirk wonder about his remark that 'it's never fate, it's always you'.

Then the circus moved south to Bournemouth for the Guinness world championship, where Higgins inspired his Irish colleagues to beat England in the final, personally beating Davis 2–0 in the clincher. (Dennis Taylor once wept in his dressing room when he lost a game for Ireland.) Higgins went on to beat Davis again a week later in the semifinal of the Benson and Hedges Irish Masters at County Kildare, becoming the first man to record four tournament victories over the world champion. Davis was cueing noticeably badly – an ominous sign just a week before his world title defence in Sheffield. A fellow pro said: 'He's bringing the cue back so far it's almost coming off his bridge and the pause at the back of his backswing is so long it isn't a pause, it's a halt.' Jimmy White beat Higgins for the £17,500 first prize, his first victory over Alex in competition.

A feature of the Irish Masters is the chance it gives players to relax before the testing fires of the Crucible. Eugene Hughes practised with a Walkman in his ear to cure snooker's equivalent of writer's 'block' – the inability to let the cue go. Tony Knowles went jogging and got lost; Eddie Charlton did a lot of sightseeing; Tony Meo visited sick children; Dennis Taylor and Ray Reardon taught Terry Griffiths how to play golf. Thorburn and Stevens went home to Canada. Steve Davis, needless to say, went back to the practice table. The bookies rated his chances of winning his third successive title at 6–4, White at 6–1, Higgins 10–1. You could get 40–1 on Dennis Taylor.

## Chapter Nine

# INTO THE CRUCIBLE

---

'SNOOKER – BLOOD MONEY' is the first sign that greets the visitor to the Crucible Theatre in Sheffield: 'The British tobacco industry kills 2000 people every week.' The crudely lettered placard is balanced precariously on a bicycle against a tree by Stuart Holmes, an anti-smoking protester who plants himself stubbornly by the stage door for the duration of the tournament, earning the grudging respect of press and players, if only for his sheer persistence in all weathers. His target is the sponsor of the world championship, Embassy cigarettes, a subsidiary of the giant Imperial Tobacco.

A more lethal drug is on everyone's mind, however, as I arrive at the theatre. The gossip from the Dulux tournament in Derby is wild in the press room. Everyone tells me the same drug story in a range of confidential whispers. I am not, therefore, completely surprised to read the same thing in the following morning's *Daily Star*. 'I Shopped Snooker Stars on Drugs,' says Francisco on page one. 'He was as High as a Kite on Dope,' he adds on page two, clearly referring to Kirk Stevens. And there's more: 'Four or five' snooker stars are known to take drugs, he says, 'most of them household names'. My press colleagues profess to be shocked by the story they themselves all told me the night before. It is one thing to gossip in the press room, apparently, quite another to put it all into print. But there it was – in very large type indeed – and it could hardly be more explicit: 'As soon as he came out, and as soon as he took his first shot, I knew there was something wrong. I looked at him. He was as high as a kite. Out of his mind on dope. Staring eyes, twitching, the lot.'

Several weeks before all this a memo had arrived on my desk

about drug-taking in snooker, naming some famous names, and referring to a major tournament in 1982 when Kirk Stevens had allegedly been put under a shower by officials while totally zonked. My source commented: 'Canadians play until one man has no money left. You need something stronger than black coffee for that.' Two other leading players were said to be hooked; my own impression is that both of those named had already chucked the habit by the time I reached the circuit. An associate of one of them confided to me late at night in the bar: 'You know him as well as I do. He can't stick at *anything*.' Peter Hildreth commented sensibly in the *Sunday Telegraph*:

> It is important, first, to distinguish between varieties of drugs. Those used in athletic sports to increase the training capacity would hardly be appropriate to snooker, where physical effort is restricted to leaning over the green baize table or fingering the chalk from a vest pocket. Do snooker players have anything to learn, though, from West German modern pentathletes, who use beta-blockers to steady their shooting arm? Or from East German gymnasts who have employed pills containing beolase and phioctacid to intensify their concentration? The drugs most likely to be used among the snooker fraternity are those which act as an after-hours escape from the competitive pressures. Those pressures have always been there, but have intensified considerably as the rewards and personal public exposure have increased.

The WPBSA had prudently introduced drug tests for Sheffield, which proved to be a timely move, even though it had been raised as an apparent afterthought by Barry Hearn under 'any other business'. As organized as ever, Hearn had even drafted the press release. But, as the *Observer* pointed out, it was not clear that the tests would show up all drugs, especially beta-blockers – a loophole later confirmed by Rex Williams, the WPBSA chairman, who admitted taking a beta-blocker himself on medical grounds.

The *Yorkshire Post* took full advantage of this heady atmosphere in a deadpan report.

Two world champions inhaled drugs in a Sheffield theatre yesterday [said Roger Cross] blatantly, shamelessly and, in one case at least, in front of women and children. He was mainlining almost nonstop. The drug was wrapped in a tube of plain white paper, placed between the lips and inhaled deeply into the lungs, causing him to close his eyes in apparent ecstasy. Further, it can be disclosed, the 'Mr Big' behind this state of affairs is one of Britain's largest and wealthiest companies operating from the cover of the comparatively sleepy west country town of Bristol.

Even in the room at the Crucible set aside for press conferences, normally the place where musical instruments are stored, the sponsor's banner behind the raised platform has to have inscribed on it: 'Smoking Can Damage Your Health'. Few of the inhabitants seem to have been deterred, however – least of all Steve Davis's father, Bill, or Terry Griffiths's father, 'Pops', who spend most of the day in the press room watching the TV monitors and inhaling gratefully from the free samples thoughtfully provided by the sponsor. Bill favours large Havana cigars: in fact, as Barry Hearn points out, smoking them seems to be his main occupation in life. The Embassy officials are clearly not amused by all this drug publicity; the wrong image altogether.

Suddenly, instead of being a reporter myself, I find that I am being interviewed – first by independent radio in Sheffield, then by my old papers, the *Star* and the *Morning Telegraph*, and finally the BBC. They seem surprised that I am writing a book on snooker, and the burden of their questions is always the same: what's a nice boy like you doing in a game like this? 'New Angle for Snooker Duffer' is the front-page headline in one Sheffield paper. The *Daily Mail*'s John Roberts, describing the Romford gang in the press room – Ron and Robbo and Bill Davis – goes on to say:

It has to be mentioned that the fourth member of the group appeared incongruous in this company. Donald Trelford, the editor of the *Observer*, has taken a break from such consider-ations as cruise missiles, teachers' pay and Tory rule and is treating himself to a liberal helping of the world's most highly publicized parlour game. He is apparently writing a book that promises to peer into the pockets and analyse the pot, following the footsteps of the *Daily Star*, so to speak, while pausing for thought. All human life is here in the potting shed.

The reference amuses Barry Hearn when he reads it and prompts him to shout across the breakfast room at the Grosvenor House Hotel: 'Donald, you're now an honorary member of the Romford mafia. Nice piece you wrote in your Colour Magazine – it's not often that somebody writes about snooker who can read and write and makes no spelling mistakes!' Janice Hale takes a similar line in *Snooker Scene*: 'Snooker seems to be attracting a better class of journalist these days. Donald Trelford, recently seen interviewing Rajiv Gandhi and, as editor of the *Observer*, usually involved in the kind of stories that shake nations . . .' etc. etc.

Most snooker journalists rarely watch any actual snooker. They prefer to stay close to their telephones (and the bar) in the press room and follow play on the monitor sets while served by the glamorous red-suited Embassy hostesses. I decide to brave it into the arena itself and wander around backstage looking for the way in, tripping over wires and cables, clambering over scaffolding, peeping round curtains until there's a break in the play and I can slip into one of the prized ringside seats between the TV cameras. Immediately the cameraman whips round accusingly and asks: 'Are you from the *News of the World*?' (who have just written a stinging attack on the BBC for wasting money in expense allowances for cameramen and other staff in covering the world championship). 'No,' I reply mildly, not sure what to think about being taken for a tabloid sleuth. In this seat I am so close to the play that I worry in case I'm in the player's eyeline as he makes a shot. It is the best seat in the house, just two feet from the table with no one between, much closer to the action than anyone in the audience. The referee, Jim Thorpe, keeps staring at me, so I stop scribbling while they play.

Steve Davis, last seen in Ireland struggling with his cueing action, is struggling again in the first round against young Neal Foulds, who forces him to 10–8 and might even have won if he had

had more belief in himself in the final frames. 'It will take a good player to beat Davis,' he says afterwards, 'but he's playing nowhere near as well as he can.' Tony Knowles, the number two seed, also struggles to win his first-round match again Tony Jones, coming back with a commendable display of guts from 5–8 down to 10–8 – and thereby destroying the hopes of the punter who had bet £1000 at 450–1 on Jones to win the title. Alasdair Ross gives Knowles, 'snooker's pin-up boy', his usual heroic write-up in the *Sun*.

Ray Reardon has been below par too, and struggles on against the Irishman, Eugene Hughes. Reardon, aged 52, has been trying out spectacles in two previous tournaments and wore a green eye shade in another. But here he has taken them off. 'I woke up this morning, saw the sun shining and asked myself: "Why do I need them?" ' he said. Reardon is playing like a man who knows how easy it is to drop out of the top six and down to fifteen to twenty in the rankings, especially at his age. His mood shifts rapidly from darkly serious to light banter at the drop of a ball – but not when it really matters.

Clive Everton was at my elbow as the match went to 9–9. 'It's fascinating, isn't it, to see a man struggling to hold himself together?' he said. 'That's what's happening there. Reardon's eyes are going. The longer the match goes on, the more it favours the younger man – and Reardon knows it. He's very tired. Even so, the young man can have temperamental problems in this class of tournament which can affect his own eyesight without him realizing it. You think you're lining up the ball, but something gets into your mind and you're not actually looking when you hit the ball. That's what just happened to young Dean Reynolds. He had made two maximum 147 breaks in practice, but in his match against Higgins he couldn't put together more than 21. Mind you, it can be even more fascinating to see a man fighting moral disintegration, which is what Higgins seems to be doing every time he plays.'

Reardon, with one last determined effort of concentration, clinches the final frame. That strength of character and the nerve to seize frame-winning openings explain why Reardon has won his six world titles. As a miner he was once buried in a roof fall for three hours, so trapped that any movement would have been fatal. He survived by replaying snooker frames in his head. As a policeman, he disarmed a man who was carrying a shotgun and, in another incident, climbed across a frosty roof to drop through a skylight on to an unsuspecting burglar. He came from a snooker-loving family at Tredegar, South Wales, playing improvised matches on his aunt's kitchen table with marbles for balls and books for cushions. He was so small when he started on full-size tables that he had to use the rest a great deal, with the result that he became the most accomplished rest player in the game. Always immaculately turned out, black hair brushed back from a widow's peak, an uncompromising competitor, Reardon is the epitome of the professional snooker player. He is known as a man of many masks, each one disguising the true self. But his MBE in the 1985 Queen's birthday honours was widely approved in the game.

Another former world champion, John Spencer, who held the title three times between 1969 and 1977, has won only two tournament matches all season. Like Reardon, he is troubled by his eyes, but in his case the problem is more serious. He has a rare ocular condition which gives him double vision and a drooping eyelid and can only be controlled by steroids. His play is marked by a nervous sniff round the table. He is a popular figure on the circuit, a gambling man who started life as a clerk in a betting shop, a practical joker who treats triumph and disaster, those twin impostors, just the same. It is hard to tell from his face after a match whether he has won it or lost it, which makes him unique in snooker. He goes out in the first round to John Parrott, aged 20, looking very strained from playing under the television lights. 'When did you realize the match was slipping away from you?' he is asked, and replies candidly to general amusement: 'In the second frame!' He will have to play in the qualifying round for next year's tournament after slipping out of the top sixteen, a bad fall from grace for the man who was the biggest name in snooker – and its most exciting player – only fifteen years ago. He also started on a makeshift table at home which was converted from a bagatelle board. At the age of 15 he made a break of 115 at Radcliffe Sunday School Institute. He won a long series of money matches before turning professional in 1969, borrowing the £100 entry fee from his bank manager. The breaking of his favourite old cue in a car accident in 1974 was a turning point in his career. He now runs a successful snooker club in Bolton.

After midnight the action moves from the press room at the Crucible to the bar in the Grosvenor House Hotel, with some members waylaid at Josephine's nightclub or Gossips, the local disco. The talk is about the Stevens-Francisco revelations. *Sun* man Ally Ross, usually first on the draw with his paper's cheque book, has been badly upstaged this time and has been heard furiously demanding that 'newsmen', as opposed to snooker writers, be banned from the press room. 'You can't do this to me,' he blusters at one point and disappears for hours on end: he is rumoured (wrongly, as it turns out) to be negotiating a big counter-deal with Stevens's management at their hotel. Few tears are shed over Ally's discomfiture.

The *Star*'s snooker man, Graham Nickless, is shrugging off any responsibility, letting the hit men from London take the credit and the blame; he has to go on living on the circuit. There is much sympathy for Kirk Stevens, who seems to be liked but not greatly admired. 'He's basically very shy,' one reporter told me, 'not at all the lady-killing sports car Romeo his image suggests. He's really a bit of a wimp.' Everybody is baffled about Francisco's role in the affair. Was he paid by the *Star* for his story? Apparently not, though he is said to have been offered £20,000. The generally accepted version is that when *Star* reporters arrived at his house Francisco was out, so they got his wife talking about the Stevens incident, claiming they knew all about it. When Francisco got home he was put in the position of either denying what his wife had said or implicitly confirming it. The paper may have said they were publishing the story anyway, whether he agreed or not and whether he was paid or not.

There is much head shaking about this among the other journalists. One reporter argues defensively that they are not there to serve snooker but the public, and these are public men, up on the screen for hours on end, deriving their wealth from the public acclaim generated by the media. My views on the ethical aspect are eagerly sought. What strikes me is that few of these reporters, watching each other warily, nervous that the other may be out on a scoop, have ever met an editor before. The rivalry among the tabloids reminds me of my period in Africa in the early 1960s. Peter Younghusband of the *Daily Mail* and John Monks of the *Daily Express* used to chase each other all over the continent. Entering a bar in Salisbury or Leopoldville, they would each look around anxiously to ensure that the other was there and not on an aeroplane. Monks once received a cable from his office: 'Younghusband shot at – why not you?'

Francisco is in action against Dennis Taylor on the morning his revelations appear in the *Star*, which is hardly conducive to his concentration. Taylor, fresh from beating Higgins for the Irish title, never lets him settle down and goes 6–0 up. Francisco pulls one frame back then goes out for a long unscheduled break – presumably not for a fix – while Taylor sits in what can only be described as mounting calm, checking his watch. Even in the morning he is formally attired in white collar, blue shirt and dark blue suit. Francisco is more casually dressed in light flannels and loose tie. Taylor, in commanding form, finishes him off 10–2.

Suddenly, there is a buzz: Francisco is holding a press conference. We wind round various corridors into a brightly lit room that is being set up for the TV cameras. Curiously, on the wall above the platform chairs, are coloured portraits of Stevens and Francisco – is this deliberate or a mad coincidence? Francisco sits looking serious, flanked by WPBSA officials Paul Hatherell and Rex Williams. 'I did not say that – it's a total lie,' he tells us. 'It was a heated final. I may have said something. It was my first major. I'd just like to apologize to Kirk and to the professional body.' Rex Williams, the bland leading the blind, looks satisfied. 'There is no evidence at all to substantiate these allegations that any players have been taking drugs or any substance. The game's high image is absolutely clear. Most of this story is fabrication. The journalist is not here – he's probably caught a boat to China.' We are left with the general impression of a whitewash: see no evil, hear no evil, speak no evil. Nothing can be proved, so nothing happened, so the WPBSA need do nothing about it. Rex, one of the most powerful back-stage figures in the game, operates a prosperous table rental business for pubs and clubs which is now on the unlisted securities market. He also built up a cue concern called Powerglide which is now run by his brother. You would never guess from his urbane manner that he was once fined £500 for bad behaviour in a billiards match.

Then Stevens's agent, Noel Miller-Cheevers, puts out a statement that 'Kirk objects very strongly to these baseless allegations and is consulting his lawyer'. But he won't say whom he is considering sueing: Francisco or the *Daily Star*? Under questioning he admits he has not actually spoken to Kirk. Nobody believes a word of either statement. So where is the story now? The hacks realize it is fading fast, that their newsrooms are not going to be vitally interested in an unconvincing and colourless denial of a rival paper's story, especially when neither Higgins nor Davis is involved. One man puts down the phone to Maxwell House and says: 'This story lacks two ingredients as far as my office is concerned: Joan Collins and the Princess of Wales.' His colleagues sympathize and turn back morosely to the actual snooker.

In the bar there is much talk of the Hagler-Hearns world title fight. Bets are being laid, with 'Racing Raymond' much in evidence. One sometimes forgets how much these people gamble. Robbo, the Romford driver – and the cheerier one of the pair who go around with Davis – tells how he won £26,000 on Steve's horse, Charming Charlie, by going round placing bets carefully with dozens of bookies. He also tells a story of how he and Barry Hearn picked up a fortune backing Steve on a Northern tour and had to carry the cash around in a suitcase that grew fatter as they went from Leeds to Manchester to Liverpool. But when Steve heard about it, his game suddenly froze at the thought of what was riding on him. Another voice offers the opinion: 'Davis isn't enjoying his snooker, he's not even enjoying being out there.' At which point Davis arrives with Ron Radley, the unsmiling one, carrying his cue case as if he has just been practising. Ron buys him half a lager and sits with him in silence while he sips it.

Willie Thorne is losing to Patsy Fagan, which causes much surprise. His corner say that he's treating Fagan with too much respect. The Irishman started his professional career with a bang in 1977, winning the UK championship and reaching the world quarter finals. He then had a car accident which left him with the 'yips'. Like a golfer who cannot use the putter, Fagan could not use the rest. He tried acupuncture, psychiatry and hypnosis, to no avail. Rex Williams, who had once had a similar problem playing through the ball, had tried to talk him out of it. Fagan slipped to thirty-seventh in the world ranking until the problem disappeared as suddenly as it came. 'I don't know how I got rid of it,' he says, 'just as I don't know how it began.' The problem took three years out of his career and forced him back to the building trade and even on the dole. Had he thought of giving up snooker? 'No,' he says, 'it's the only thing in the world I can do well. The game was giving me up.' Fagan had been a formidable money player. He was once taken up by a London builder called Peter Careswell, who gave him a nominal job as a plumber's mate but really took him on to play for wagers all over the country. Fagan beats Thorne 10–6 to re-establish himself on the circuit, but goes out to Reardon in the next round.

The next press sensation is from Big Bill Werbeniuk, the giant Canadian, who attacks Higgins and Knowles in the *Sun*. He has evidently talked to a local correspondent who, much to Werbeniuk's annoyance, has passed the story on to the *Sun*, where it gets much bigger play than he ever intended. He comes out of his dressing room, tells the referee he is not quite ready, returns for two more quick lagers, slips on the steps and drops his chalk as he enters the arena, then scores 143, the biggest break of the tournament. This gives him a prize of £6000. 'How many cans of lager is that?' quips one reporter. 'One hundred and forty three is more points than he had scored all season,' says another. Werbeniuk beats Joe Johnson 10–8, but is crushed 13–3 by his friend Thorburn in the next round.

Thorburn nearly did not get that far, dicing with sudden death against Mike Hallett of Grimsby. He was 1–6 and 3–7 down; first man to ten wins. Hallett is a bit like a school prefect with neat fair hair, a charcoal grey suit and shiny black shoes on flat feet. He looks fresh faced against the grizzled Thorburn. Grimsby is a strong snooker town and Hallett has beaten most of the good players, including Davis, but has found it difficult to string two winning matches together at this level. At 7–4 Hallett goes 51 ahead and one senses that this could be make or break for

Thorburn. He wanders perplexed round the table for minutes on end, deliberately slowing the game down, then finally turns to the crowd and asks: 'Any ideas?' When Hallett mutters something, Thorburn says: 'Yeah, I know *you* have!' He flukes a red ('I fluke about three balls a season,' he jokes laconically afterwards) and lands on the black. He takes four reds and blacks, then the yellow, but misses the green. Hallett flukes the green, but finishes too close to pot the brown, which would have given him the frame. Thorburn needs all the colours and spars for an opening. This is real cat-and-mouse defensive stuff, with the brown being shifted from the top cushion to the side and back again to make it impossible for the other man to pot. The atmosphere is tense and the Crucible seems hotter than ever. If Hallett loses this frame after being 51 up, his game may crumble. Finally he loses patience and goes for the brown and leaves it on for Thorburn. He returns slowly to his chair. Thorburn sinks brown, blue, pink and black and clenches his fist in a victory salute. He is still 5–7 down but he knows he has stopped the rot and – even more important – got to the other man.

Thorburn's concentration is potent as he bends low over the cue, almost seeming to guide the tip with his moustache. He uses the cue like a lecturer pointing at a blackboard. In Davis's hands, when he's going well, it looks like a needle threading its way through the balls. White uses the cue like a rapier, Higgins like a gun. Most amateurs stand side on to the table. Pros stand almost foursquare (or certainly at 45 degrees), with the right leg stiff, left knee bent, and the cue running tight along the waistcoat and under the chin (and in some cases, as with Thorburn), rubbing the bristle as it comes through.

Unsurprisingly, the Grinder takes the next frame too. It's 6–7. Thorburn immediately lets Hallett in with a bad break-off – it's surprising how often this happens with professionals. You would think that they would have perfected this part of the game. Still, it makes things more lively. Thorburn finds himself 42 behind with 51 on the table, gets an extraordinary fluky red, then misses the blue from off the cushion. More cat and mouse. Thorburn gets a bad cough, splutters and says: 'What a great advert for Embassy!' – then sits down to sip more water. He misses and lets Hallett in.

That coughing may have lost him the frame. He is 48 behind, with only 35 on the table – he needs at least three snookers. He gets one, but Hallett runs away with the frame. It's 6–8.

Will it go to 6–9 or 7–8? The difference could be crucial. First blood to Thorburn. He makes a break of 39 and wins the frame. It is 7–8. Hallett goes 43 ahead with everything to play for, but misses a simple red. Thorburn recovers to 45. Cat and mouse again. A great pot by Hallett but he just fails to split the reds on the side cushion by a whisker. The score is 50–45. Hallett just misses a brave attempt at a double to the middle pocket, which catches the edge and rebounds to where Thorburn can pot it. He clears both remaining reds, but twice misses chances for the yellow; the second time it nearly goes in two different pockets. Hallett lays a canny snooker which Cliff gets out of neatly. Then a chance for Cliff on the yellow, which he gets, plus the green, but is not perfect on the brown. He gets it anyway and nudges the blue, billiards-style, towards the top pocket, then clears blue and pink to go level 8–8.

Between frames Thorburn sits there, staring ahead. You can feel the force. First red to Thorburn, but he comes back too far. 'Shucks,' he says. Hallett gets a triple plant (making one ball hit another and the second knocks the third ball into the pocket). He can't get on a colour and leaves the reds widely dispersed. But Cliff leaves a red over the pocket, letting Hallett in for 49. He is then guilty of a push shot (nudging the cue ball instead of striking it) in a tight position. Thorburn raps the table with one hand to applaud the break (or the referee's decision – I think the former). Thorburn gets to 12 points behind, then decides he's too close to the cushion to risk what looks like a safe black. Back to cat and mouse, both laying snookers. Hallett gets the yellow, but misses a fairly straightforward green, leaning too far across the table and falling off the shot. It's now 52–38 to Hallett. Cliff takes the green and brown, but misses the blue. 52–45. Hallett misses a long blue and leaves it. Cliff leans a long way to reach it, eschewing the rest, and gets it, screwing back for an awkward pink, which he puts in the middle pocket. But he still needs the black and takes it. Houdini has survived again. For the first time in the match Thorburn is ahead, 9–8.

Is Hallett finished? I suspect he may be when he starts chatting with the audience near his chair, ruefully shaking his head at the missed opportunities. In the early frames, when he had been on a winning streak, he had just sat quietly in his chair, totally self-possessed, waiting to get on with it. Now he seems to feel a need to connect with other people that he did not feel before. He is chatting with the referee and a bit more jaunty than usual. It is as though he knows he is going to lose when he could have won and needs the reassurance of company: he wants to share the pressure of all this because he can no longer cope with it on his own. He is looking red-rimmed round the eyes, which isn't surprising as it's nearly midnight. It is probably past his bedtime; it is certainly past mine.

A bad sign of nerves from Hallett early on when he doesn't go for a pot when there seemed to be two reds on. He would not have hesitated before. Then he misses a red altogether, so Cliff puts him in again, and he misses again. 'It wasn't easy,' Cliff says consolingly as the crowd gasp. On Hallett's next shot, he goes in-off. So in four successive trips to the table he has shied away from a pottable red, missed twice and gone in-off. Surely now it's only a matter of time for Cliff to clean up. Hallett goes in-off again. 'Should have been over an hour ago,' Hallett mutters to the press bench as he passes, suggesting that he too is conscious of feeling tired and is offering this as his excuse. There is no doubt that the late hour favours Thorburn, the old night owl.

All the balls congregate at the top, rather like on my table at home, which sags at one end. One finally drops for Hallett, but he can't make enough of it. It's 37–16 to Thorburn. More cat and mouse, then Hallett sinks another, and this time makes 26 to put him 42–37 ahead. A brave rally. Thorburn just misses going in-off, the cue ball wobbling in the jaws; had it dropped, Hallett would have been back with a chance to clean up from the position the balls were then in. But 'the run of the balls', as the pros say, always goes one way. This is proved again a moment later when Hallett goes for a brave, brilliant cut on a red which hovers on the edge of the pocket and stays out. Thorburn pots it, but misses the yellow, then gets it but goes in-off at the same time. The crowd are holding their breath and no wonder. Now it is Hallett's chance. He gets the yellow, but pushes the green near the hole for Thornburn to pot it. 48–43 to Hallett. Thorburn puts down the blue and pink to win the match. 'That's about it,' says Hallett as Thorburn lines up the winning pink. Clive Everton, elated by the match, says to me in the press room afterwards: 'You see, this game's about character.'

After the match Thorburn says: 'I don't want to say much' (meaning we guess, that he doesn't want to be trapped into commenting on the Kirk Stevens affair). Did he think he was going to lose at 3–7 down? 'I always feel I'm on for a 10–9 win when I'm 0–9 down,' he jokes. 'I felt a bit numb early on, not as though I was in the world championship. The tables feel different here from other tournaments for some reason – maybe it's the money!' He agreed that the twelfth frame was crucial. 'He went a bit at the end, but he really stuck it to me.' Hallett, subdued but by no means looking crushed, said: 'My manager warned me that he'd come out grinding. Still, he knows he's been in a game. He brought off some fantastic pots – about 95 per cent of them. I was buzzing yesterday, but I started shooting from the hip towards the end – you can't take those risks with these guys. I missed the key balls and he didn't.'

Waiting for Kirk Stevens is like waiting for the entry of the gladiator. The crowd is buzzing. Will he turn up? Everybody wants to know how he will cope after all the publicity: will he crack up, as Francisco did against Taylor? I spot him in the corridor backstage, looking pale but chirpy. He enters the arena to great applause, an elf compared with the gigantic Werbeniuk, his fellow-Canadian, who is playing at the next table. Stevens's opponent is Ray Edmonds of Cleethorpes, a bulky dark-haired man who seems to have strayed in from the earlier, less trendy, sergeants' mess days of the snooker era – or rather billiards, at which he is the current world champion. He owns a club and has a share in a table manufacturing business, but he has never won so much prize money as he has this year. When he was proudly showing the snaps of a baby in the press room, I assumed it must be a grandchild, but I was wrong: it was his own. (I then notice, to my chagrin, that he is the same age as I am!) The Kirk Stevens fan club is in evidence in the front row, including a pair of dark-haired twins, one wearing KIRK across her white T-shirt, the other presumably STEVENS, but the first and last letters of the surname are lost under her armpits, so all we can see is KIRK EVEN – which might be an oblique comment on his row with Francisco.

It is a scrappy match, Kirk using power as a substitute for guile, without much success, crashing the ball off the table at one point in frustration. 'Come on, Kirk,' the girls shout loyally. When he loses the first frame, Stevens lights up a cigarette. 'Will someone please analyse that substance?' says a voice in the press box. Edmonds's feelings are spread across his pleasant old face, unlike the younger men, who keep their faces under control. He has a certain swagger when a good shot goes in. But there aren't too many of those. Stevens's cue looks curiously long in relation to his height. This is because he likes to play through the ball a long way to achieve great cue power and send the ball spinning all round the table for position. His cuff links get in the way of one shot – I saw the same thing happen to Werbeniuk. Stevens cracks in a red that Edmonds acknowledges with a wry grin, misses the black, which flukes into the middle pocket: Edmonds's grin is even wryer. Next shot Stevens's cue ball drops in, so justice is served. When Kirk's fans cry out, referee John Williams calls: 'Gentlemen, please', even though at least half of them are women. A lifetime's habit in male snooker clubs is hard to break. Williams, the senior referee, is self-effacing to the point of invisibility, his hands behind his back, fading on soft shoes into the background – a contrast with Len Ganley at the next table, who struts around like a sergeant major on parade. Even so, Williams goes up to the press bench and slaps a reporter on the wrist: 'Keep your hand still,' he hisses.

Even though the Stevens–Edmonds match is boring, with too many shots being missed, it still contrives to reach a thrilling climax at 9–8 to Kirk. Edmonds comes back from 36 behind and pots the green but misses a crucial cut on the brown which would almost certainly have drawn him level 9–9. Stevens doubles the brown dramatically into the middle pocket to wild applause from his fans, with the blue to follow on the edge of the pocket. He pots the pink flamboyantly after sending the cue ball twice round the table, and it's all over. They embrace each other warmly afterwards. 'Shakin' Stevens, as the press have cruelly dubbed him, bounces into the news conference afterwards: 'OK class, hello boys and girls, how are you all today? Now what did I do now – or what didn't I do?'

Did he take illegal drugs?

'I can't answer that.'

Has he hard feelings towards Francisco?

'I'm numb about the whole thing.'

What is he going to do about it?

'This won't be left – I'm really disgusted. It was very anti-climactic going into the tournament – I really didn't feel like being there. I didn't feel the excitement you're supposed to feel at the Crucible. It's usually Alex under fire from you guys – now I know how he feels.'

Play stops during the Stevens match when Werbeniuk, on the next table, approaches the end of his big break. Stevens peeps round the room divider. Big Bill and referee Len Ganley look evenly matched for the heavyweight title. Werbeniuk, gulping lager between shots and wheezing and snorting a good deal, makes hard work of beating Joe Johnson of Bradford 10–8. At one point he misses badly, the cue ball leaps in the air, lands by accident on a red, which dashes into the hole like a startled rabbit. Big Bill roars to the crowd: 'It's great when it happens to you!' On another occasion he misses and cries out: 'I used to do this for a living!' At his press conference he is cross with the *Daily Star* and the *Sun* and refuses to talk to them. He is a big soft thing like a teddy bear, says Janice Hale, really a very nice man, but badly off form this season. 'I've had a bad year,' he admits. 'Things got caught up in my own brain. The pressure was on me and I collapsed. But there's nobody out there whom I regard as a better player than me,' he adds defiantly. Exit clutching a pint. 'At least he won't have any trouble giving a sample for the drug test,' says the girl from Ceefax.

Meanwhile, back in the press room, the snooker hacks decide to get their own back on one of the *Star*'s 'newsmen', that dangerous breed, who had worked on the Francisco/Stevens story and made them all run around after it. He is sitting at a desk when the *Star*'s phone rings. He picks it up, listens for a while, then leans closer to the mouthpiece, putting his hand round it conspiratorially and sneaking a furtive look round the room to see if he can be overheard. The fact is that everybody is straining to hear every word, but you would never guess that from their carefully composed straight faces. It's a deliberate set-up and everybody is in on the secret except the poor benighted victim. Steve Acteson, the Press Association's man on the circuit – a gentle, uxorious fellow whose main worry is that the snooker keeps him away from his family too much – does a marvellous Ray Reardon imitation and is putting it to good use. In a lilting Welsh accent on the telephone 'Reardon' is offering the *Star* the full inside story of the snooker world – 'girls, drugs, homo-sexuals, the lot – you name it, boyo'. The news hawk cannot believe his luck. His eyes grow wider and his pen races across the pages of his notebook. A meeting is arranged over breakfast the next day. He sits back as the telephone goes down, his eyes shining with barely suppressed excitement. He picks up the phone again to dial the *Star* news desk and pass on the good news. As he does so, Graham Nickless, the *Star*'s snooker cor-respondent, walks over and cuts off the connection, gently direc-ting his attention at the rest of the room, which is falling about in hysterics. The poor man sits back and closes his eyes as he realizes how he has been wound up and how willingly he has been conned. To his credit, he takes it very well.

The bar at the Grosvenor House Hotel is even livelier than usual after all that. Terry Griffiths appears in a salmon-pink jacket – 'that must be Barry's idea', says a wag. The players and press need time to wind down after an exciting match, so it is not surprising to learn that they sometimes stay in the bar until 5 a.m. before going to bed and sleeping till noon. It is such a self-enclosed and self-absorbed world that they make up their own rules. 'What about the snooker groupies?' people ask me. There are certainly women sitting around in pairs in the bars of the hotels, as there are in any large town when there's a big event going on; some of them may be professionals, others enthusiastic amateurs. I met some girls who give up their holidays to go all over the country to watch the snooker; but they seem to be as genuinely interested in the play as the players. Barry Hearn turned to them on one occasion and asked out of genuine interest: 'Who's number one for you kids? Still Alex? Then who – Jimmy White?' There was certainly one rich woman who plucked a top player by helicopter – said to be Tony Knowles – and dropped him back the next morning. There are always girls in discos and night clubs who are attracted to athletic young men with plenty of money to splash. And of course the players spend a lonely time away from home in dreary hotels. If there's much more to it than that, then I am afraid it escaped this reporter.

Another canard about snooker is perpetrated in Bob Geldof's unspeakably bad film, *Number One*, starring the Boomtown Rat himself as a bent player and Mel Smith as his crooked backer. The message of this 'dunderheaded tale' (*Financial Times*) is that the whole tournament is rigged. Incredibly, Geldof himself turned up in Sheffield to see the première in the presence of some of the game's top players and officials. As Victor Davis said in the *Daily Express*, the fact that he 'didn't end up pocketed in a drainpipe with a cue wrapped round his neck is some sort of tribute to the self-control of snooker's brothers of the green baize'.

You can become so involved in the tournament, living with the players on and off the stage, sharing their tensions, hopes and disappointments, that you tend to forget everything else. One journalist said: 'When you go away and then come back, you realize these people are so wrapped up in a private world that nothing else breaks in.' Janice Hale tells a story against herself about this. Paul Callan had been attending a championship when he was suddenly called away by the *Daily Mirror*. 'Where are you going?' she asked. 'I'm being sent to Cambodia,' he replied. 'Cambodia?' she thought, very puzzled. 'They don't play snooker in Cambodia.'

By this time, well into the tournament, even Steve Davis seems less forbidding. He exchanges a few words in the bar as he sits with Ron Radley sipping a lager. Had he seen Werbeniuk's 143? 'No, one break doesn't mean much anyway.' I said Thorburn had taken a long time to warm up. 'The trouble with the first round is that by the time you've warmed up you may be out.' He mentions that he once saw Joe Davis in the gents at Wembley. Joe did not speak. He makes a jokey self-deprecating reference to his chances of still being in the tournament next week. 'There's no danger,' say I. 'There's always danger,' says he. I sense that Steve, for all that he needs and welcomes company, is still uneasy with a journalist, so I make my excuses and leave, with a guilty feeling that the harder men of Fleet Street might have made more of the opportunity. He had gone through easily to the quarter final, beating David Taylor, 'The Silver Fox', 13–4. When somebody tells Clive Everton in the press room, 'You know, Clive, you look a bit like the Silver Fox yourself,' Barry Hearn whips round and says: 'Right, the Silver Hamster!' Taylor, in his rimless glasses, looks less like a fox than a pedagogue or the doctor, Chebutykin, in Chekhov's *Three Sisters*. (In fact, he was a hairdresser in Manchester.)

The match becomes a contest of defensive play, which means one of two things: either sending the cue ball up the table, clipping the reds and running back as close as possible to the baulk cushion; or stunning the white ball and hitting a red in the middle so that the white rolls tight on the top cushion. The point of being tight on the cushion is that your opponent can only hit the top of the ball, which gives him a harder shot to control. A variation, if you cannot put the cue ball tight on a cushion, is to rebound close to one of the baulk colours (yellow, green and brown) to snooker your opponent. Both are good defensive players, but Davis is usually that vital inch or two closer to the cushion, forcing Taylor into marginal errors which let Davis in. He looks cool, slightly coiled, every nerve alert, and makes breaks of 100 and 105.

At Davis's press conference Barry Hearn stands by the door – 'just to make sure none of you leave before you've written down every word'. Steve is relaxed. 'In the first round you're panicking a bit, everybody is. If you enjoy a tournament you get better.' Had he any preference between Griffiths and Higgins for his next match. 'No, they both smoke!' he replies, forgetting himself for a moment. The Embassy man in the chair leans forward and jokes: 'This conference is now closed!' Taylor praises Davis's safety play but adds, 'I think he's vulnerable. He's vulnerable if you can stay with him and capitalize on his mistakes. He has tremendous mental ability, but he has holes in his game which players playing well (which I wasn't) can exploit.'

Higgins goes out 13–7 to Griffiths in an anticlimax. The crowd, who always reserve their biggest cheer for Alex, are plainly disappointed. Griffiths professes surprise at winning: 'When I saw the draw I only brought one shirt with me.' Higgins is dressed in a smart grey suit and white shirt. There had been rumours of a punch-up in the hotel the night before, with Higgins allegedly falling down the stairs, but there always are such rumours whenever he is around and no reliable means of checking them. He sends out for a pint of lager, drinks it, then demands a chilled orange juice – ice-cold for Alex. He saves his best play until the position is irrecoverable. Even when he is 95 behind with only 22 left on the table, he refuses to concede and goes on bashing the ball around as if he had paid for the lights. But he did one thing I had not seen before. He potted the blue and deliberately left the cue ball on the blue spot so that it had to be respotted on the black, so that he could get among the top reds – the pink and black balls being unusable on the cushion. He says afterwards: 'I didn't enjoy the whole razzmatazz of the Crucible. I'm looking over my shoulder all the time. There are press men everywhere. This is the festival of snooker and it has taken some of the gloss away.' He objects to the way the drug tests were suddenly introduced (though his first response had been: 'If they want to test me for rabies they are more than welcome'). He is fed up with the £1500 fine he received for swearing at Wembley and with the fact that players cannot wear advertising logos. 'I'm considering proposing a vote of no confidence in the board.' In conclusion he declares to the assembled press: 'I feel like John McEnroe at Wimbledon' – and gives a two-fingered salute to prove it.

Reardon beats Fagan, borrowing Fagan's cue for the *coup de grâce* after his own tip came off – a rare sporting gesture. He goes through to play young John Parrott, who disposes of a pale and dispirited Kirk Stevens. Stevens joins Higgins in complaining about the professional body – in this case for failing to give him adequate protection from the media. John Virgo, the bearded

WPBSA vice-chairman, replies with a lugubrious look implying that players are old enough and rich enough – even if they are not clever enough – to look after themselves. They also have managers to look after them. Kirk has borrowed a suit of black and silver stripes from Jimmy White and bounds into the press room like a parody of himself: 'Hi, folks! What's doing, guys?' He admits that the situation was 'a bit of a moral disappointment', especially for his father, who was travelling with him. 'I kind of let myself down.' He evidently cheers up later in the bar and opens a bottle of Moët et Chandon.

White beats Meo, his old truancy partner, 13–11 in one of the best matches of the tournament. The surface of Meo's moon face ripples with pleasure when he makes a 130 break. He is tailored more smartly than White, whose creased and let-down trouser bottoms catch on his heels and nearly trip him up. By contrast, Meo is resplendent in what looks like natty grey mohair with an expensive shine on it – perhaps another mark of better management. Off stage he favours spangled pinks, yellows and purples, like a pop star. Neither looks like a morning player to me, and I feel like an intruder at their hangovers. Knowles goes on a winning streak to destroy Doug Mountjoy 13–6. There is a ferocious intensity about the Welshman's long potting, as if it is directed by the determined muscular strength of a rugby prop forward. When Knowles misses a shot, which isn't often in this match, he stares hard at the green baize or at the cue ball as if they must be to blame rather than himself. Afterwards, as Marilyn Monroe and Robert Mitchum fight it out in *River of No Return* on the TV, the young Romeo dates his first blonde of the night in the press room.

Between matches a young man with long fair hair, who looks a bit like a hairdresser, comes out and brushes and irons the tables, redraws the lines and checks that the spots are still visible. I have noticed him backstage, wincing proprietorially at some abuse of the cloth by Higgins or Werbeniuk. When Spencer plays a shot with his cue almost vertical, exerting a downward squeeze on the ball to twist it out of a snooker, the boy hardly dares to look.

It is send-up time for Barry Hearn. Sharon, the girl who looks after the bookstall, calls him up saying someone wants to see him. When Barry gets there he finds that she has set out a display of coloured photographs of him and the crowds are rushing forward for autographed copies. Robbo says he once bought Barry a JR hat in Dallas for 67 dollars. Barry does, in fact, have the same wide face as actor Larry Hagman. Sharon ticks me off for calling Robbo a 'minder'. 'They're not minders,' she says. 'They're just nice fellas.'

Dennis Taylor, continuing his fine form, beats Eddie Charlton 13–6. The Australian veteran has come tantalizingly close to the world title twice – both times against Reardon – in the 1970s, losing by a single frame (31–30) in 1975 and after leading 7–0 in 1973. Now, at 55, it seems unlikely that he will make it. 'Steady Eddie' is indignant at the idea that he plays unusually slowly: 'Back in Australia I'm known as an attacking player!' he says. For twenty years he has dominated the game in Australia, where he is revered as their Joe Davis. As a boy of 11, he played an exhibition against the legendary Walter Lindrum, at 15 he scored his first century at billiards, and at 17 his first at snooker. He was also a surfing champion and accomplished at roller-skating, cricket, athletics, boxing and tennis. In 1956 he carried the torch at the Melbourne Olympics. With his dour, unyielding face, his unhurried play, his ruthless potting and disdain for side and spin, Eddie Charlton is the ultimate 'never say die' man. In the 1978 world championship he beat Willie Thorne from three frames down and four to play and Cliff Thorburn from four behind and five to play. He fought as hard as ever against Dennis Taylor, but missed the vital balls. As Clive James once pointed out: 'The champions lose when they miss the easy ones. The snooker player, like the ballet dancer, sadly attains his fullest knowledge just as his body begins no longer to obey him.'

Meanwhile, Stuart Holmes, the anti-smoking campaigner, has been keeping up his vigil outside the players' entrance. He thrusts into my hand a cutting from *The Times* reporting a survey on child smokers and a copy of a letter he has sent to Sheffield City Council calling for a ban on this 'tobacco promotion'. He is hoping to get the many churches around the Crucible to condemn the tournament jointly. 'It's disgraceful,' he told me. 'They are trying to associate smoking with this popular game, with these glamorous people, knowing that it will appeal especially to the young. I've talked to the churches and told them that they condemn alcohol but invest in tobacco companies, which kill many more people. But I can't get them interested. One of them nearly threw me out. I've talked to the Environmental Health people, who agree that it negates their work if the Crucible, which the council supports, runs a tobacco-sponsored event like this. But when the press ring them, they clam up. The Lord Mayor's just the same. The trouble is there's so much money at stake. They should insist on a different sponsor.'

He has been working full time at this since November 1983 – 'I can't think of anything more important to do.' Before that he was a draughtsman. He has been living rough since he was thrown out of his bedsitter for non-payment of rent. He is buoyed up by hope and little victories such as getting people like me to stop and talk. 'The vicar may be issuing a press statement,' he says earnestly as I move on.

In the first quarter final the unthinkable happens: Terry Griffiths goes into a 4–0 lead over Steve Davis. Davis finds something wrong with the cue ball even before they start. A dour 47-minute opening frame ends with Davis going in-off the black. In the next frame a TV cameraman has a coughing fit as Davis goes for a winning pink. He misses it. Barry Hearn, who is drinking coffee thoughtfully in the press room with Steve's father, rises and goes out, presumably to give Steve a pep talk. Robbo tells me later: 'I saw Steve was 4–0 down, so I thought I'd pop along to his dressing room to give him a lively' (which is presumably Romford slang for cheering him up). 'As I reached the door, I thought to myself "Better go carefully, it might be a nasty scene in there", so I turned the handle very slowly and had a peep inside. There he was, standing straight as a guardsman, just staring at himself in the mirror. Eerie it was, so I closed the door quietly and tiptoed away.' Whatever Davis was doing, it seemed to work, for he soon caught up.

'Terry is harder than he's ever been,' says Hearn. But he didn't look hard. For all his carefully cultivated good looks – the hair, the shoes, the rings – he seems just a bit soft to me, going slightly podgy and round-shouldered. I preferred his hair flopping around as it did when he won the world title at the first attempt in 1978; now it is rather too elaborately coiffeured. One senses that the money, the house, the Mercedes, have all blunted the edge of his ambition and softened the will to win. He was always a rather reluctant professional, preferring to be at home with his wife and sons, and took a long time before making up his mind to join the circuit. He learned to play really well during a postal strike when he was working as a postman in Llanelli. He was also an apprentice blacksmith, a bus conductor and an insurance salesman. At one stage he felt that the life of the professional snooker player had trapped him in a cage – all the travelling, the staying in strange hotels, the lifeless exhibition matches, the repetitive trick shots. 'I used to go to bed and I'd think, Jesus, what are you doing? But I'd have to get up the next day and do it all again and again and that went on for months. I felt the people were like woodpeckers pecking away at me all the time.' He rebuilt his snooker action and plays now with a conspicuously loose grip. He also took up aikido, one of the martial arts, and releases tension by riding a 750cc motorbike. Under Barry Hearn's stewardship he has found financial security and strikes one now as a well-adjusted man, extremely courteous, sharp and brightly curious. His very niceness tells against him in his match against Davis, for he owns up to fouling the ball with his waistcoat and lets Steve in for a break of 80 that sets him up for victory.

Reardon *v.* Parrott is the archetypal confrontation of Experience and Youth, the Sorcerer and the Apprentice. There are more than thirty years between them. Both are tall and dark and might be taken for father and son. Parrott has a more middle-class bearing than most snooker players, with a neatly barbered mop of hair, untrendy grey flannels and heavy brogues. He speaks with a light Merseyside accent and rushes off between matches to support Everton at Goodison Park. Living in the Penny Lane area, he is as recognizably Liverpudlian as Cilla Black, Jimmy Tarbuck or the Beatles. His father has nursed his career, which started by accident. When they couldn't play bowls one evening because of rain they tried snooker instead. Some say he is ready for more aggressive career management of the Barry Hearn type.

He has the boyishly handsome looks and the personality for easy commercial exploitation and is most people's favourite as the one most likely to succeed among the younger generation – even, some believe, as Steve Davis's natural successor. His 'million dollar cue action', as Clive Everton called it, has been polished by Davis's own guru, Frank Callan of Blackpool. I was in the hotel lift with Parrott and Jimmy White on the night before his match with Reardon. When it stopped at the second floor White got out and invited him to the bar. 'I think I'll have an early night,' he replied firmly. 'Match tomorrow' – and carried on up to his room. 'Are you in form?' I asked him. 'Well, I'm keen for the game and that's what matters,' he said.

His keenness took him to a quick 4–0 lead. Reardon kept shaking his head at Parrott's run of the ball. His face goes through many contortions of pain, pleasure and disbelief, especially when a spectator comes crashing down the aisle, right in his line of vision, carrying a plate of sandwiches and a pint of beer. 'Have you any sauce on that?' he says to the man, then turns to the referee: 'You can't believe what some people do these days!' Reardon keeps pulling back vital frames when Parrott seems about to go into an unassailable lead. At the formal dress evening session, which Reardon clearly relishes, he wins five frames on the trot to lead 12–9. But Parrott comes back level at 12–12 for a last-frame decider. The atmosphere is tense. The young man edges ahead but the old magician, using all his tablecraft, leaves a devastating snooker on the last red, extracts a free ball from it and runs away with the match.

'When I saw that snooker,' Parrott says afterwards, 'I wondered if he had a father!' He takes his defeat very calmly: 'I'll wake up kicking myself tomorrow, but tonight I feel great.' He is delighted that he has shown he can fight back under pressure. He once said to Janice Hale as she rummaged in her handbag: 'Can you get me some confidence pills?' He and his father are determined to develop his game at the right pace and not be rushed: 'The press and the media are expecting me to win too soon,' he says. One wonders if this easygoing boy, for all his talent, is too soft to go all the lonely way to the top. It will be good for snooker if he does. A girl from the BBC asks him innocently: 'Do you find it easier or more difficult coming from the behind?' 'What a question!' says Parrott with mock primness as the room dissolves in mirth.

The other quarter finals – Taylor *v.* Thorburn and Knowles *v.* White – were a demonstration of snooker's infinite variety. The first was a long gruelling affair, hours of rugged defensive play by seasoned campaigners, while the other was an exhibition of attacking potting by the glamour boys of the circuit. 'Let's get this straight,' says Thorburn affably after his match. 'I wasn't the only one who played safe. If I'd played well, this would have been the longest match ever. But he had an answer to everything I tried.' It was long enough anyway – four and a quarter hours in the first session, five and a half at night, finishing at 1.20 a.m. Taylor clears up the next morning 13–5, having taken on Thorburn, his best friend on the circuit, at his own game and comprehensively beaten him. The game is marked by the exchange of amiable Irish and Canadian banter. Taylor had popped over to Ireland between matches to make a TV commercial for crisps, which suggests that he had not been confident of reaching this stage of the competition – a lack of confidence shared by the bookies, who were still offering 33–1. But there were other opinions. I saw Barry Hearn watching Taylor closely on the TV monitor during his match against Thorburn. 'Dennis is a new man, isn't he?' he said quietly, almost to himself. 'He always gives Steve a hard time. He'll be the man to beat.'

Knowles and White play high-quality snooker, both making century breaks (whereas in the Taylor-Thorburn marathon there was only one break of over fifty and that in the last frame). The old pros like Jimmy White, whom they regard as the most natural genius on the circuit, compared with whom Davis is a forced flower. 'He'd make a wonderful billiards player,' says Rex Williams, as if that was the highest accolade he could confer. They are less keen on Knowles, whose dedication is suspect. They say he does not take his cue out of his case for weeks on end. One feels, though, that deep down it's his sexual exploits they find hardest to take. Knowles has a chance to beat Werbeniuk's 143 for the £6000 prize, but misses an awkward

thin cut on the black, having gone for a flashy positional shot
off the pink which seems superfluous. When Knowles is on
song he looks unbeatable, but he gets easily upset when something goes wrong and glares like a spoilt child instead of analys-
ing the problem. 'You can't teach him anything,' says one of the
old pros. Taylor, faced with the speedy Knowles for the semifinal after Thorburn and Charlton, says: 'I'll never be able to
get used to an early night.'

Jean Rook in the *Daily Express* describes the pack of four
semifinalists as King of Diamonds (Davis), King of Hearts
(Knowles), King of Clubs (Taylor), and King of Spades (Reardon). The King of Diamonds quickly overpowers the King of
Spades 16–5 with a session to spare – the bane of the television
companies, who have to pad out with feature items, old film
and exhibition matches. Robbo is pleased, though, having wagered £400 on the exact frame score. Reardon's experience has
seen him through tight matches against Hughes and Parrott, but
Davis is equally knowledgeable at the tactics of the game and as
used to the pressure of a big event. 'He showed me great respect
in there,' says Reardon afterwards. 'He never gave me a
chance!' Davis's safety play is so precise and so positive that
Reardon is left with only half chances that are risky to take on.
His long potting for the first red also lets him down, usually
because Davis has forced him to play from tight on the cushion.
He describes Davis as the greatest player of the past decade.
'Professionally, I enjoyed seeing him play so well.' Reardon
feels the fates are against him: 'When I went in-off early on, I
thought to myself this is going to be an against-the-wind job.'
Did he fancy Davis's chances for the title? 'He's going to take
some stopping.'

The only players left to stop him are Dennis Taylor and
Tony Knowles. Much to everyone's surprise – and to his own
considerable annoyance – Knowles is completely outplayed.
Taylor wins by the same easy margin as Davis over Reardon,
16–5 – and again the BBC people are dismayed by the loss of
another evening session, not to mention the crowd of a thousand people who have paid £6.50 each for a ticket. It is beginning to look as if the championship might be a TV disaster.

John Hennessey writes in the *Daily Mail*: 'What should be the most exciting climax to the sport's premier event is in danger of becoming reduced to a farce.' Trevor East, his ITV rival, quips to Nick Hunter in the corridor: 'If you're running out of old film, I've got some in the boot of my car!'

Knowles cannot understand why he was playing so much worse than in his match against White and gets angry with himself. 'He started throwing his cue at the ball, which never works,' says Taylor. Knowles had gone out on the attack because he thought the Irishman might not have recovered from his hard match against Thorburn. But Taylor responds in kind, playing different tactics from those he had used against the Canadian. 'Knowles can't face the fact that he tried to outpot Taylor and that on the day Taylor was a far superior potter,' says Clive Everton. As usual, Knowles blames everything but himself. He complains about a spotlight shining in his eyes and calls for a chair to be brought into the arena so that he can move his seating position. Taylor cannot resist a joke as he glances back at Knowles from the table. 'Are you sitting comfortably? Perhaps you'd like an armchair – I could have used a double bed the other night' (for his Thorburn night marathon). Knowles glares surlily around him, unamused. He is not amused either – though the crowd are – when Taylor seems to catch himself in an embarrassing place while climbing on to the table and makes a cabaret act of it. 'How do I explain it? You can't. I never got into the match,' says Knowles afterwards. He relapses as ever into minute frame-by-frame analysis: 'I missed a red to the right-hand pocket in the third frame. If I'd got that I might have gone 3–0 up.' He isn't unduly gracious towards his opponent. 'Dennis went out and potted everything,' he complains, as if this was some breach of snooker etiquette. 'To beat Steve he'll need to play as well as that, have the run of the ball and have a lot of luck besides.'

Taylor, with a century break under his belt, rates his chances higher than that. 'It won't be as easy as that against Steve,' he tells the press. '16–6 perhaps,' he adds with a roar of engaging laughter. To a reporter who says he'd never given him a chance against Knowles, Taylor responds cheerily to another roar of laughter: 'I always knew you were bloody stupid!' Then, on a more serious note, he adds: 'If I could make it tough for Steve when he was winning everything, I must stand a chance now. I know that and Steve knows that. Barry won't let him think like that, but it'll be in there somewhere.'

*Chapter Ten*

# A BIT OF A MATCH

Exactly an hour before every session in which Steve Davis is playing, an unusual cortège gathers at the Grosvenor House Hotel and makes its way in procession to the Crucible Theatre. There are three men in the lead: Steve himself with his cue case, usually looking tense; Barry Hearn, his manager, usually looking cheerful; and Robbo, the tall Romford club assistant, in his double-breasted pin stripe with single-breasted revers, his bouffant hair, ruby ring and white co-respondent shoes. After that the order may vary, but the procession normally includes Bill Davis, Steve's father, clenching a huge cigar; Ron Radley, the karate expert, carrying Steve's bag; Mark Lazarus, the former Queens Park Rangers soccer star, with his son, a keen snooker player; plus assorted friends and hangers-on. I once heard Barry misquote Julius Caesar with approval: 'Let me have men about me that are lean.' Here they are – and they look like a mafia hit squad on their way to a funeral.

They always take exactly the same route. Outside the hotel's front door in Charter Square they turn right past Bobby's Takeaway and the Pizza Hut and Henry's trendy café; over the road into Cross Burgess Street, keeping Cole's department store and the Salvation Army Citadel on the left; over the busy main thoroughfare of Pinfold Street, towards the new Town Hall. Then down an alley containing a herbal store and shop called Blisters which has posters in the window for various pop groups: the Sub-Humans, Toxic Toys, Dead Meat and Hole in the Wall. Next comes the cobbled walk under the Town Hall extension, where fountains keep alive the memory of Samuel Holberry, the Chartist leader who died in jail after the Sheffield Rising of 1840.

There is also a notable bronze statue by George Fullard of a 'Walking Man', into whose mouth someone has inserted a fag end which may or may not be an Embassy.

They have now reached the top of Norfolk Street, with all its churches, the Art Shop, Leonie's Pizza Parlour, Ruskin's (founded 1785) and the Brown Bear public house, where they all ritually stamp on the beer delivery cover. Past the cluster of BBC caravans, Stuart Holmes and his anti-smoking placards, and into the Crucible's stage-door entrance. The route is unvarying because Steve likes it that way and says it puts him in the right frame of mind.

The cosseting continues right up to the door of the arena. Barry escorts him from his dressing room along the corridors back stage, past the signs for the Green Room, the Rehearsal Room and the Quick Change Room – all redolent of greasepaint and showbiz – past the tripwire cables and the scaffolding, and stands with him while the introductions are made inside. Robbo is called up for a last cheery word – to 'give him a lively', as they say. 'Be good' is Barry's final shout as Steve goes though the orange curtain and into the bright lights and the applause. He is given no time to brood on his own.

Whatever the psychological purpose behind all this, it seems to work as Davis builds up an early lead. Taylor starts with a 50 break, but misses the last red to the middle pocket, letting Davis in. In the next frame Davis scores 87. Both men sense that the third frame is crucial, Steve licking his lips in nervous concentration. His safety shots stay magnetically on the baulk cushion, his potting is sure, and he makes hardly any mistakes. 'That shot was unbelievable,' says Robbo in the press room. Taylor, ever the humourist, tiptoes round the table as a ball hovers on the edge of the pocket. Steve takes this frame and the next, as Taylor misses a crucial red with the old snatch at the back of his cueing action. It is snowing outside but you can feel the heat in the Crucible.

'Scar tissue forms on boxers' eyebrows but in snooker players' minds.' Clive Everton opines thus about the final of the Jameson tournament of 1981, when Davis whitewashed Taylor 9–0. Could this be nagging at the Irishman's memory? He is so nervous he misses the pack of reds completely and hits the black.

His back hand is about a foot from the end of the cue, which leads him to snatch. 0–5. His luck is so far out that he goes in-off, which sets Davis up for a break of 66. 0–6. Taylor sits helplessly in his chair with the shrugs, smirks and self-conscious grimaces that are all this cruel game leaves for the loser. A brave long red in the seventh gives him a chance at last, but again his luck is out as the reds split badly. He manages to fluke one and makes a joke about it, pretending to examine his shoe to see if there's dog dirt on it. Davis comes back with a break of 58, so it's 0–7 at the end of the afternoon session and the bookies reduce the odds on a whitewash from 300–1 to 100–1.

'He looks three inches shorter. His head has sunk into his neck,' Clive Everton says in the interval. Taylor is certainly looking red in the face with suppressed rage or shame (he tells me afterwards he was more embarrassed than angry at this point). 'Even if he gets a chance now, he won't be able to take it,' says Everton. 'He's lost belief in himself – every shot will look horribly difficult for him.' Robbo and Bill Davis, cigar glowing, sit watching the slaughter. 'Another case of the nice guy coming second,' I say to Hugh McIlvanney. 'He'll come third if he goes on like this,' says McIlvanney, ruefully re-phrasing his article for the *Observer*'s later editions. What he wrote bears repetition:

> Davis brings to his work the inviolable singlemindedness that sets apart such champions as Nicklaus and Fangio, of whom it was said that he could drive through a crowd who were throwing beer bottles at his head without missing a gear change. What that singlemindedness inflicted on Taylor last night was painful to behold. Red-faced and seeming to sink even lower in his chair, looking more and more like a sick owl resigned to being savaged by an eagle, he was humiliated beyond anything a nice man should be asked to suffer.

As I return to the Crucible for the evening session, I hear running steps behind me on the cobbled stones. Trevor East pants past shouting: 'I must catch Dennis in his dressing room before the start.' Taylor is one of his ITV commentators and they have become good friends. Trevor's cheery directness may be just what he needs.

But the eighth frame looks like being his worst yet. He retreats to his chair, after a miss, with his head in his hands. 'Perhaps he's saying a prayer,' somebody says. As if it had been answered, Davis misses a straightforward shot, leaving a red on. 'Davis has gone,' quips Robbo in surprise. But Taylor misses the red and dawdles back to his chair again. 'His head's in a jam jar,' says Robbo. 'He doesn't know what's going on. To be fair, though, he hasn't had a chance. Steve's left him nothing much to aim at. Every safety shot tight on a cushion. Even when he misses a pot he leaves the white safe up the table. That shot's got a six-inch nail in it,' he adds quickly in appreciation as Davis sinks a long red to begin yet another break. He wins the frame 121–0, the biggest margin so far: 0–8.

It takes Dennis 38 minutes to pot a single ball in this session and six hours 20 minutes from the start before he scrambles the ninth frame. Davis gets the next, then Taylor takes another. By now his complexion is returning to normal and his stroke is recovering the smoothness of the past two weeks. 'Here comes Dennis,' Willie Thorne in a red blazer jokingly warns Steve's father. When a TV camera squeaks loudly as it moves, Dennis stops on his stroke and goes over and pretends to oil it with his cue – much to the enjoyment of the crowd. The joke and the laughter seem to release some tension in him and he makes a break of 61. Davis concedes the frame reluctantly, just sitting in his chair and staring ahead, making no acknowledgement of the referee's interrogative look.

Could it be that the champion has some unhealed scar tissue in his memory too? In the final of the 1983 Coral UK he had been overhauled by Alex Higgins after leading 7–0. This had a searing effect on him – 'it was as if', said Clive Everton, 'he could no longer rely on life's fundamental certainties'.

As if to confirm this, Taylor makes a break of 98 to go 4–9. He staggers around pretend drunk as a red bobbles around the pocket before going down. Davis is allowed only one point in the next – it's 5–9. Steve looks embarrassed when he misses a shot, showing a red-haired flush of annoyance, as though he hates to lose control of his facial expression. When he is going well, however, he is tall, proud, nostrils extended, a bit like Christopher Dean in his Spanish matador routine. This time he breaks off badly, scattering the reds and leaving the cue ball among them, which is most untidy for him and a sure sign that the pressure is reaching him. Taylor is looking altogether more fluent and sure of himself, a different man: what did Trevor East say to him, I wonder? His confidence is such that when he pots seven reds and seven blacks he senses that a maximum break may be on, and deliberately opts for a risky plant to the middle pocket to stay on the black rather than take an open red leading to one of the lower baulk colours. 'Snooker's gods generally punish such presumption,' Everton comments, but he gets away with it to close 6–9. Davis hasn't scored a point. He has also played safe when possible pots were on, which Taylor observes with some satisfaction.

Now it's the last frame of the session and both men know it will make the crucial difference between a four-frame and a two-frame deficit overnight. The previously silent Irish contingent are making themselves heard in the crowd. Steve starts with another loose shot, but recovers with a break of 44. After some cat-and-mouse play the score is 48–43 to Davis. Dennis then flukes a really vicious snooker, leaving the white on the edge of a pocket and tight against the brown. Steve fails to get out of the snooker by an inch, and Dennis goes clear to the brown. He needs the blue for the frame; Steve needs all three remaining colours. Steve goes in-off – to shameful jeers in the crowd. This leaves Taylor with a straight blue and a long slow pink for the frame and 7–9. The crowd go wild with applause for an impossibly brave comeback. Steve walks off stiffly, his face a mask.

Meanwhile, back on the wet pavement outside, Stuart Holmes has struck gold. 'SMOKE BOMB HITS SNOOKER' is the front-page lead in the *Star*. 'Sheffield's Lord Mayor today dropped a snooker final shocker by saying the city should not play host to the Embassy-sponsored world championship. Non-smoker Councillor Roy Munn has called for government legislation to halt a tobacco company's sponsorship of the £300,000 event.' The paper went on to say that the council might threaten to withdraw its annual grant to the Crucible. Embassy's marketing director, Brian Wray, and the head of events, Peter Dyke, seem unperturbed when I see them at the sponsors' lunch the next day. Wray had actually passed Stuart Holmes on the pavement but decided against introducing himself. Embassy have committed more than £3 million to snooker over the next five years. Terms have also been agreed with the Crucible until 1990. Even if the sports sponsorship agreement is not maintained by the government after 1986, the snooker event could pass to a less controversial part of Imperial Tobacco's empire.

The sponsors cannot easily quantify the commercial value of the event, but they argue that it promotes their brand name against rivals rather than persuading nonsmokers to take up the habit. As it happens, Davis and Taylor do not smoke. Embassy say it is no different from supporting the opera at Glyndebourne or Covent Garden – where, one suspects, Brian Wray would feel more naturally at home. Not so Peter Dyke, an outgoing man with a look of the late Eric Morecambe, who has been a key figure in the growth of the world snooker championship since 1976. That was the year the promoter vanished before all the bills had been paid and was later seen in Canada. Rex Williams remembers going to the man's apparently deserted house and calling through the letter-box: 'Come on out, we know you're in there!' After that the players – led by Williams, Pulman, Reardon and Spencer – decided to phase out all promoters over a period and deal direct with the sponsor, but not before promoter Mike Watterson had taken them to the Crucible, an inspired move. There was a chance meeting at the races in the late 1970s which brought together Williams, Pulman, Dyke and Nick Hunter and they set the future pattern for the event, which is now effectively run by the WPBSA (Del Simmons), Embassy (Peter Dyke) and the BBC (Nick Hunter). According to my back-of- envelope calculations, the professional body must be left with a handsome surplus.

When the players resume on Sunday afternoon, Dennis plays an imprecise first shot, leaving a possible red into the middle from the top cushion. Steve elects not to take it, but to play for safety instead. Dennis, hard-pressed, leaves another loose red, which Davis takes. But when he pots the black and scatters the reds, he is on the cushion, so plays again for safety, leaving a possible long red for Dennis. Will he go for it? After a long look around he does – and misses, leaving another red on to the middle pocket, which Steve gets. But still there is no way through. More safety, up and down, until Dennis can see a long red near the pocket, which he gets. But still the balls don't fall right. It is utterly gripping in the arena, like seeing boxers sparring for the first blow or professional cyclists watching each other warily before making a burst. Taylor makes a carefully executed break of 53, just failing to tip the last red off the cushion. But Steve needs snookers, one of which he immediately gets. Taylor is 42 ahead with 35 on the table. Taylor flukes the last red and Steve concedes: 8–9, the vital first frame to Dennis.

Steve misses a straight red to the middle, which Dennis accepts gratefully and is off again on a break of 38. As Joe Davis said, according to Ted Lowe over lunch, 'It's the easy ones that are difficult.' Steve pots one at last, but the run of the balls is against him and he has to leave the cue ball cunningly behind the yellow. 'I've got him on the run,' says Taylor. Steve doesn't laugh. Taylor can't get out of the snooker and hits the black. More important, he leaves a red into the middle. Steve makes 46. Taylor takes a good red down the cushion, cannoning off another red near the pocket, but the other red rolls across to another pocket, stopping on the edge and preventing Dennis's planned follow up with the pink. Instead, he has to go for a long green. He gets it, pots the hanging red, then comes back unluckily to touch the brown with the cue ball. 'Touching ball,' says referee John Williams, meaning that he can only play away without moving it. 'Both of them?' jokes Taylor. Steve gets in again when Taylor pots the brown in error, and cleans up the colours: 10–8.

Early on in the next frame Steve doesn't take a straightforward black along the top cushion and elects for safety. But Taylor finds a way in and takes 40, which Steve then matches. It's 41–40 to Davis with two reds left on the table. Steve misses a pot, Dennis takes it, but gets an unlucky kiss on the last red. Dennis has another chance but misses a simple red. 'Come on, Steve,' shouts someone in the crowd. Steve stays in his seat, takes a sip of water, and proceeds to clean up the colours while Dennis is sitting there kicking himself. But Steve misses the brown, then Dennis misses the blue. A nervy game. Steve takes the blue, but misses the pink with the rest. Dennis takes the long half-butt down the length of the table, gets the pink, but misses the black. It's 59–58, a black ball game. Steve stays in his chair a very long time, then comes out and clips in the black to win. Dennis had three good chances, two of which Steve gave back to him. There is a stern crowd warning from referee John Williams, still addressed exclusively to 'Gentlemen' (who are, of course, exclusively to blame for the noise). The referee's parting begins half an inch above his left ear, and his hair (what there is of it) is then coiled round the scalp in an anti-clockwise direction.

There is much safety play in the next frame, including eight successive little pushes among the reds, none of them moving the cue ball more than an inch. Steve's effort at concentration is such that he actually grits his teeth as he plays his shot. He grunts loudly as he finds himself snookered behind the yellow. Although he gets out of it, Taylor is in. There is a crowd of reds at the top of the table, so Dennis has to keep the black out of the way and use the pink, which he does to run up a 42 break. Davis appears to miss for a second foul shot, but complains to the referee, who looks up to the scorers. No foul. The odd thing is that the referee is much closer than either Davis or the scorers, but he accepts their verdict. Dennis, being Dennis, says nothing. Steve goes in-off for two successive shots. Dennis pretends to place the white jokingly behind the brown, then makes Steve play again. He misses and has to play yet again. Next Steve fouls a pink, which makes four fouls altogether. Dennis only needs a simple brown to make Steve need snookers – instead, he elects for a much more difficult black, and gets it to go into a useful lead. More cat and mouse until Steve snookers himself on the yellow and mutters 'blast': 9–11

Steve breaks and leaves a red. Dennis rolls a long slow black along the cushion that just drops. But he can't go much further. Then Dennis leaves a red and Steve goes back to his chair for a drink of water before potting it. He gets stuck among the reds.

Steve misses a straightforward green to the middle pocket and lets Dennis in for a frame-winning break of 57: 10–11. There is so much palpable pressure in the arena that you would think victory qualified the winner to a place in the Kingdom of Heaven.

The real test in this game, I note, is not just of talent, or even courage: it's having the self-perception and self-honesty to recognize your errors and correct them. Taylor's touch by now is exquisite and his confidence is pumping away, willing the balls to fall right. Steve's action is looking a bit crooked, twisted to the left, a bit uncomfortable. A long red wobbles in the pocket, letting Dennis in briefly before he gets tangled in a net of reds. Suddenly there are reds all over the table and Dennis clears them up, at first with difficulty, then more easily as the table becomes less crowded. A break of 55 is enough to bring him level 11–11, to loud applause and general satisfaction. The owl has landed! We really have a match on now.

There are reds all over the place again in the twenty-third frame – the first man in must prosper. But the jockeying for position goes on for a long time. They play many 'shots for nothing' – meaning difficult pots that can be attempted because the cue ball will go safe anyway if they miss. Both men miss narrowly in an attempted break out before Dennis gets in. He nearly falters on a pink close to the cue ball, but somehow conjures it in and goes on to make 44. Davis grins wryly and mutters to himself as he muffs a red. Dennis pretends to kick the table to knock in a ball that seems to go in and out again. Davis gets the last two reds and the yellow to go 11 behind with 25 on the table. Taylor gets the green but is touching the brown, so he cannot play it. Davis is now 14 behind with 22 on the table. He wipes his hands slowly before rising from his seat to pot brown, blue and pink. But he still needs the black, so he stands up to his full height to study the line and takes a deep breath before putting it safely down. As he does so, he gathers his fist as if to punch the sky but decides not to follow through. Instead, he turns sharply and goes back to his seat with a spring in his step. He knows it was a vital frame, 12–11, especially from 50 behind.

Lights reflect from the shiny black doors as they open and shut at the back of the hall; also from the cameramen's watches and from Taylor's rings and the gold chain on his wrist and his big gold cuff links (Davis wears no rings). A replacement cameraman sneaks in soundlessly from behind the arras and takes over the headphones. People cough and whisper nervously between shots. The Cup stands gleaming on a table.

A young man with no arms, evidently a thalidomide victim, appears in the front row, wearing a grey jumper with no arms.

A long period of attrition in the next frame. Davis lays a clever snooker, Taylor fouls, leaving a red on to the middle pocket. Davis moves away smoothly, but the last red is on the top cushion. He swerves back for it, but the pot sticks in the jaws – perhaps an important miss. Davis is 19 ahead with 35 on the table. Taylor scores 13, including yellow, green and brown, but the cue ball is knocked off line by touching the pink. He tries a left-handed crack at the blue into the middle, but misses, leaving it for Steve who is 11 ahead with 13 on the table. Davis fails to double the pink but leaves it apparently safe on the top cushion. But Taylor, remarkably, pots it with massive side spin. So it is a black ball game again. Taylor hits it too thin, leaving it possibly on to the baulk pocket. Again Davis takes his time leaving the chair, sips his water, wipes his hands, and comes out to pot it: 13–11.

They shake hands at the end of the session, but as Taylor passes me in my seat next to Trevor East he mutters: 'He's a lucky old bugger, I'll tell you that.' Taylor has been ahead in every frame today, with a good break in all but one – and even that one he won. I ask Knowles's manager who is going to win: 'Dennis Taylor,' he says firmly. Clive Everton thinks Dennis will be downcast, though – having played at his best and still finding himself two frames behind. Until now I have been moving between the arena, the press room, the sponsors' room and WPBSA room to see the match from all the angles. From now on, however, the only place to be is in a ringside seat in the Crucible itself, just two feet from the table, for all human life is here – the hopes, the frustration, the courage, the humour and despair. The players and officials are all in black tie for the

evening session, which adds a solemnity to the rituals being
enacted there. Even the TV cameraman, I'm amazed to see, has
made a brave effort in a blue cord jacket, jeans, sneakers and a red
bow tie. Officials, including the off-duty referees, are ready for
trouble and fan out to watch the audience. 'Is that a camera?' one
of them shouts. 'No,' says another after checking, 'it's only opera
glasses.' The players are twelve minutes late because the BBC has
gone backstage to televise the ceremonial walk from the dressing
room. In the hall the stage lights are switched on, which height-
ens the dramatic effect.

As Davis breaks off, clipping the triangle of reds very neatly
and bringing the cue ball back down the table, an attractive girl
with long blonde hair and a yellow anorak pushes along the front
row, drawing all eyes. 'How can people be late for the world
championship?' my peeved neighbour hisses. 'Because she was in
the hotel bar until five this morning,' someone replies. Davis
moves efficiently to 86 to win the frame. 11–14: a psychological
plus for the reigning champion.

Taylor crashes the ball into the reds, leaving them scattered,
and retires to his chair, banging his thigh in annoyance. Davis
moves in again. He is stopped, but Taylor fouls the black and
gives him another chance, which he declines. Then Davis fouls
the black, but as usual leaves nothing on. A prolonged bout of
safety play follows, in which Davis appears to spin the more
intricate webs. For this part of the game you lay traps for your
opponent and hope that he will leave himself exposed by doing
something rash as he tries to escape. Davis fouls – his ball going
right through the pack without touching any reds – giving Taylor
a slim chance, which he accepts. Taylor blinks owlishly up at the
scoreboard through his ludicrous glasses, trying to calculate if he
is safe, and amuses the crowd by pretending to count on his
fingers. He makes a break of 61, which leaves Davis needing a
snooker. He misses the last red unaccountably and leaves a lucky
snooker of his own. Taylor escapes but Davis leaves another, this
one deliberate and dangerous. Taylor misses. Davis can now win
the frame by one point if he takes all 35 left on the table. But
Taylor gets the red, misses the yellow, and Davis concedes:
12–14. So Taylor has not given up.

He smacks the balls around as he misses a red, narrowly avoiding an in-off (which might have been safer, as it happens). Davis has a real cherry orchard to pick from now, but scores only 12 then goes in-off himself. Can Taylor enjoy the rich pickings instead? He only gets to 13, leaving a red on for Davis, who tries again, this time with more success. He makes 66 to clinch the frame: 12–15.

The next frame starts slowly, both men pushing the cue ball into the pack for safety or retreating behind the black. While this is going on, they lean alternately against the press bench. Davis is silent, of course, but Taylor mutters: 'I've had the opportunities.' Davis misses a red to the middle, giving Taylor a similar half chance, which he takes, but only as far as 14. Taylor looks cross with himself for leaving Davis a path to a red, but he jokes to John Dee, editor of *Cue World*: 'I've tried to tempt him into a pot here!' Davis makes 27, then misses an easy one. Taylor is disturbed by someone moving and squeaking backstage, looks up and says: 'Quasimodo?' Taylor wins with a 70 break. It's 13–15 and they come off for an interval. As he passes, referee John Williams says: 'It's like he's dead and he won't lie down.' I bump into Bill Davis and ask how he's feeling: 'All right. He's still two frames ahead.' John Dee enthuses: 'This is the best snooker match since Griffiths beat Higgins 13–12 in the quarter-final in 1979.'

Just before they resume, the eye-catching girl in the audience bites an apple: for a moment I thought she had swallowed the green ball. There is a big policy argument behind the scenes about letting a spare cameraman into the arena. David Vine is interviewing the players backstage, so they are late again. It is a wonder he doesn't get a cue over his head as he knocks on their door. The atmosphere in the crowd has heightened appreciably. 'Come on, Alex,' somebody shouts, and gets a big laugh.

Taylor pots the first red, but is badly placed on the black and makes a hash of his escape, giving Steve a chance of a red, which he takes, but only one. There is now absolute stillness in the arena, broken only by a man munching crisps. I spot Robbo, who crosses his fingers and nods gravely. A long pot for Dennis, followed by the blue, then he screws back the full length of the table on to a red. He takes the spider to reach the black, but he can't see another red, so goes up the table for safety. Steve gets a pink, then sighs ruefully towards the referee as he leaves the next red. Dennis takes it and many more to score 57: 14–15. It is getting warmer all the time.

Davis misses a long pot straightaway, leaving an opening, but Taylor can't take full advantage. Steve's tongue literally comes out in relief as he pots a tight black and goes on to build a break of 17 before deciding he doesn't fancy a red on the cushion and sneaks away to safety. Eventually he gets a long pot, after hesitating over it for some time, and is perked up by his success. He still misses a simple one, though, a couple of shots later. As Dennis clears the reds and forces Steve into needing snookers, he bashes the palm of his hand hard with the cue in satisfaction. He makes 79 to go level 15–15 and clenches his teeth. 'Have you ever seen a man so determined?' asks Trevor East next to me. 'Yes,' I say, 'Steve Davis over there.'

Taylor, a strong family man, must know that victory tonight should solve their financial problems for the foreseeable future. Would such a thought help or hinder him in his task tonight? Davis is rich whether he wins or loses: does *that* thought help or hinder him? Taylor makes one brave long pot from behind the baulk line, but finishes too close to the blue to exploit it. Then Davis fouls, and he can't exploit that either. Taylor misses a blue across the table because he's too tight on the cushion and lets Davis in. He gets to 48, but the remaining reds are all nestling impossibly with the black in a line along the top cushion. He gets back with another chance to win the frame and takes it: 16–15 to Davis. Six frames to go. 'Exciting isn't it?' says Davis to the press bench as he goes off for a short break, during which, I am told later, Dennis is persuaded to take a slug of brandy in the dressing room.

Davis is first in with a cracking pot which picks out the black and urges it nearer the hole. Taylor sits hunched, knowing he has to win this frame. Both are now playing so well they are missing very little – neither can afford any mistakes. Davis doesn't make any until he reaches 46, then it's cat and mouse as they spar for position. Neither dares to take a risk. Davis has a red to the middle, but the cue ball is tight on the cushion. He risks it nonetheless and is rewarded with a clinching break of 35. Like all true champions, he seems to have a higher gear. I notice that his Perrier bottle, which was previously visible, is now snookered behind the ice bucket, presumably at the BBC's request.

The next frame is vital for Taylor, who has to win three frames to Davis's one. Still people wander in and out with pints, even while play is at its fiercest. They should surely be kept out during frames, as in a concert. Taylor gets in with a brave pot, but then overstretches when he might have used a rest and lets Davis loose again for 25. He's soon back in again, this time only for 8, but edging ahead all the time. He is like Sebastian Coe; you think he is flat out when suddenly he manages another spurt round the last bend. There is a girl in the audience in black tie, white shirt and academic gown – for all the world like a lawyer in full fig. Someone behind me jokes coarsely about her professional fees. Davis comes back yet again but, unbelievably, a straight brown hits the jaws of the middle pocket. Taylor realizes what an escape he has had and moves quietly towards the table on soft shoes. He stops and frowns as other squeaky feet, probably cameramen overhead on changeover, disturb his concentration. He sets off on his last stand, a small lonely figure in the spotlight – and he does it – a bold break of 42, ending with a devastating snooker, to cheers all round. Someone whistles in the crowd and the referee cries: 'Escort that whistler to the door.' (Afterwards Taylor tells me that the whistler was his brother-in-law, who could not control his excitement.) There are six balls between the cue ball and the last red, but Davis gets to it and leaves a long, just possible, very difficult pot down the cushion. 'This could be the one,' says Trevor East beside me. Taylor misses. 'Stretching too far again,' says Trevor sadly. To everyone's amazement, Davis, playing slowly across the nap, leaves this simple pot on the edge of the pocket. The crowd stirs in disbelief, and Davis stays down and closes his eyes.

Taylor gets the yellow, but the green is out of position. He misses it but leaves the cue ball safe. Nothing is really safe from Davis, however. After a couple of snookers, he picks off the green into the centre pocket, but is snookered on the brown. He smiles through thin lips. It's now 60–42 to Taylor – 18 ahead, 22 on the table. Taylor sinks the brown up the full length of the table, but snookers himself in turn on the blue. He is now 22 ahead, 18 on the table. Davis needs a snooker and gets it, Taylor missing the blue. Davis can win if he pots all three colours. They stalk the blue. Taylor misses a long pot but goes safe. Davis tries a snooker but leaves a long blue on, and quietly stabs the carpet with his cue. Taylor gets it and pots a tantalizing slow pink into the middle to go 16–17. In the hall people are breathless, on the edge of their seats; they hardly believe it can be so exciting.

'It's all about who keeps his brain together now,' says Trevor. Davis keeps his together by serenely disdaining a risky long pot. His safety is as precise as ever, right on the back cushion, giving Taylor nothing to aim at. It will be sudden death for the first mistake, one feels. Taylor makes it, leaving a red on a pocket, but Davis misses it to gasps all round. He chalks his cue in silence, his face expressionless – his thoughts, however, easily guessable. Taylor takes a red, then cuts the black into the corner from a very oblique angle. 'What a shot that was,' says Trevor. 'Jesus Christ, it's going to be a last frame job.' Taylor goes for a very difficult red on the cushion – 'he's got everything on the top rail in this tournament,' says Trevor. He reaches 57 with six reds left on the table. Davis plays a safety shot too 'fat', as they say in golf. 'Davis is twitching,' says Trevor. He goes for a hard pot and leaves a red for Taylor, who pockets it and goes on to get 14, making Davis need snookers. Another (by his standards) poor shot by Davis, but Taylor also misses and Davis tries to stave off disaster, starting 71 behind with four reds on the table (a possible 59) plus snookers. He takes the four reds, but then concedes. It's 17-all – and everything is on the final frame, the first time this has happened for a decade in the final of the world championship.

Taylor comes off, motioning Trevor East to join him in his dressing room. 'Dennis has won this,' says Trevor as he goes out. The audience stand up to stretch their legs. The buzz is electric. Palms are even sweating in the press box. Both players get a standing ovation as they return. And all this is going out live on TV. In fact, the audience of 18.5 million has broken all records: the biggest-ever British viewing figure for a sporting event; the highest-ever BBC2 audience; and the highest British audience after midnight. Some of them have switched on to see an episode of the BBC's dramatization of Dickens's *Bleak House* and have become too involved to switch off again. There is nothing bleak about the Crucible.

 Taylor starts the final frame at 11.15 pm with a miss. Davis plays safe. Taylor gets an unlucky rebound, which sends Davis away briefly. A long, brave red by Taylor, but no colour to follow. There are eight balls now on the top cushion – it's going to be a messy game. Taylor has a whack – not the thing to do in the final frame of a world championship – but finishes safe. Now there are ten balls on the top cushion, the cue ball among them. Another Taylor red, but no easy colour. He misses a long blue. 'This is going to be a bloody long game,' says Trevor. A rare Davis defensive error after 'bending' one ball round another, but Taylor cannot exploit it and leaves a half chance. Davis folds his arms on his chest to decide whether to risk the pot. He decides against. He then misses altogether, and Taylor goes in-off – such is the tension. Davis smiles ruefully to someone above the press seats – Barry, Ron, Robbo, his dad? He taps the table to acknowledge a brilliantly judged escape shot by Taylor. The game of patience goes on for about a dozen shots before Davis pops a red out and Taylor pots it well, going on to make 22. Davis responds immediately with a red and blue, but is out of position. 'Yes,' he says to himself ironically. He uses the big spider, scatters balls everywhere, but gets away with it. 'He's been jammy all through the match,' Trevor comments. Taylor waits a long time before playing, then goes in-off, leaving Davis a long pot which he makes, but he misses a straight blue off the pink spot. He stares at the shot in disbelief, as well he might, for in retrospect this was the shot that could have determined the match. There were six reds left, most of them easily pottable. Taylor gets one of them, but then he gets stuck among the balls on the top cushion and lays a good snooker. Davis misses. 'That was no way a genuine attempt,' says Trevor. Another good snooker from Taylor. Davis misses and is put in again. This time he makes amends but misses the next one. The score is 44–24 to Taylor, 67 on the table.

Taylor gets a lucky rebound that nearly goes in-off the pink but ends in a perfect snooker. 'Ugh!' says Davis, then gets outs of it. After many more ups and downs of high skill, Taylor misses, Davis knocks in a red, then skilfully lifts the other reds off the top cushion while potting a blue. The balls are suddenly wide open. Is this it, the *coup de grâce*? Dennis's head goes down briefly. Davis makes 25 then fails to get position after the last red. It's now 53–44 to Davis, with a snooker on the yellow that Taylor doesn't like the look of. He has to go all the way up the table and back, and misses, but safely. Taylor almost doubles the yellow, but leaves it on. Davis screws back the full length of the table for the green on the bottom cushion, but misses it. Davis's luck holds again, however, as it snookers behind the pink. 59–44. Davis then flukes the green: 62–44.

Taylor must take all four colours to win: Davis needs only the brown. As Clive Everton was to write: 'It was a time for bravery; it was a time for caution; it was a time for hope; it was a time for fear. It was the commencement of the ten-shot sequence which brought the championship to a climax and will for ever be counted among the great moments in sport.'

Taylor misses a long pot and leaves it possible for Davis, who also misses. Taylor stays in his chair smiling as he contemplates the awkward pot this leaves him with. He misses, and the crowd will the cue ball behind the blue for a snooker. Another long, awkward brown for Taylor. He's in agony over whether to try, keeps getting up and down on the shot. In the end he plays fairly safe, leaving Davis with a hard pot which he misses. Another long brown for Taylor, again with the cue ball close to the cushion, but this time he gets it – to wild applause. This is the turning-point. He explains afterwards that he went for the pot, even though it was awkward and risky, because he could see no way to play safe. 'Come on my son,' the press box mutters in unison. The blue is an angled cut, but possible. He makes it – again to excited applause. 62–55. He needs both balls and he's tight on the cushion again for the pink. But he gets it – and goes over to the trophy with a shaky hand, as if to say – so near, yet so far!

All on the black in the final frame – what a climax to a world championship! £25,000 riding on a single shot (£60,000 for the winner, £35,000 for the loser – and no deals in advance). Taylor could play safe, but he goes for a double to the middle pocket which he lined up when he sank the pink. The black hits the jaw of the middle pocket and rebounds to safety. Cruelly, he thought it had gone in, and so did the crowd. Davis, with no hope of a pot, plays a superb safety shot, leaving the two balls at opposite ends of the table. Taylor has almost exactly the same safety shot to play, but an outside chance of a double into a top pocket. He misses it and the black just creeps safely past the middle pocket. Davis then does something remarkable for him. He goes for a rebound into the middle pocket off the top cushion – known as a 'cocked hat'. Afterwards all the commentators were to say he simply miscued a safety shot, leaving a long black on for Taylor. In fact, as I confirmed with him, he was going for the double – something he would never have attempted in a million years at such a stage of a world final, except that Taylor had psyched him into it with two attempted doubles of his own. He gets a double kiss on the black, leaving Taylor with a good chance. When he misses it Taylor clearly thinks he has lost. He goes straight back to his chair without daring to look at the table. Only when he gets there does he realize that the black is not a formality for Davis, requiring a very fine cut into the top pocket. Seven times out of ten, Davis says later, he would get it, but perhaps only three times out of ten under such pressure. The white is close to the cushion, so he has to play down on it, which tends to magnify the slightest error. The pocket he is aiming for is out of his direct vision. As he says later: 'It's not difficult, but it's not easy.' In the event he makes too thin a contact on the black, which rebounds a few inches away from the pocket, leaving Taylor a relatively straightforward shot for the championship. It's all over. I reflect that, curiously, the black puts him ahead for the first time in the entire match. Taylor raises his cue triumphantly over his head in two hands, like a stave, shakes hands, then points a finger at Trevor East and at his wife, Trish, and his family in the crowd. Trevor grabs me in a bear hug.

David Vine described it as 'one of the greatest sporting

moments of all time'. Frank Keating wrote in the *Guardian*: 'The climax, off the last ball of the last shot of the last gasp, was tumultuous in its almost dotty fulfilment of dramatic unities . . . It was like Sergeant Bilko beating Ali over the full 15 rounds.' Clive Everton enthused afterwards in *Snooker Scene*: 'It was a demonstration of all that was finest in snooker. When the bewildering kaleidoscope of skill, fortitude, heart, nerve, fear, will and courage finally settled to reveal Taylor as the winner on the final black, there was grace and sportsmanship not only from the highly popular new champion but from the deposed champion, Steve Davis.' Some people would challenge that last tribute, for Davis was clearly overwhelmed when he spoke to David Vine moments after his defeat. Asked if he could believe what had happened to him – a tough question in the circumstances – he replied: 'It happened. You've seen it – in black and white.' It struck me as a goodish, even witty response on TV from a man *in extremis* who had, in Everton's words, 'worn his nerve endings down so utterly by the end of the match that he could make it to the dressing room with dignity only by cutting himself off from his emotions'.

Emotions are certainly red-raw in the Romford camp – and not only because of the money they have surrendered to the bookies. They are not accustomed to losing at Romford. Barry Hearn is shielding his eyes, almost in tears, but still has the presence of mind, I notice, to stuff Steve's cheque into his jacket pocket. Robbo bangs the scaffolding painfully with his bare fist. Only Ron is cool, carefully taking charge of Steve's cue and putting it in its case. Steve comes over to the Romford group and Barry's wife, Susan, puts an arm round his shoulder as Dennis receives the cup. Steve is clearly in a state of shock, walking out stiffly, zombie-like. Brian Wray tells me that Steve was looking rocky backstage during the last interval. Trevor East had £10 on Dennis at 40–1 and proudly shows me the betting slip. Mike Watterson says: 'I had three grand on Davis, but I'm glad I lost my money.' Taylor's wife, a blonde homely lady in a silver-grey dress, who used to act as his manager and booking agent, comes down with their teenage daughter, Denise, to kiss the new world champion. 'We've done it,' they say to each other.

Taylor walks in triumph into the press room with an arm round Trevor East, who has clearly given him the same kind of psychological boost that Hearn and his team provide for Davis – but for free! There is spontaneous applause from the journalists as he enters. He is introduced as 'the new Embassy World Champion'. Dennis grins: 'Say that again – it sounds good!' He looks at the press and the press look at him, no one knowing where to begin. 'A bit of a match that,' he says finally, in the understatement of the year. There had been thirteen breaks of over 50, the mark of a real class encounter, which clearly pleases the professional in him. He points out that Steve had won three frames on the black which could obviously have gone the other way. 'Where's Clive Everton?' he suddenly asks. 'I didn't snatch in the last frame, did I?' Was he sorry for Steve? 'I can't honestly say that I am – after all, he has dominated the game for the past three or four years.' He had thought Davis would cut in that crucial black. A journalist stands up and announces that the *Irish Times* has held its presses for the first time in its history to carry the result. Dennis looks suitably impressed by this signal honour and goes out to join the official Embassy party in the arena, where Trevor East takes me to meet him. He looks to me like a man who is eager to get away among his own folk and really let his hair down – which, after a polite interval, he duly does, taking a minibus to transport his extended family – champagne corks popping and Irish songs in full flow – to his hotel, where the knees-up lasts till dawn.

Davis's press interview is a more subdued and rather embarrassing affair, for we are intruding on private grief. Hearn, as ever, is at his side, looking heavy-eyed and clutching a pint.

'How do you feel, Steve?'

'Great.'

Silence.

'I feel devastated.'

'Is that the worst you've ever felt?'

'Yes.'

'What about that cut on the black?'

'I fancied it, but I overcut it.'

'You looked at the trophy a long time tonight when you'd finished.'

'Yeah.'

Barry chips in: 'He's been through the pain barrier. I'd like to put him through it again – backwards. The worst thing about being number one all the time is that there's nowhere to go but to stay there. Still, it could have been worse – it could have been Marvin Hagler! If he can pick himself up in twenty-four hours, you'll see a much improved player. Now we're going to drown ourselves in champagne.'

You can't keep a man like Barry Hearn down for long. Within a week he had found a way to continue being manager of the world champion: he had signed up Taylor for the Romford camp. If you can't beat them, get them to join you.

## Chapter Eleven

# THE MAN FROM COALISLAND

When Dennis Taylor, aged nine, first peeped through the door at Gervin's Hall in Coalisland, County Tyrone, and saw the coloured balls whizzing around, he could never have imagined that he had found his own private road to Eldorado. Still less could he have imagined that he would one day become the source and inspiration of the extraordinary scenes that took place in the streets of his home town in the early hours of Monday, 29 April 1985. The moment he potted the black at the Crucible Theatre in Sheffield to win the world title he clenched his cue in two hands over his head in an exultant release of emotion. His countrymen, however, were used to releasing their emotions in less inhibited ways.

The people of Coalisland poured out of their houses and clubs in a spontaneous mood of joy that overran into Monday morning. They came as they were – some in pyjamas and dressing gowns and many with small children in tow – and paraded around the town, too excited to go to bed. Many got into their cars and pumped their horns as they proceeded around the town square. The local band got together for an impromptu and somewhat inebriated performance. Some people went in reverential pilgrimage to the Taylor household in Mourne Crescent, where the telephone rang till dawn. It was like a Mediterranean night as whole families took to the streets. Children climbed on their fathers' shoulders to see the circus more clearly. None of them would forget that night as long as they lived. People greeted their neighbours with a friendliness unknown for forty years, since the end of the Second World War.

At first sight Dennis Taylor might seem an unlikely focus for this complex web of emotions. He is not built like a hero, even a local hero. The early pictures show a freckled youth of middle height with a potato face and little obvious personality. Even now his outsize glasses – like the back of a Cortina or the front of a shop – suggest a comedian rather than a sporting superstar – Eddie Charlton said he looked like Mickey Mouse with a welding shield on. Yet he attracted the biggest television audience that any sport has ever known and the public reaction to him is one of unqualified admiration and affection – which is more, much more, than can be said of either Alex Higgins or Steve Davis, the only other snooker champions since Joe Davis to reach his level of popular fame. How has he achieved this?

The first answer is: slowly. 'It's taken you thirteen years to become an overnight success,' Barry Hearn joked to him after the world championship. In fact, this is almost literally true. He became a paid professional player in 1972 and did not win a major British (as opposed to Irish) tournament until the Rothmans Grand Prix in 1984. He had always been there or thereabouts, consistently high in the merit table, and before 1985 he had reached three world semifinals and one final, losing to Terry Griffiths in 1979. Yet he seemed destined to be snooker's Nearly Man, outgunned and overshadowed by younger players like Steve Davis and Jimmy White, and especially by his more flamboyant Irish contemporary, Alex Higgins.

He first crossed swords with Higgins in the 1960s when they met on the amateur club circuit in Northern Ireland. Higgins is a Protestant, Taylor a Catholic, but both had left for England before the resurgence of the troubles. Coalisland is a strong Republican area and was the scene of the first civil rights march in 1968. It is no secret that Alex and Dennis are hardly the best of friends, but their differences have more to do with temperament than politics or religion (though there was an edge to the relationship when Alex once had the nerve to court Dennis's pretty sister Molly, who finally hid under the stairs to escape his attentions). Dennis did not drink in the early days and he has always been careful with money; neither of these characteristics would be likely to commend him to Alex. They nearly had a punch up at the Tolly Cobbold tournament in 1980 when Higgins contested a refereeing decision and then muttered 'bloody cheat' as he passed Taylor's chair. Taylor was so upset he lost the match from a winning position. One of his standard jokes now is to say at exhibitions 'Alex Higgins should have been here tonight, but he was launching a ship in Belfast and he wouldn't let go of the bottle.'

But in 1968 Alex had followed him to Blackburn, where they practised a good deal together at the Old Post Office Club – 'Alex played phenomenal snooker in those days,' he recalls. Dennis, who was then driving a van for a rental company, actually supplied him with a TV set and helped to install him in a flat. Dennis has stayed in Blackburn, where he lives with his wife, Patricia, their daughter Denise and sons Damien and Brendan in a large, specially designed house on a hill next to a golf course, with a magnificent snooker room underneath. The night Denise was born he lost a match because he kept seeing the baby's face whenever he looked at the ball and his eyes filled with tears.

Taylor and Higgins were both born in 1949. In 1968 Higgins won the Northern Ireland amateur snooker title and Taylor the British junior billiards. But Higgins was first to break through into the big time, winning the world professional snooker championship at his first attempt in 1972. It was this that finally decided Taylor to join the professional ranks, which he did with the help of John Spencer. He earned very little on the circuit in the early years and became manager of a snooker hall in Preston. Higgins used to give him a 21 handicap at that time, but the margin came down quickly over the years.

Taylor first made his professional mark on a tour of Canada, where he reached the final of the Canadian Open in 1974, and even caught the great Joe Davis's eye with twenty-four centuries in a fortnight, six of them over 130. He also scored 349 points in three frames without missing a shot. This was enough to get him into the BBC's *Pot Black*, where he lost two finals. He reached the semifinal of the world championship in 1975 and 1977 before losing the 1979 final, which he felt he should have won, to Griffiths, who thereafter became a close friend. He finally toppled Higgins in the Irish Championship in 1980 to clinch his first major title. Three things then combined to lift him to a new level of fame and fortune: his cue, his glasses and his mother.

His cue had previously been a three parter which he used instead of the standard half butt to reach long shots. But he found one day that if he screwed two of the parts together he had a cue that was two inches longer than the one he was used to. He found that it suited him. He had always been short-sighted – 'my eyes were so bad', he says, 'that as a schoolboy I needed glasses even to find the front row in the classroom'. He had tried contact lenses and swivel lenses before Jack Karnehm, the snooker coach and commentator, called on his training as a manufacturer of spectacle frames to design the outsize Joe 90 glasses that he wears today. Dennis watched in fascination as Karnehm got out his tiny old optician's tools and made the glasses himself in his garage over a weekend. The size is not for effect, but to ensure that he gets the right degree of focus as he bends to play a shot. The result, he says, was both miraculous and instantaneous. It was as if he had previously been playing the game in miniature. For the first time, he remembers vividly, he could see the ferrule shining on the end of the rest. His play improved dramatically. 'The glasses have made all the difference to my game,' he said. 'I now have the confidence to take on and beat anyone in the world.' That was six months before he did exactly that.

The third impact on his game was more tragic: it came with the death of his mother in October 1984, during the Jameson tournament in Newcastle. Annie Taylor was a powerful personality who had followed his career proudly, ringing the local paper with every scrap of news about his successes on the mainland. Her sudden death at the age of 62 was a shattering blow to the family, who had always been close. He has two brothers, four sisters and three children of his own. After his mother's death the family persuaded him to go back and win a tournament for her, which he duly did at the Rothmans Grand Prix in Reading, a tear-stained evening in the history of the game. He beat his old friend Cliff Thorburn 10–2. *Snooker Scene* wrote:

> So close-knit and loving is Taylor's family that his wish to unite them in joy as they had been in sadness transcended any

other factor. Frequently a player shrivels under another's force
of personality or seizes up when victory and its rewards loom
tantalizingly close, but Taylor, who has suffered from both
maladies in the past, overrode them this time through his
irresistible sense of mission . . . Recognized for so long as a
genuine entertainer and a true professional, he became at last a
major winner through producing the best snooker of his life.

Dennis himself said: 'It was just the family and my wife Patricia
who made me do it. They motivated me. We had a chat after the
funeral and my dad told me to come back and get stuck in.' His
prize of £45,000 was nearly three times his total earnings in the
year before. Friends say that he had previously tried too hard,
had been too eager to win, but that his mother's death gave him a
new attitude to the vicissitudes of the snooker hall and a more
relaxed attitude to winning or losing that actually made him
more likely to win. 'What really happened,' he says, 'is that the
enormity of my mother's death put snooker into its proper
perspective. It brought home to me the fundamental truth that
what matters in life is life – and that life is about people,
especially family and friends. Nothing can be more sacred than
that, certainly not a game. This revelation perhaps made me
realize who I was and what I wanted from life. That was my
mother's legacy.'

The family had been very poor, brought up in a damp house
by a canal, the children (three boys and four girls) sharing a
bedroom. His father drove a lorry for an egg company. Dennis
would beg and borrow sixpences to play snooker at Gervin's
snooker hall, which rapidly became his home from home. When
he began he stood on a lemonade box. The owner, Jim-Joe
Gervin, was a great Irish character who wandered about in a
shopkeeper's brown coat and whacked the boys with a feather
duster when they missed a shot. Dennis used to be allowed in the
club early to set up the balls and hold the rest and seized every
chance he could get for practice, sometimes wearing gloves
before the heating came on. Once, when he lost a match and
couldn't pay, he escaped through the lavatory window.

I was with him when he returned to play at Gervin's for the

first time since he had won the world title. He had earlier attended a wild civic reception at which the Lord Mayor had made him wear his red gown. There were herograms on walls all over the town, including one saying 'Dennis for President'. First he played an exhibition for the youngsters of Coalisland, who kept up a happy chant throughout, many of them running around the room screaming like kids at a Saturday matinée. In spite of the noise and the flash bulbs popping in front of his glasses, Dennis made breaks of 96 and 112, the second of which might have been his first-ever maximum break if the fifteenth red had stayed in the hole instead of popping out. He then played a series of exhibition frames against local amateurs, including the son of Jack Rea, the old Irish champion. The warmth and genuine love in his reception are hard to describe.

I counted five priests in the hall, one of whom stopped me and said to be sure to mention Dennis's early prowess at Gaelic football. He was evidently very good indeed and was once chaired through the town by the rest of the team after scoring the match-winning goal in a keenly contested local Derby. He also won two boxing bouts and, as a full-back at soccer, was recommended to Blackburn Rovers. For all the seedy connotations of the game, snooker champions tend to be fairly athletic, or at least were in their youth, which is not so surprising when you consider that the same hand-eye coordination is needed in most sports. Charlton was an all-Australian champion at several sports; Thorburn's father threw him into all games; Spencer played cricket in the RAF; Steve Davis played soccer; Meo table tennis; Knowles is a water sports fanatic; even Higgins, with the archetypal pallor of the misspent youth, was once a jockey.

Taylor has always been devout, starting as an altar boy in childhood. He and his family attended mass at St Marie's Cathedral in Sheffield, opposite the Crucible, on the Sunday morning of his world final. The priest wished him luck in front of the congregation. His sisters say they were conscious of the power of their dead mother's presence at the final. 'It was Annie willing the balls in the hole,' one of them told me. 'When Dennis was under real pressure, I turned away and begged her to help.' His mother had said shortly before she died: 'I know Dennis will win a title, but I may not be here to see it.' The memory of his mother's personality was such a force in Coalisland that when he returned for the civic reception after his victory, the editor of the local paper told me: 'It was raining all morning, but everybody said Annie would persuade the Almighty to give us sunshine as soon as Dennis appeared. And He did, just as the car came round the bend into Coalisland.'

Taylor has developed such an easy comic patter, full of Irish jokes as he demonstrates his trick shots or sits with Terry Wogan on TV, that it is hard to believe he was once so tongue-tied that he couldn't even join in rumbustious family debates, and when visitors came he would sit in a corner saying nothing. He was too shy to ask his future wife, Patricia, to a dance and could only demonstrate his affection by writing 'I love you' with his finger on a steamed-up car windscreen. Yet he is now one of the most witty and accomplished speakers on the snooker circuit, always ready with a joke, especially while he is playing. 'If someone had told me I'd be telling Irish gags in front of millions of people, I'd have laughed at them,' he says. It has been suggested that it was his impish sense of humour that gave him a crucial edge over Steve Davis in their epic final. Davis, coiled up almost to breaking-point under the pressure, found himself locked in a do-or-die battle with a man who, disconcertingly, seemed to have something to spare. It was not that Taylor didn't feel the pressure – far from it – but that this was his method of releasing it.

How did he feel when he was 0–8 down to Davis on that traumatic Saturday night? Did he really believe he could make up so much lost ground on the champion? His answer is prosaically typical: 'I had been cueing well all week, especially against Thorburn and Knowles, so I knew I had to come good some time. I also knew that if I could only get close to Steve and stay with him, he might be vulnerable.' And so, of course, it proved. Taylor's victory has undoubtedly done snooker a great deal of good. Not only did it provide a TV spectacular, introducing millions of viewers to the excitement of the game, but it created an attractive and mature new folk hero in a less severe mould than Steve Davis. The Taylor victory distracted attention from the drugs scandal which had threatened to stain the image of the game, and of course it has not done the Taylor family fortunes any harm. With Barry Hearn as his manager, negotiating his contracts, he can expect to earn about £250,000 in his championship year; in one hectic week in Ireland he earned £15,000. Will success spoil Dennis Taylor? No chance, I'd say.

As an Irish-born world champion, Dennis faced some of the same pressures as boxer Barry McGuigan, who had to be equally careful to address his appeal to both Irish communities, and not to alienate either. While I was with Dennis in his father's house in Coalisland, a message was delivered from Long Kesh, the IRA internment camp. It had been smuggled out in someone's tooth and we unrolled the crumpled letter, the size of an aspirin, over the kitchen table. The writing could just be deciphered. It read:

Dennis O chara, on behalf of all the republican POWs I'd like to thank you for scaring the life out off us!!? At this point and time it might be useless information to you but we sweated, groaned and sunk into a terrible depression late on Saturday – I think you know what I mean!! We had confidence in you surely, *But* 8–0??? Ha-HA. All us POWs had been keeping an eye on you in the early rounds (particularly us Tyrone men). But it was at the semis that the grip really took hold of us – even those who don't like snooker – some of the screws were not amused at you winning, and on Saturday they were like the cats who got the cream. However you fixed their wagons for them and at about 12.30a.m. Monday morning there was a terrible din + banging round this camp as the lads got on to the doors, hammering to acknowledge your *fantastic* victory. Maith thu a chara, it's a while since we've had an opportunity to 'Bang' in such good news. May you repeat your success soon. Good luck in the future and please know that our prayers (sweat + nerves too!!!) are behind you always. Slan is Beannach Mo Chara

H-Block, Long Kesh.

I was reminded of a chilling story told about Terry Griffiths when he visited Coalisland and introduced a trick shot called 'the machine gun', in which a white is struck off slowly towards a pocket and a handful of reds are then fired off in rapid succession to beat it there. Terry said: 'The only trouble is that I haven't got a machine gun' – to which an Irish voice in the crowd replied: 'Don't you worry, Terry, we'll soon fix that up for you!' When I returned from Coalisland to my hotel at Dungannon, the car was stopped at two Ulster Defence Regiment road-blocks. There were marksmen behind the trees, ready to throw a chain across the road at the first suspicious move. The week after his great victory Dennis played an exhibition at a Protestant club in Belfast. It pleases him that his reception there was equally warm and enthusiastic. He left Ireland before the troubles began. At his homecoming in Coalisland he was feted by Catholics and Protestants alike, with no political or religious barriers on view. He says, 'I know it will take more than sport to heal the wounds of Ireland, but I am glad that – like my friend Barry McGuigan – I can offer something in which both communities in Ireland take equal pride and enjoyment.'

Dennis was present at the ringside to see McGuigan's challenge for the world title against the Puerto Rican holder, and saw him in his dressing room after the fight. Earlier he had been asked by a reporter if he had any advice to offer McGuigan from one Irish world champion to another. Quick as a flash, Dennis replied, 'I hope he sinks the black quicker than I could!' As he says in his book, 'If I've brought anything to this game, I hope it's a sense of humour and a touch of common humanity. If I'm to be remembered for anything at all, I'd like it to be as the man who put the smile back into snooker.'

## Chapter Twelve
# TOMORROW THE WORLD

As soon as he had recovered from the loss of his world title, Steve Davis was whisked off by Barry Hearn to somewhere more exotic than Sheffield, or even Romford – to São Paulo, where they play a game called Brazilian snooker on an eight-foot table with a single red. The undisputed champion at this game is a man known as Rui Chapeu. He plays in a white hat and has never been seen without it. He has said he will remove it only when he is beaten. When he invited Steve to a series of three challenge matches for a substantial fee and expenses, it was an offer Barry couldn't refuse, especially as the third match was to be seen on an eleven-hour sports programme before 40 million television viewers – more than twice as many people as watched the world final at the Crucible.

The two of them arrived in Brazil with only one day to get used to the table and the complicated rules, so it was hardly surprising that Steve went 0–3 down straightaway and seemed about to be whitewashed. But he persevered gamely, mastering the tactics and the scoring like the chess player he is, until he finally achieved the impossible and beat the Brazilian champion 6–5 at his own game. But Chapeu kept his head – and his almost eponymous hat – and threw out the second challenge: this time they would play snooker on a full-size table under British rules. Steve won a ding-dong thriller on the final black.

Then came the big one, the TV spectacular, at which Steve immediately went 1–3 down. The TV commentators began to apologize for the Englishman's performance – the long flight, unaccustomed to the rules, and so on. But again Steve fought back to win 4–3 before the Latin millions. Still the Brazilian refused to expose his naked cranium, however, and presented Barry and Steve with white hats of their own instead.

As a result of the trip, Brazil is expected to affiliate to the International Billiards and Snooker Federation and may become the first South American country to compete in the World Amateur Snooker Championship. Hearn is trying to make similar contacts in Chile, Paraguay, Argentina and Ecuador, all of which play cue games. The commercial follow-up would be sales of TV snooker programmes and possibly tables and equipment.

Hearn is a great enthusiast for exporting the game to wider markets abroad and takes a group of players on a Far East tour that is fast becoming a fixed part of snooker's calendar year. They play to large and enthusiastic audiences in Singapore, Malaysia, Thailand and Hong Kong. The highlight of the 1985 tour was a repeat of the world final between Davis and Taylor in Communist China, another first for the game. When I was in China a decade ago, I remember seeing hundreds of children in a huge hall being drilled at table tennis. The tables stretched as far as the eye could see and each child, like a clone, was being coached in exactly the same stroke. Are we about to see the same technique applied to the green baize, with the Chinese equivalent of Frank Callan calling the shots? Sales of snooker tables to Hong Kong and Thailand, in particular, have risen at an astonishing rate in recent years, and one of the Thai players, Sakchai Sim-Ngarm, has actually beaten Steve Davis, albeit in a best-of-three. In Hong Kong the star is Gary Kwok: apart from working as an actor and a horse-race commentator on TV, he also managed to find time once to beat Jimmy White on the snooker table. Kwok beat Sakchai Sim-Ngarm to become Asian champion in 1985. This tournament produced two new young stars of the East in 15–year-old Wattana Pu-Oborn from Thailand and Lim Koon Guan, aged 19, from Singapore, who scored a century break.

It was fitting that the world amateur snooker champion should come from India, where it all began. O.B. Agrawal, a bearded player from Bombay, was a surprise winner, following in the tradition of great Indian billiards players like Wilson Jones and Michael Ferreira. Agrawal says he thinks the word 'float' whenever he feels the pressure, but since he works in a dairy it isn't entirely clear if this means that he goes transcendental or is merely thinking of a milk float. Tony Drago, a flamboyant and ambitious young Maltese who is clearly going far, had been the favourite. Players from twenty-two countries took part, an encouraging sign for the future of the game. Lord Killanin, the former President of the International Olympic Committee, has opened new horizons by suggesting that snooker might become an Olympic sport. It surely has at least as strong a claim as, say, synchronized swimming or rhythmic callisthenics.

The game has flourished most naturally in the former colonies, led by Australia, Canada and South Africa, though Australia has been a commercial disappointment and South Africa is politically off-limits. But in the biggest potential market, the United States, pool has a clear edge on snooker because more tables can be fitted into a club room. Rex Williams, the WPBSA chairman, would compromise by reducing the size of the snooker table for the American market, but that idea horrifies purists, one of whom said to me: 'Rex doesn't mind because the strength of his own play is his short game around the black, so a small table would suit him just as well.' Barry Hearn doubts if the average American viewer would appreciate the slow subtleties of snooker. He is looking East rather than West for the game's development and sees more points to be gained there. The involvement of Black countries seems a long way off, though an amiable dock worker from Mauritius called Christian D'Avoine (shortened by the press to 'Christy Divine') turned up at the world amateur tournament and made a break of 38.

It is a mystery why women's snooker – another obvious area for development – has never taken off as a commercial spectacle. The quality of the women's play has always finally defeated the many attempts to put money behind their game. And yet there is no logical or physical reason why women should not be as good as men – though it is sometimes pointed out in this context that there are no female Grand Masters at chess. The reasons may be similar in both cases – that there is no incentive for women to spend several hours of every day of their lives in acquiring the necessary skills. Women have been discouraged in snooker by the traditional male exclusiveness of many clubs – and by the

seedy environment – though this may now be breaking down as
the smart new snooker complexes welcome family membership.
Joe Davis once thought he could turn Lind Joyce, the actress
from ITMA, into a women's snooker champion, but reckoned it
would take 'fifteen years or so – the time I considered necessary
to turn a good amateur into a top pro'. His final word on the
subject: 'My advice to Mrs Worthington is – don't put your
daughter into snooker.'

A women's association was formed as long ago as 1931, and
three good players quickly emerged – Thelma Carpenter, Ruth
Harrison and Joyce Gardner – who rotated the championship
among themselves until it lapsed in 1950. Several attempts have
been made to reactivate the women's game since the 1970s. In
1976 Embassy sponsored a women's world championship in
parallel with the men's, and in 1980 it was Guinness who put up
the cash. In 1984 National Express, the nationalized bus company, put up about £100,000 of public money for a tournament,
and a women's circuit, Ladies Snooker International Ltd, has had
a brief and controversial burst of life.

The trouble has been that the audiences have usually been so
small – there were only twenty or thirty at the National Express
matches, despite free admission – and that television promotion,
which is needed to boost public support, is unlikely to be forth-
coming until the standard of women's play is consistently higher.
This standard is unlikely to improve until there are more competitive players and a greater incentive for them to take up the
game as a living. It is an almost perfect circle leading nowhere
very fast. The situation has been made even worse by the division
of the hundred or so serious women players into amateurs and
professionals – a totally artificial divide since both are allowed to
keep money prizes.

The National Express Women's Grand Prix of 1984 was the
best showcase the women's game has ever had. The winner,
Mandy Fisher, left with £14,000. But, as Michael Gouge of the
*Daily Express* wrote after seeing the women at the Armley Sports
and Leisure Centre in Leeds: 'Row upon row of empty seats
greeted the competitors as they strode proudly into the revam-
ped multi-purpose games hall, and it was impossible not to feel

sympathy for them. They were playing for the biggest prize their game has yet been able to offer but, it seemed, nobody wanted to know.' His conclusion was disappointing: 'My brief excursion to Leeds did not leave me with any great expectations that women's snooker will ever capture the public's imagination, even on a proportional scale, as the men's game has done.' This is the general view within the snooker world. Steve Davis said: 'The girls have made some big steps forward, but they have some giant steps to go before they can challenge men on equal terms.'

Against that, it has to be said that women's tennis has been a huge international success without the need to 'challenge men on equal terms'. Martina Navratilova, probably the best women player in the history of tennis, would admit that she could not beat any of the best hundred men; it has even been suggested that she would have difficulty beating any of the first *five* hundred. Yet women's tennis stands up independently on its own qualities. It is claimed that women's snooker has a special problem, as opposed to tennis, in that it is a numerical game in which direct comparisons – of break scores, for example – can easily be made with men. On the other hand, women's athletics does not seem to suffer unduly from this; public interest in Zola Budd or Tessa Sanderson is not lessened by the knowledge that men can run faster or throw farther than they can. The real problem in snooker is the number of women who can find the time, place and inclination to practise; they usually prefer something more productive and, as they see it, more demonstrably adult to do than knocking little balls around a table all day on their own.

Ironically, this period of gloom and stifled hope for the women's game has produced a brilliant new star in Allison Fisher, who is arguably the best female player ever to hold a snooker cue. She has already, at the age of seventeen, beaten several of the top male amateurs, who in turn are as good as some of the lowest ranked professionals. When I rang her the first time to make an appointment, she said: 'Can we talk later? I'm just on a big break at the moment!' She has scored 103 in practice and 88 in competition. She picked up the game by watching it on television. Her father, who doesn't play much himself, has added an extension to the family home at Peacehaven to accommodate a snooker room, where she spends most of her time practising. She also spends two days a week at college on a youth training course in leisure industries. She plays exhibitions twice a year in Ireland and also at holiday camps, but she finds it expensive to travel far from home, especially to the north, where women are still barred from many snooker clubs. She finds it a lonely existence, struggling to perfect an art in which nobody shows much interest. She feels she won't improve a great deal within the women's game because there are not enough people to push her, and she now aims to be the first woman on the professional male circuit. 'It's depressing sometimes,' she admits, 'just practising and practising and not knowing if it's going to lead anywhere, always with this nagging feeling that no woman has ever made it to the top and maybe there's some reason for that. But last night I was playing well and I thought to myself: "Why *can't* I be as good as Steve Davis if I work at it hard enough?"'

Willie Thorne predicted after the National Express tournament in July 1984 that it would take no more than five years for a woman to make a century break in competition. It is a mark of the speed at which the women's game is developing that 15-year-old Stacey Hillyard made a break of 114 in the Bournemouth League just seven months later – before taking her O-levels at Highcliffe Comprehensive School, Christchurch, Dorset. She beat Allison Fisher in the women's world amateur championship in a match that provoked the fighter/boxer comparison often made between Jimmy White and Steve Davis. Fisher is the one with the steady all-round game, but *Snooker Scene* reported that 'the crowds are drawn towards Hillyard's table as the pistol cracks of her long potting echo around the hall'. At this same tournament, incidentally, a Canadian player called Maureen Seto won two matches while sitting in a wheelchair after a serious car crash. Allison Fisher has since beaten Stacey Hillyard, and these two are now the country's leading women players, having taken over from Mandy Fisher (no relation) and Vera Selby, who has captained a men's team in the Gateshead League.

It is hard to quarrel with Clive Everton's verdict that 'for all its present problems, women's snooker may yet prove one of the game's great growth areas of the 1980s, but only if it grows steadily and organically, rather than through the artificial stimulants of hype and over-pricing'. The WPBSA, which now has ample funds to spare for investment in the game, should take a more active interest in women's snooker, perhaps appointing someone to work part time in this area. They should also use their influence to arrange a women's open event, breaking down the false distinction between amateurs and professionals which is holding back the game's development. As happened with the men's game in the 1970s, it will probably need the combined forces of the professional body, a reliable sponsor and serious TV interest to turn the women's game into the popular entertainment it surely deserves to be. Until then women's snooker will be a ripe subject for sexist cartoons and will suffer from the same kind of male condescension Dr Johnson showed towards women preachers: 'Sir, a woman's preaching is like a dog's walking on its hinder legs. It is not done well; but you are surprised to see it done at all.'

Billiards has had more persistent efforts at rehabilitation, perhaps because the men professionals (and therefore more money) are involved. The WPBSA, Strachan the clothmakers, and Channel 4 have all created new tournaments which have the makings of a professional billiards circuit. The problem, as ever, is how to make the game interesting as a television entertainment without destroying it as a sport. They have not gone as far yet as Kerry Packer's blue and yellow pyjamas for floodlit cricket in Australia. But some of the variations being tried would make the old pros like Tom Reece go as green as the cloth (though not, perhaps, his old sparring partner, Melbourne Inman, who once opened a club beneath the Criterion in Piccadilly Circus which featured the first billiards Bunny girls in pink satin breeches, black silk stockings and perky little hats).

In one billiards tournament the matches are settled by five games of 400 up. In another they play three games of 200 up. Some matches are against the clock for either a half-hour or an hour. One final is over five hours – and even that is not enough for the purists. Others are 1500 up. In the Channel 4 game no player may occupy the table for more than fifteen minutes at a time. These devices are justified on the cricket analogy – that it was the more entertaining one-day game that kept the 'real' game alive. The problem is that there is no way an exciting climax can be guaranteed. Clive Everton, who has done as much as anyone to promote billiards, is nothing if not realistic about its prospects: 'It is anyone's guess how billiards – in any form – will turn out as a television entertainment, but unless it can be entertainingly presented on television its commercial potentialities are clearly limited. It is this which justifies a degree of experimentation in the overall best interests of the game.' No one believes billiards can ever generate the same excitement as snooker. Although I enjoy playing the game myself, I find it curiously flat on television, even when played by vivid characters like Fred Davis and Alex Higgins or the game's leading virtuosos, Rex Williams and Mark Wildman.

Snooker itself is clearly riding a boom and it is hard to see what, if anything, can halt its momentum now. It is true that professional billiards suddenly died in the 1930s when Walter Lindrum left the scene, just as it seemed to have reached a peak of popular acclaim; and professional snooker died twenty years later when Joe Davis quit the stage. It is tempting fate to assume that public taste will not be fickle again, or that some rival new craze will not emerge to repeat this historic cycle of boom and collapse. It does not seem likely, however. Having spent many years overcoming the problem of failure, the game now has to cope with the more congenial – and infinitely more manageable – problems of success. It seems well equipped for this task, with a commercial management that is both skilled and highly motivated. If there were more men like Barry Hearn and Del Simmons in the boardrooms of British industry, we would all have less to worry about.

A new generation of players has come bursting through to ensure that the public will not be allowed to tire of the old familiar faces, as happened once in the past. Youngest of all is Stephen Hendry, who has broken all records by turning professional at the age of sixteen, a few months after leaving school. He started at twelve on a small table his grandparents bought him for Christmas. He has twice won the Scottish amateur title. When he won junior *Pot Black* he could barely see over the top of the table, though he has shot up a few inches since then. He plays some local exhibitions, for which his fee is £150 a night, but he cannot travel far from Edinburgh because his father has to go with him. When I asked to speak to the player himself, his manager – Ron Clover of Fourleaf Promotions – said the lad was too shy.

It is a fair bet that other young players will have rather more to say for themselves in the years ahead, especially about the administration of the game. In fact, if professional snooker faces any serious problems with the players, it may take the form of a youth *v.* age confrontation. Already there is some resentment at the disciplinary process, especially at the inconsistency of the criteria applied to that hoary old offence of 'bringing the game into disrepute'. This seems to be applied as a random, catch-all punishment, rather as the Army used to accuse people of 'conduct prejudicial to good order and Service discipline' when they could not nail them for any specific abuse. It is certainly difficult to apportion financial sanctions equitably for offences as diverse as being late for tournaments, swearing at the crowd, urinating in flower pots and writing about the more interesting personal habits – chiefly sex, drugs and drink – of fellow players. But there has to be a sense of equity and justice if the WPBSA's writ is to run. How, for example, can Silvino Francisco be guilty of bringing the game into disrepute for, among other things, telling the *Daily Star* what appears to be the truth about Kirk Stevens's drug addiction – when Stevens himself escapes any serious punishment? If it is argued – as I have heard it argued – that Stevens has brought only himself into disrepute, isn't that equally true of Higgins's several misdemeanours?

Rex Williams's televised statement that beta-blockers (which steady the hands and reduce stress) are acceptable in snooker, and that only 'illegal substances' are banned, runs counter to Sports Council guidelines and to most modern thinking on drugs in sport. As the *Sunday Times* put it, 'At the end of the day it is an ethical issue for snooker. Is it cheating or is it not?' Dennis Taylor surely had matters in the right perspective when he wrote:

What people like about snooker are the best things in it, not the worst. They like the skill, the subtlety, the formality, the colour, the clash of personality, the gladiatorial contest. The drugs, the sex, the drink, the fights, the jealousies and the tantrums are bound to catch the headlines from time to time, because snooker players are human like everybody else. They often come from less privileged backgrounds and many have had the proverbial misspent youth. They also work late at night in an alcoholic atmosphere, often under great personal strain, away from their wives and families. And there'll always be a market for dirt.

What matters above all is that the governing body should be seen to be dealing openly and honestly with such 'dirt', not hiding it under the carpet.

There is clearly a problem of justice being seen to be done when some members of the disciplinary body may stand to benefit personally and financially from the punishment they mete out. This is especially so where the offending player loses ranking points for future tournaments, as Francisco did, thereby allowing others (possibly including members of the disciplinary committee) to go ahead of him. This surely cannot be right. No matter how honourable the individuals concerned, there are too many apparent conflicts of interest for the system to *look* convincing. There is always the risk that personal scores will be settled in this way. If someone writes a newspaper article that is critical of another player – or, as in a recent case, says that a venerable and much-liked member of the snooker hierarchy drinks a bottle of scotch a day – can he expect a fair hearing from the friends of those under attack (especially if the offender is a foreigner or excluded for some other reason from the small group at the top)? It is time for the WPBSA to frame a more closely defined and generally accepted code of conduct, especially in relation to newspaper revelations, and a carefully prepared scheme of punishments, taking precedents, comparisons and a player's previous record into account. It is much too arbitrary at present. There should also be a proper appeals procedure and, ideally, a lay element on the judging panel, bringing to bear experience of other sports or other walks of life. If the governing body loses touch with the younger players, or fails to convince them of its reasonableness or even-handedness, it risks a split like the one that brought the WPBSA itself into being in 1971.

However, these are relatively small matters of internal housekeeping which simply happen to have caught a stranger's passing eye. They are important only in as far as they cast any shadow over this glorious game. One of snooker's problems, in a way, is that there are so few of these shadows – compared, say, with professional soccer – that each one gets a disproportionate amount of public attention. It is the price of fame. A folk sport has suddenly become big business and that requires an adjustment by all those taking part. Some of this adjustment may be painful. 'All the fun's gone out of it,' Ray Reardon complained. 'There's too much money. We're in a world of agents and managers now. There are so many professionals now we are having to play these short matches.' In a sense, of course, Reardon is right. It is a tougher life for circuit professionals than it was when he started, but it is also a much more rewarding one, as he knows well enough. Anyway, that must have been a passing mood: the old magician seemed to me to be having plenty of fun when he beat John Parrott at Sheffield in the final frame. And I do not suppose he complained about getting 'too much money' for it.

But the atmosphere on the circuit has definitely been soured a bit by the new pressures induced by the money. And the incessant publicity can be wearing, intrusive and divisive. It saddens a newspaperman to admit that, while television has undoubtedly served snooker well, the press has generally served it badly. As Janice Hale wrote in the *Observer*: 'There is a breed of newspapers, and of reporters who work for them, who are not interested in sport, human endeavour or even human interest. What they are here for is smut.' In a curious way, though, snooker cannot afford a saintly or sanitized image: a hint of the old Adam is *de rigeur*. That is why people will always perversely prefer watching Alex Higgins to Steve Davis. They like a sense of living dangerously, and Steve does not show the signs of a misspent youth.

*

After a late-night conversation with some of the world's leading players, I remember saying: 'I thought I was writing a book about snooker. Now I find I'm writing about life and death.'

'Oh no,' one of them laughed. 'It's much more important than that.'

# BIBLIOGRAPHY

Davis, Joe, *The Breaks Came My Way* (W. H. Allen)

Davis, Steve, *Frame and Fortune* (Arthur Barker)

Devi, Gayatri and Rama Ran, Santha, *A Princess Remembers* (Century)

Everton, Clive, *The Guinness Book of Snooker* (Guinness Superlatives Ltd)

Everton, Clive , *The Story of Billiards and Snooker* (Cassell)

Fishlock, Trevor, *India File* (John Murray)

Higgins, Alex with Patmore, Angela, *'Hurricane Higgins' Snooker Scrapbook* (Souvenir Press)

Lowe, Ted, *Between Frames* (A. & C. Black)

Perrin, Reg, *Pot Black* (BBC Publications)

Priestley, J. B., 'At Thurston's' in *Saturday Review*

Rafferty, Jean, *The Cruel Game* (Elm Tree Books)

Redford, Brian, *Steve Davis, Snooker Champion* (Arthur Barker)

Scholes, Percy A., *The Oxford Companion to Music* (Oxford University Press)

Taylor, Dennis, *Frame by Frame* (Queen Anne Press)

Taylor, Dennis, *Natural Break* (Queen Anne Press)